If There Hadn't Been You

By J.R. Zimmer

Book one

Fisher/Lafayette Saga

Badlanders Press

If There Hadn't Been You

©2024 by Janette Walker

This copy has been corrected of previous errors.

Previously published ©2017
By Janette Walker

ISBN: 978-1-7345789-8-0

Cover design by Janette Walker

For my son,

David C. Walker

Chapter One

June 10th, 1962
New York City

There was a bounce in Colten's step as he walked into the office where his boss, Cadman Benson, currently sat behind a desk, speaking on the phone. When the man signaled for him to have a seat, he did.

The wooden-back chair was not built for comfort, but Colten did not care. He would not be here long enough to get comfortable. After this unexpected summons to Cadman's office, he would be on his way to North Dakota.

As he waited for Cadman to finish the conversation with whoever was on the other line, he wondered what his boss wanted. He assumed, however, it was to tell him to have a good time while on his vacation, so he settled in and waited for Cadman's conversation to end.

Cadman hung up the phone and cleared his throat as he stood up. Placing his hands behind his back, he delivered the news. "They have revoked your time off."

Colten blinked. "Excuse me?" Hell to the no on that, he thought to himself. He'd been planning this trip for almost a year.

"The president has a special request for you." And with that Cadman clarified what the favor entailed.

"He wants me to do what?!" Colten's voice boomed as he jettisoned out of the chair, nearly knocking it over in his haste. "Is he out of his goddamn mind?!"

He began to pace, though it looked more like a prowl as his six-foot, two-inch frame circled the room.

"I can assure you he is serious about this."

Colten stopped and pinned Cadman with a glare that was frightening enough to peel paint.

Cadman shrugged, ignoring the lethal expression. He knew Colten would not be happy about this turn of events, but it was out of his hands. "Listen, I'm only the messenger."

Colten continued to stare. Perhaps he believed if he looked at his boss long enough, the man would suddenly break out in laughter and tell him this was a joke.

"He announced it during this morning's briefing. And by the way, everyone is still talking about the splendid work you did in January, stopping that counterfeiting ring."

Colten waived the compliment away. He did not consider having broken up that west coast counterfeit operation as anything more than having done his job. It had printed a half-million dollars worth of counterfeit money since August of last year and it needed to be stopped. He did not want compliments; he wanted his damn vacation.

Through clenched teeth, Colten said, "I don't care what the president wants me to do; he'll have to find someone else. He approved my time off, damn it! I'm going home."

2

Cadman's hazel-colored eyes roamed his office. He knew nothing he said would appease the man standing before him, so he remained silent.

Colten exploded with a string of curses. "God damn it!" He kicked the chair he had been sitting on earlier, launching it a few feet away from him and into the wall. It hit the innocent wall with a resounding crunch. Without a doubt, the chair would need to be replaced.

It had not survived Colten's wrath.

"Why me?" Colten exclaimed, spinning on the heels of his dusty cowboy boots as he, once again, faced his boss. He considered Cadman a friend and would want him protecting his back if the need arose. "Why me?" he repeated, striking his right hand over his heart with a hard slap. "There are countless agents who would love, and I do mean love this whole assignment. Why would the president pick me, for God's sake?"

Crap.

His grandfather was turning 96 in a few weeks, and even though the ancient man was spry and had his wits about him, Colten wanted to see him before that was no longer the case. The man was a walking history book. The stories he told about his childhood, growing up in North Dakota's Badlands, kept Colten riveted to his storytelling. He and his grandfather shared a love for the state of their birth and a passion for quarter horses.

Colten planned one day to build a home in the Badlands and open a tourist spot, one which would offer trail rides into that rugged land. The scenery was a breathtaking kaleidoscope of color at sunup and sunset. There was no place on earth to enjoy such a spectacular view more than in its heart while on horseback. He wanted to retire from this job and hoped to do so before his 40th birthday. That was in ten years, but time had a way of speeding by. Then, suddenly, dreams were only that, vanished without having the chance to flourish.

Colten repeated, "Why me?"

Cadman shook his head as though he could not believe Colten was not jumping at the opportunity they had handed him. "I can't believe you're not excited about this. Rosalinda Vallombrosa is a babe."

"You do it then," Colten replied. "I wouldn't care if she were Marilyn Monroe or Jean Shrimpton. I am not a goddamn babysitter!"

Cadman, damn him, had the balls to chuckle, "Well, honestly, that's what we are. We just have a more glorified name." He used his fingers to place quotation marks around his next words, "Secret Service; we babysit diplomats."

"Rosalinda Vallombrosa is not a diplomat!" Colten snapped. "She's an actress from France-" He paused, frowning. Something about that last name seemed familiar, but he brushed the thought aside.

Strolling past Cadman, Colten stopped at the large window and looked out. New York City stretched out before him, and he grimaced. Honest to God, he hated this city. Wall-to-wall people and the population continued to grow as fast as breeding rabbits in the wild. For the millionth time, he wondered how he wound up here, employed by the United States government. He wanted solitude and far less adventure. Colten knew he was too young to be feeling melancholy, and he wondered if the time to retire from the Secret Service was sooner than expected.

Wasn't it funny? Dreams had a way of turning around on a person. Once, he desired to be away from the heartache, but now he yearned to go back home, and wasn't that a laugh? He left North Dakota almost six years ago because he could not bear the memories of what he lost, but now all he wanted was to go back and have a fresh start. As though that was possible because no matter what, Caroline would still be six feet under and Clinton....

He closed his eyes, feeling remorse. When he made the trip back to the state of his birth, he spent more time with his grandfather than his own son because he did not know how to relate to Clinton.

He told himself it was better for the child to live with his grandparents. He believed Clinton didn't need him in his life because, after all, what did he have to offer him? Colten was never around, and Clinton needed a stable home.

Throughout the positive pep talk he gave himself Colten knew it for the lie it was. He stayed away from Clinton because he could not handle the fact that he had fathered a retarded child. Harder still was not to hate that child for having been born the night Caroline died.

He knew it was not Clinton's fault to have a slow-developing brain. Nor was it the child's fault that the umbilical cord had been wrapped around his neck, cutting off his air supply during the birth. For all Colten knew, had that not happened, Clinton would have been normal.

And yes, Colten loathed himself for his shallowness.

With a will of iron, he pushed the dreadful thoughts from his mind and switched back to the subject at hand. Turning back to Cadman, he sighed and asked one more time, "Why me? Surely there must be someone who would be more than willing to look out for the overrated star?"

Cadman's eyebrows shot up as his eyes widened in disbelief. "Are you telling me you have never seen her perform?!" he exclaimed. "She's a very talented woman. Some say she has more talent than Monroe."

"That's not saying much," Colten mumbled under his breath. He honestly did not think Marilyn had any more talent than a tree frog spinning around on a wire. Others found her beautiful; he thought she was a bubblehead.

Benson ignored the comment. "The fact is, we all thought Rosalinda wouldn't mind having an agent who had something in common with her."

For the second time that day, Colten's jaw dropped as his eyebrows flew skyward. "I don't have a damn thing in common with her!" Seriously, had there been drugs at the meeting today with the president?

"Well, sure, you do." Cadman drawled. "You're good friends with her distant cousin, Antoine Vallombrosa."

"Tony!" Colten roared, staring disbelievingly. No wonder the last name sounded familiar. "We are not good friends."

"But you know him."

"Yes. Tony's grandparents spent time in the Badlands of North Dakota. My grandfather worked for them during that time, but we aren't best buddies." Tony Vallombrosa was on his list of strange ducks, regardless of him being the current Duke of Vallombrosa since the man's father passed away a few years earlier.

"You're telling me," Colten clarified, almost calmly, "that the only reason the president gave me this assignment is because I know Tony Vallombrosa?" It was another reason not to like the man, Colten thought with annoyance.

Cadman shrugged. "Yep. That about sums it up, you lucky dog."

"Lucky!" The word boomed out. "This is a joke, right? During this morning's meeting, all of you, including the president, thought it would be side-splitting to tell me I had to guard Miss Fancy Pants. Well, ha, ha. I hope all of you bust a gut when you report back to him what my reaction was." He spun around, grabbed his black cowboy hat with its gold-tone-accented hatband, and headed for the door.

"Colten, this isn't a joke. Rosalinda is being hassled by some crazy nut, and Kennedy wants you shadowing her for the duration of her stay in America. The fact you know her cousin was simply icing on the cake."

Colten stopped short of the door. Turning, he looked at Cadman and uttered a sound from his throat that could only be described as a growl, "Then if she is being bothered by some loony, which might I add, isn't unusual given the fact that she's a celebrity, shouldn't she have her own bodyguards? Since when does the president demand protection for a celebrity?"

"She has security. You'll want to report to the person responsible for that, but it doesn't matter. You know Kennedy. When it comes to women, he's a goner. Besides, it's at the request of President de Gaulle. I'm afraid France's president is quite a fan of Miss Vallombrosa."

Colten rolled his eyes. With two of the world's most powerful leaders involved in this ridiculous affair, there would be no way he could get out of this ludicrous assignment. He closed his eyes, took a deep breath, and tried to resign himself to the fact that he was going to babysit some stupid actress, for God knew how long.

Oh, he was angry. Pissed as hell. But he was a servant of the United States, so he would do the job. However, when this was over, he planned to go to the White House and have a long talk with JFK.

After getting the address from Cadman of where Rosalinda Vallombrosa was staying, along with the name of the person supposedly in charge of her security; J.M. Grymes, Colten walked the distance instead of finding a taxi or using the government vehicle at his disposal. He needed to walk off his anger before meeting the starlet.

The sun was shining. That, at least, was a bright spot in his otherwise dismal day. The temperature was not too bad either. He grew up where it could still snow in June if it had a mind to. Usually, the weather stayed in the lower 70s, so this New York high of 79 felt perfectly acceptable to him.

As usual, the streets were crowded and the traffic insane. Taxi horns blared as vehicles wove around each other as though participating in a race, and pedestrians flipped them the bird.

Colten saw the crime happen before the unsuspecting victim knew what hit him. Cool as you please, a young hoodlum bumped into a well-dressed man, and with the stealth of a magician, managed to snatch his wallet from his pocket without a trace and kept on walking down the sidewalk.

For a brief second, Colten thought of letting the little pickpocketer go. After all, if the man in business attire was too foolish to realize his pocket had been picked, he deserved to lose whatever money he had on him. But then, in a split second, Colten changed his mind and headed after the kid who appeared to be around fourteen years old, and certainly no older than fifteen.

"Hold it right there!" Colten ordered as he caught up to the thief. Of course, the kid didn't comply, instead, he ran like a gazelle.

Well, shit.

Colten took off after the young pickpocket, weaving through the population as they cursed him for his recklessness. He finally grabbed the teenager by the shirt collar, twisted him around, and shoved him up against the wall of a dry cleaner store.

"Hey, you dick, what's your hassle?!" the teenager screeched, trying to break the hold and wiggle free.

"You've got something that doesn't belong to you," Colten told him, pushing him farther into the wall, letting the kid know he was not going anywhere.

"Are you in la-la land?!" the teenager shouted. "I was just walking along, and you started chasing me!" His eyes darted around the now-gathering crowd. Apparently deciding to take advantage of the moment, he shouted, "I thought you were going to kill me!" He let his eyes bulge as he pleaded with someone, anyone, to step in and help him get away from this guy. He had already lifted six other wallets, and the day was still young.

"Hey now," some brave soul said, stepping forward. "What's going on here?"

Colten narrowed his eyes at the would-be hero, and the man faltered.

"Kid, just make it easy on yourself and give me the wallet. I'll return it to the owner."

"Wallet? Are you crazy, mister? I ain't got no wallet except my own."

"Oh yeah? What's your name?"

The teenager licked his lips nervously. At the end of the block, from the starting point of the whole chase, a voice raised in panic, "Hey, someone stole my wallet!"

Colten's grin was evil as he watched the kid squirm. "I just bet'cha, you can't give me a name that matches any of the wallets you've got hidden in that coat of yours. I also bet that guy down there-" he jerked his chin toward the end of the block, "would be more than happy to give me his name because it will match one of those wallets."

By now, the fellow who had gotten his pocket picked was heading their way.

Leaning into the teenager's ear, Colten growled, "I'm Secret Service, kid. Do you want to go to jail? I'll make that happen if that's what you want. I'll make it so you won't see the outside world for a very long time." He looked directly into those now honest-to-God, scared shitless eyes and asked, "So, what's it gonna be?"

The teenager laughed nervously, "Hey man, I didn't mean no harm." He quickly rummaged in his jacket and pulled out a wallet. Without delay he handed it to Colten just as the victim stopped beside them.

Colten held the young man in place with one hand and grabbed the wallet with the other. After flipping open the leather holder, he gave the suited man a questioning glance and inquired, "Is your name Mary Ana Maria Gonzalez?"

Business suit sputtered, "I am most certainly not! My name is Jonathan Emmanuel Williams," he said. And as though it were a second thought, added, "the third," in a snooty tone that had Colten wanting to adjust it right up the man's superior nose. Instead, Colten looked back at the kid. "Would you like to try again? Another wallet, perhaps?"

It took three more tries before the teenager pulled the right wallet from the inside of his coat pocket. Colten handed the wallet to Mr. Williams, the third, before patting the teenager down for the rest.

"Busy guy, aren't ya kid?" Colten said, as he handed the stolen property over to the police officer who had shown up somewhere along the line. "I'll cut you a break 'cause I don't have time to write up a report. But I'm warning you. You take another wallet, and I'll hunt you down and cut your balls off. Got it?"

The teenager's eyes filled with tears, "You're... You're letting me go?"

Colten nodded, "Just remember, if you want to keep your manhood, you won't take any more wallets."

"I won't!" The teenager promised, wrapping his arms around Colten in a grateful hug. "Oh, thank you, Mister!" He took off down the street as fast as his legs would carry him.

The officer shook his head, "Now, why would you let the kid go? You know as well as I do, he will get another wallet in under an hour."

Colten shrugged and headed back down the street. He wasn't sure why he didn't give the kid a harder time for stealing the wallets. Maybe it was because he remembered what it was like to be that age, or perhaps it was just because he hadn't wanted to bother further than he had. The stolen wallets would be returned to their rightful owners and the rest was history.

Chapter Two

The long walk did him a world of good. By the time he reached his destination, Colten calmed down enough to be civil to people who greeted him in passing on the street. His temper remained, however, at being denied a vacation. He'd be professional enough to get the job done then leave for his long-awaited break. He just hoped it would still be an option; if not, Colten had plans of punching his boss in the face.

When the hotel came into sight, he was certain he would have located it without Cadman's directions. The entrance of the building drew a crowd of at least one hundred people. Undoubtedly, there to catch a glimpse of the famous visitor from France. Honestly, Colten thought, people needed something else to occupy all the time they seemed to have rather than gawk at another person just because they were a popular movie star.

He paused on the pavement, taking in the scenario. It didn't seem like there was anyone controlling who could enter the building. To test whether this was indeed the case, he strolled forward and blended into the people already present. As if he had every right to be there, he stepped through the doorway with assurance.

As he walked in, Colten could see the shining marble floors and tall white columns with plants growing around them. He admired the bright colors on the walls for a moment before his attention shifted away to something else. Security was evidently lax – not a soul seemed to take notice of him as he browsed around, so he made his way over to the front desk and asked where Vallombrosa's room was, although he already knew the answer. The query was just another test of the hotel's lack of security.

The young man behind the counter appeared to be around twenty-five, but he could have been younger. He shook his head and said, "Sorry, bub. Can't tell you that."

Colten placed a hand in the upper pocket of his shirt, and before he congratulated the man for staying quiet about the room number, he pulled out a fifty-dollar bill and laid it on the counter. He raised an eyebrow as he posed his question: "How 'bout now?"

The young man's gaze lingered for a second, only a second, on the bill with President Ulysses S. Grant's portrait before he shrugged and pocketed it. He muttered "409." Then, as if nothing had happened, the guy turned his back and walked into the backroom.

Colten's lips pressed into a thin line, and he spun on his heel, heading for the stairs. It was obvious to him that the woman's life meant little to the desk attendant. Colten had already made up his mind: by the end of the day, that guy would be done with this hotel. Meanwhile, J.M. Grymes—the one Cadman had said was in charge of Vallombrosa's security—was not doing a great job either, if you asked Colten. Not a single guard was keeping watch over the fourth-floor hallway, so without hesitation or fear of repercussions, Colten made his way down it until he arrived at room 409 and gave the door three solid knocks.

As Colten raised his hand to knock once more, the door suddenly swung open, and he found himself staring at a woman. She wasn't the stunning Rosalinda Vallombrosa that he was expecting. He might not have ever seen the actress perform, but he had seen enough pictures of her over the years to know this lady was not her. However, there was something striking about her appearance that caught his attention.

The most striking thing about her were her Bristol blue eyes, almond-shaped and inviting. Colten imagined he could get lost in their depths for an eternity. Her dark blonde hair was tied behind her head with a satin ribbon of a lighter corporate blue which highlighted her eyes and made them stand out even more. He wondered if she'd intentionally done that to capture his attention.

Mentally, he shook himself.

Coming out of his trance, he realized his fist was still up and ready to knock. He sheepishly lowered it back to his side, embarrassed that he had been so taken aback by the woman's good looks. He didn't know her, nor was there any reason for her to have put on such a figure-hugging dress and styled her hair specifically in that way to attract him. Despite himself, however, his gaze dropped down to her lips. Lips that were small but still kissable. And what-in-the-hell was he thinking? He quickly raised his eyes to hers and saw she had been staring, too. Slowly, one of her brows rose as she asked, "Monsieur, que voulez-vous?"

Colten blinked.

She sighed. "Mister, what do you want?" she asked, this time in English, but the slight French accent had him going weak in the knees.

Colten shook off his confusion and got straight to the point, "I'm Colten Fisher, President Kennedy sent me. I want to speak with J.M. Grymes because he is an incompetent fool."

The woman's eyes narrowed, "Incompetent?" She spoke the word slowly, with a lot of heat behind it.

He ignored the irritated tone as he ranted on about J.M. Grymes' inadequate safety protocols, "The security for Miss Vallombrosa is the sorriest excuse for protection I have seen. Ever!" Suddenly, he felt something hard and cold press against his stomach and heard the click of a gun's hammer being cocked back. He could have kicked himself for walking right into this situation, whatever it was.

It surprised him to feel the pressure of another weapon against his lower back, wondering how he had not noticed the second person coming up from behind.

It was those damn eyes of hers that had ensnared him; he thought and decided the woman before him was a witch. She was a pretty witch, but he felt like she possessed magical powers for having been able to pull his attention away from everything else.

"Do you want your fifty bucks back, mister?" the person behind him breathed into his ear.

Well, hell, Colten thought as he recognized the voice. The desk guy was in on this whole thing. "That depends," he said in a voice that was calmer than he was feeling at this point. "If this isn't Rosalinda Vallombrosa's room, I'll take the refund."

The woman's lips twitched as though she were trying to suppress a smile.

"If you have identification," she told him, "we'll see whether this is Rosalinda's room or where you die."

Colten pursed his lips together to stop himself from telling her what she could do with her request. "Back pocket," grumbled, feeling the heat of embarrassment swell up inside him. Some Secret Service agent he was.

"You're a funny guy," the person behind him said. "There ain't no wallet."

Colten's mind suddenly went blank. Where in the hell was his wallet?

A deep fury sparked in his chest as he made a silent promise to himself that he'd kill the kid if he ever saw him again. "For the love of Mike," he mumbled, almost too low to be heard. "Call Cadman Benson; he'll vouch for me." He was embarrassed beyond words.

The woman seemed satisfied when Colten mentioned the name of the Government official who was sending protection for Rosalinda. She removed the gun from Colten's belly and motioned for him to enter the room, stepping out of his way so he could come in.

The shove from the person behind Colten forced him to take a step forward. The urge to turn and punch the man in the face was strong.

The door closed without anyone bothering to lock it. Colten rolled his eyes and couldn't help but shake his head in disapproval. He was in no position to reprimand such ignorance, although he wanted to point out how ridiculous it was that they left the door unsecured.

"So," the blue-eyed beauty said, carefully placing the uncocked colt .45 on the maple wood table in the middle of the room. She fixed him with a stern gaze and asked, "Do you still believe J.M. Grymes is a bumbling fool?"

If he said yes, would she pick that gun back up and shoot him where he stood? Probably, the little bitch. "Could you just tell the man I'm here and I'll share my thoughts with him."

She laughed, and Colten tried to resist the urge to find her laughter attractive, but he couldn't help it. He wanted to grab the gun and shoot himself; when had a woman ever been able to mess with his senses like this? Caroline, who was once the love of his life, hadn't had a laugh like that.

The woman invited him to take a seat before turning to the desk boy and saying, "Ralph, thank you. You can go now."

The guy bowed in acknowledgment, and Colten rolled his eyes as he watched Ralph open the door and leave. What a suck-up, he thought to himself.

"I'll be just outside the door," Ralph announced, then gave Colten a look that conveyed his doubts over Colten's expertise in anything.

Once the door was firmly shut Colten shifted his gaze towards the woman who stood not far away from him. He was staring at her with a fierce anger, and it was far more intense than what he'd directed at Cadman earlier.

The woman seemed unbothered by Colten's stance; she moved to a chair and with an indifferent shrug then sat down. She remarked in a low voice, "Mr. Fisher, It seems we have made you speechless."

"Not speechless," he all but snarled. "Just get Grymes for me, and we'll forget the whole thing." Her grin had his heart doing a somersault, despite his ill humor, which really pissed him off.

"Would you like to have a seat?" She suggested once more, and when he shook his head no, she sighed heavily. "Okay then." Taking in a deep breath, she continued, "Mr. Fisher, J.M. Grymes is already here in the room."

Call him slow-witted, but he glanced around the hotel room. He was looking for someone else, even though he knew there were only the two of them in the room. When he eventually understood her point, he silently accepted his defeat. She had rendered him speechless.

"You're J.M. Grymes?" his eyebrows raised in surprise. He slowly lowered himself onto the chair, attempting to process how a person as small as her, barely coming up to his chin and didn't look as though she could kill a fly, had been appointed to the security personnel of Vallombrosa's safety.

She nodded.

Disbelief tasted bitter on his tongue.

"Jacqueline Medora Grymes," she admitted.

He stared at her; mouth slightly agape. "Medora," he said slowly, as if the name was strange to him. The day had taken a very peculiar turn. Not only was Tony Vallombrosa a part of it, but J.M. Grymes also had Medora as her middle name. It was the same name given to the small town in North Dakota where he called home.

Somewhere along the line, between getting out of bed this morning and his meeting with Cadman, he had fallen down a rabbit hole. Undoubtedly, the Mad Hatter would pop in at any moment.

Jacqueline leaned back against the plush wing-back chair. "Rosalinda and I share an ancestor whose name is my middle name," she told him. For some reason, she felt compelled to explain her family history to the government official who was sent to assist them with the problem they had gotten into.

Colten removed his cowboy hat, hit it on his pants leg as though removing dust and snidely said, "Let me guess, that ancestor wouldn't be Medora Van Hoffman Vallombrosa, Marquise de Morès; the wife of Antoine-Amédée-Marie-Vincent Manca de Vallombrosa, the Marquis de Morès?"

Jacqueline's eyes widened with astonishment, "How would you know...?"

Colten dismissed the question with a gesture and said, "Never mind that. What can you tell me about this individual who's been bothering Rosalinda?"

Just then, Rosalinda Vallombrosa walked through the connecting doorway. Colten couldn't help but admire her beauty. She seemed quite petite, likely just a bit over five feet tall. Her midnight black hair was pulled into a bun, and her emerald-green eyes captivated his attention. It was clear why she had been labeled a twenty-five-year-old beauty.

"The truth iz," Rosalinda's accent, although heavier than Jacqueline's, wasn't nearly as sexy to Colten's ears, "I am not zee one who iz in danger." She nodded toward the woman sitting in the chair. "Jacqueline iz zee one in need of your protection."

Chapter Three

Jacqueline watched Colten bolt out of his seat as though he had been pricked by a pitchfork. She could not help but wince. Rosalinda had thought up this plan to deceive the United States government into granting her protection from Pierre Belle-feuille, and Jacqueline had pleaded with her otherwise. But Rosalinda was determined. Pierre was merciless and showed no mercy to those who crossed him, so if he found her, she would be doomed for sure. The thought of death terrified Jacqueline, making her feel nauseous.

Colten strode towards Rosalinda, his eyes blazing. His de-meanor was eerily composed, but his body language clearly conveyed he was anything but. In Jacqueline's eyes, Colten re-sembled a panther- agile, sleek, and most certainly on the hunt. "Let me understand this correctly," he said. "You had the Pres-ident of the United States believe you needed protection from someone demented, when really what you needed was protec-tion for is her?" - he asked, pointing at Jacqueline.

Jacqueline felt her muscles tense. Was he suggesting her life was of lesser value than Rosalinda's? What a jerk, she thought. Rosalinda spoke up and called him an ass; if she hadn't, Jacqueline would have.

Colten ran a hand through his hair in agitation and replaced the Stetson with a firm push, "Whatever the trouble is, hire yourself a bodyguard." He glanced toward Jacqueline, "Good God. Do you have any idea? Any idea at all the trouble you'll be in if the president realizes you duped him?"

Rosalinda shrugged carelessly. "John Kennedy happenz to like me." The way she said it left Colten with many mental pictures of what kind of appreciation the president had for her. "I knew he would send me his best Secret Service man to help. He would have no consideration for Jacqueline and would be as narrow-minded as you to suggest an average person oversee her safety."

They glared at each other, neither of them willing to give an inch.

Jacqueline shook her head, feeling exasperated with Mr. Fisher's constant dismissal of her concerns. "Look," she said in a measured tone, rising to her feet, "I know we don't exactly see eye-to-eye on this, but I need you to hear me out. If I'm caught by this man, I will die." She kept herself from trembling visibly, but inside her anxiety was at an all-time high. There was no exaggeration here; the danger was very real.

Colten gave her his full attention. The prolonged quiet set Jacqueline's nerves on edge. Even with the anger looming over him, he was still a very attractive man. When she opened the hotel room door and found him there, fist raised to knock again, all sensible thinking flew out of her mind. His appearance had taken her by surprise. Sure, she had seen good-looking guys before in her twenty-three years of living, but something about Colten Fisher left her speechless. She couldn't figure out if it was because of those deep black eyes that held her gaze so intently, or because of his aura of sexual attraction that drew her in like a moth to a flame. Plus, she was a sucker for a man wearing a cowboy hat.

He was waiting for her to say something. She had no choice but to tell him the whole story. Taking a deep breath, she braced herself. It was strange how she could face down a man with a gun without being scared, ready to pull the trigger if necessary. But talking about what had pushed her into such danger made her tremble. She should never have gotten Rosalinda involved in this mess, but that didn't change the fact that she was now just as much in danger as she was.

Taking a deep breath, she once again met Colten's eyes, "Have you heard of the Sancy Diamond?"

He raised his eyebrows skeptically. "Some," he replied. He knew it had been taken from the Astor family a week before, one of the most influential families in New York City. People often called them "The Landlords of New York".

Jacqueline turned away from Colten as she stood at the window, giving him an unobstructed view of her long, dark-brown hair. It cascaded past her shoulder blades and down to just above her waist.

He snapped his eyes back up when they began admiring her firm and shapely buttocks. It was not his fault; Colten tried to convince himself that he admired the silhouette of her behind. He was a man, after all. He would have had to be made from stone not to notice.

She peered out of the window and observed people going about their business without a worry in the world. She longed to be that carefree again, although she could not help but think of her foolishness. Her gaze shifted to the deserted building across the street—five floors filled with mystery. What would become of it in years ahead? Would it be a motel, apartment building, or store? The future was ever-changing, as this situation served as evidence. For a fleeting second, she thought she detected motion from behind one window in the structure opposite from the one she was gazing out from—a ghostly silhouette like a butterfly's kiss rippling through the glass.

"The Sancy Diamond is a pale-yellow, shield-shaped diamond, weighing 55.23 carats," she said, her eyes shifting away from the building and settling on Colten. "I'm sure you heard it was stolen one week ago—it made all the headlines." He didn't respond verbally, but he nodded in acknowledgement, and she continued. "I was at the party at Astor's home the night some-one lifted the gem."

Despite himself, he could not contain the sardonic smirk on his face as he asked in a mocking tone, "Are you about to admit that you are the thief?"

She emitted laughter, but its hollow sound betrayed the un-derlying sorrow. Colten felt an absurd urge to offer some kind of comfort, which he normally wouldn't do. He used to be more caring when his wife was alive, but after her death, that part of him seemed to go with her.

He suppressed the impulse to embrace Jacqueline, instead asking her with a hint of impatience in his voice: "Well?"

She inhaled deeply, her breath trembling as she spoke. "Did I take the Sancy Diamond from the Astors?" She paused be-fore shaking her head. "No, but I took it from the person who did."

"You what?!" he was incredulous. His mind struggled to wrap around the claim. "Well then," he said, "I suppose I'll have to take you in. It's the surest way to keep you safe."

This time it was Rosalinda who laughed, "People are hurt and killed in jail all ze time, and it would certainly not stop Pierre Bellefeuille from going after her there."

Colten swiveled his gaze to the stage actress, wondering who Pierre Bellefeuille was. The name vaguely seemed familiar, as if a distant memory were trying to come back to the surface.

Jacqueline hesitated and nervously licked her lips, "He is my stepbrother."

And now, Colten did laugh, "Well damn, this story keeps getting better and better." He ran a hand over his face, tired of this bullshit day.

"She iz telling the truth!" Rosalinda exclaimed.

Jacqueline exhaled in exasperation. Frustrated and weary, she began moving back toward the chair she sat in earlier when suddenly, the window behind her shattered into millions of tiny pieces.

Rosalinda and Jacqueline's ear-piercing screams joined the clamor.

Colten reacted instinctively, diving towards Jacqueline and pushing Rosalinda out of the way in one swift motion. He threw his arms around Jacqueline, tumbling to the floor with her at his center. Rolling away from the shattered window, Colten felt fragments of glass raining down on the room. They blasted into the sky-blue rug, high-back chairs, furniture, and even piercing flesh.

"Stay down!" he ordered Rosalinda as it wasn't possible for him to be in two places at once and a person only had two arms. At that moment, he was hunched over Jacqueline, acting as a shield, protecting her from whatever else might come their way.

In an instant, the door to the hotel room flew open and Ralph rushed in. A red spot suddenly bloomed on his forehead, and he dropped like a rock to the floor. His eyes were wide and unblinking as Rosalinda cowered nearby, and she let out another scream before retching onto the rug.

Colten locked gazes with Jacqueline, feeling a pang of sympathy as he saw the terror that consumed her. "Don't move and stay down," he advised her, earning a nod in response before he wriggled across the carpet to where she had put down her gun. All was peaceful again, apart from Rosalinda's retching and Jacqueline's sobs.

He gave Ralph a quick glance. The man had entered the room without thinking of any peril; he had come in with no regard for his own safety and received a bullet in response.

Dumb bastard.

But Colten also blamed himself for the circumstances. He had disregarded what the two women had said to him, instead blinded by his frustration at being forced to forgo a much-anticipated vacation in order to look after an actress. His anger blurred his judgment.

Dumb shit. He chastised himself for being so foolish as he reached out to the table, searching for the gun that Jacqueline left there earlier. He wouldn't be caught off guard again. Although there were no gunshots ringing out now, he wasn't willing to risk his life by exposing himself if someone started shooting. He needed to be ready in case something happened.

This room was on the fourth floor of the building, and it was clear the shot came from across the street. Whoever had pulled the trigger was no doubt waiting for someone in this room to reveal themselves. Or perhaps they were on their way to this hotel to see if their shots hit their mark. Though Colten doubted it, he did not discard it. He figured, with the attention the shattering glass would have caused on the street below, there were bound to be people coming up here to check things out. And he heard police sirens through the now gaping hole in the window which were getting closer by the second. Hopefully, that meant somebody had been kind enough to call the authorities and they would arrive soon.

Colten glanced over at Jacqueline and noticed the drops of blood staining her shirt. His heart stopped for a moment. Had whoever fired the gun injured her? He crawled forward, inching his way back toward her. "Were you hit?" he asked, voice grim.

She looked at him, those radiant blue eyes large with fear. "No," she shook her head.

"You're hurt," he said, moving closer and inspecting the wound on her arm. She hadn't been shot, but a large shard of glass was lodged in her forearm. As carefully as possible, he extracted it from her flesh and searched for something to use as a bandage. He felt Rosalinda move into position beside him, pale-faced and looking almost drained of life. Determination tugging down her lips, she handed him a hand towel. "Use thiz," she instructed him. Colten admitted, if only to himself, that unless she was a brilliant actress, Rosalinda must have had nerves of steel.

Mumbling his thanks, Colten pressed the towel against the wound on Jacqueline's arm as his eyes did a quick survey to see if there were any other signs of glass that needed attention.

Jacqueline's eyes met Rosalinda's. "I am so sorry!" She sobbed. "I never meant to lead Pierre here. I never thought he would..."

"It iz alright mon amie," Rosalinda soothed. "It iz alright." She looked at Colten and narrowed her eyes, "And now perhaps, you zee the truth!"

He didn't necessarily want to, but the reality of Jacqueline needing protection started to sink in for Colten. Both women were in jeopardy. So how was he supposed to keep them secure, when one of them was a world-famous actress?

He had just started to feel the beginnings of a headache gripping the back of his head when New York's finest stormed in with their weapons drawn. His migraine instantly transformed into a full-blown sledgehammer of pain when it was obvious to them, he was guilty of the crime. He was holding the gun, and there was a corpse sprawled out on the floor in front of him.

Yep, it had turned into one hell of a day.

Chapter Four

Cadman Benson stepped into the police interrogation room. Pausing in the doorway, he took a moment to assess the two women, who both appeared exhausted and uneasy, seated at the long table in the center of the room. Then his gaze shifted to Colten, and he noticed that his expression was one of immense anger. Cadman's expression stayed neutral as he asked the other man, "Rough day?" before proceeding into the room.

Colten told him what to do with himself, no matter if the act was anatomically impossible. "Just get us out of here. I don't want to look at your ugly face any longer than I have to. Twice in one day is asking too much." Though Cadman was five years older and technically Colten's superior, he didn't care. It was hard to contain his anger, so he held onto the bottom of the chair he sat on to keep from lashing out at Cadman for the amusement dancing in his eyes. He couldn't believe that the police had arrested him.

Cadman chuckled, simultaneously confused and bemused. He pulled out the chair opposite Colten and plopped down. "So, you want to let me in on it?" he said. "I don't often hear from one of my men that he's been accused of murder."

At that, Jacqueline's, Rosalinda's, and Colten's voices raised in heated anger. The three of them began recounting what happened in the hotel room earlier that day.

Cadman held up a hand, "Hold it, just hold it!" He pointed a finger at Colten, "You can have the honors."

On a heavy exhale, Colten relayed the incident that happened in the starlet's room beforehand. He reached the part of the story where the police barged into the place and finished with, "They arrested me even though Jacqueline and Rosalinda here tried to explain I was only holding the gun! Despite what they said, the officers just brought us here to wait until you showed up. Instead of jailing me."

"Why didn't you show them your government I.D.?" Cadman wanted to know. "That would have saved you all from taking a trip down here, not to mention pulling me from a crucial meeting."

Red splotches instantly appeared along Colten's high cheekbones, and suddenly he seemed to find more interest in playing with the Stetson he'd whipped off his head and tossed carelessly on the table the moment an officer brought them to this room. "They," he refused to tell Cadman about the kid lifting his wallet, "they cuffed me before I could show them." Even in his own mind, he sounded like a child excusing some misdeed.

Cadman raised a brow, "They told me you didn't have any identification on you at all."

Bastards, Colten thought.

"Where's your I.D.?" Cadman's voice had an edge to it.

With a sigh and through gritted teeth, Colten told his boss all about the damn kid.

Cadman shook his head, "I don't believe it." But his lips twitched with humor.

"Neither do I."

Cadman let out a deep breath and promised to have replacements for the items taken by the thief by evening. Switching his focus to Jacqueline, he said, "So, you have the Sancy Diamond?" He had gathered that information from Colten's short phone conversation.

She shook her head, "I had it."

Both men stared at her.

"It is safe," she assured them, but her brows drew together, and a frown crossed her lips. She was not positive the diamond was safe. She hoped it was, but she could not be sure.

"Where's the diamond, Jacqueline?" Colten asked, almost conversationally. It thrilled her the way her name rolled off his tongue, as though it was an endearment. His face, however, told her it was not an endearment, and he was livid as hell.

"Well," she said, clearing her throat. She reached out and grabbed the glass of water that an officer had given her earlier. She took a sip to steady her nerves before speaking. "I mailed it to one of my friends who lives in Pennsylvania."

"Mailed it!" Cadman's eyes bulged.

Colten roared with laughter, tears streaming down his face. She had entrusted the Post Office to deliver a valuable diamond, worth more than half-a-million dollars, to somewhere in Pennsylvania. He struggled to contain himself between fits of mirth and questioned incredulously, "Why didn't you just mail it back to the Astor family?" This was by far the funniest thing he ever heard.

Jacqueline and Rosalinda exchanged looks, then Jacqueline blushed.

"I did not think of that," Jacqueline offered sheepishly. "When I took it from Pierre, I was so afraid..." She shook her head. "I did not think."

Rosalinda reached out her small hand and covered the top of her childhood friend's, "It would not have made a difference, mon amie. Pierre would still be after you."

Colten's laughter subsided, his face turning serious, "You said Pierre is your stepbrother. Want to fill in the blanks?"

Jacqucline did not pretend she did not understand his question. "My father passed away two years ago. I was attending college as an exchange student at Clarion University of Pennsylvania at the time." She waved that fact away. "My mother met Jon Bellefeuille four months later. He is a wonderful man, but his son," she shuttered, "Pierre is a criminal; always in trouble with the authorities."

Cadman sucked in his breath, "Pierre Bellefeuille is your stepbrother?"

Colten raised an inquisitive brow.

"You recall Colt, don't you? He cut the head off our agent in Paris a few months back while he was playing a part in that counterfeit business over there."

The reminder jogged Colten's fuzzy brain, "That's the guy we're talking about?" Jesus H. Christ. "I remembered the Paris police got the bastard, but he escaped. No one's been able to pick up his trail since then."

Cadman's eyes turned once more on Jacqueline, "How did you get the diamond?"

"I saw him at the Astor home; at the party the night the diamond was taken."

"How do you know Pierre was the one who took it?"

She chuckled, "Mr. Benson, if Pierre can get his hands on a diamond or drugs, you better believe he'll take advantage of the opportunity." She adjusted her posture before continuing to recount the events of that night at the Astor's party. "I saw him sneak into the library. When he came out, his right hand was tucked in his pocket—a sure sign that he had taken something. Pierre will tell you to your face that he is innocent and make it sound convincing with his melodic voice, but his left eye gives him away every time; it twitches when he lies."

"But how did you get the diamond?"

"Before he left the gathering, Pierre paused to address me." She had always felt an eerie presence whenever he was around. He had the face of an angel and caused women to swoon at the sight of him, but she noticed a malign air surrounding him the first time she met him. Obviously, she had not been wrong to be wary of him from what she just heard Cadman Benson say.

"Someone bumped into him," she continued, "He then bumped into me. That was my chance to snatch whatever it was he had taken from his pocket. I didn't think he'd noticed what I'd done." Both men looked about to interrupt and tell her it wasn't a smart thing to do, but she cut them off with a stern, "I know it was stupid! He must've figured out that I took what he had stolen soon after he left the Astor's home. We went our separate ways, and I checked into my hotel." It wasn't until she was alone and had locked her door that she realized what she had taken from him. She was terrified and immediately put it in a box and shipped it as soon as possible for safekeeping. Of course, she didn't tell them that she had fled the motel in a panic that night. She had no way of knowing if Pierre knew where she was staying and hadn't been willing to risk finding out. To stay safe from him, she changed locations every day, confident in her ability to remain hidden – until today.

"But you didn't return it to the Astor family, nor did you contact the authorities. Why not?"

"I do not know!" she exclaimed. "I was frightened. I only acted out of fear and mailed it to Uncle Digger." She shook her head in frustration. "When I heard Rosalinda was in New York, I went to her. It was her idea to get help from the president of this country."

Colten shook his head. It was the craziest story he had ever heard, but he believed her.

"Tell me about Ralph," he said quietly. He understood they were still in shock and terribly upset after witnessing his untimely death at the hands of a gunman right before their eyes.

"He," Rosalinda said sadly, her voice trembling, "was my bodyguard. He volunteered to help us, but now," she bowed her head, tears filling her eyes as she clutched her hands in her lap, "now he iz dead."

Cadman released a sigh as he reclined in his chair, and assured her, "I'll make sure it's all taken care of. Please don't worry - just tell me what information you have regarding next of kin and I'll contact them." He held her hand for a moment before turning to Jacqueline. "Let's give your uncle a call and find out if the package arrived." With that, he stood up.

Jacqueline coughed, "He does not have a phone."

"Then we'll call someone who you trust, who can ask him if he received your package," Cadman said with confidence.

"Uncle Digger lives in the center of Allegheny National Forest. The only way to reach his place is on horseback. He receives his mail through the park service. Either they take it to him once a month, or he comes in for supplies and gets it then."

Again, both men stared at her.

Cadman's eyes widened. "So, you're telling me that the diamond could be just sitting in some Park Ranger's office, buried under stacks of paperwork?" he exclaimed.

She nodded.

"For the love of Mike," Colten grumbled under his breath. No one in their right mind would believe this story if he ever told the tale in his old age.

Cadman let out a deep breath, pondering something for a few seconds. He then slowly tilted his head in an inquisitive manner. "On horseback?" he asked with a raise of his eyebrow, mulling it over.

Colten looked at his boss. "Don't even think it," he said.

But Cadman, damn the man, merely glanced back with a wide smirk and said, "Well now, that's right up your alley, Colt."

"Cadman," Colten's voice had a slow warning in it.

Cadman grinned. Colten's sigh was long and drawn out.

Cadman regarded Jacqueline, "Have you been to your uncle's cabin?"

She nodded, "He isn't really my uncle. He's a sweet old man who's related to the family I lived with while in college."

"That sounds great," Cadman said with delight. "You and Colten will go to Pennsylvania. Not only will it get you out of New York City for a while and away from Pierre Bellefeuille, but the two of you can retrieve the diamond and bring it back." Two birds, one stone, he thought to himself. Jacqueline still needed protection. Colten was an expert horseman, and she could lead him to the diamond. The perfect solution.

Turning to Rosalinda, Cadman knew he could not expect Colten to keep his eye on both women. And now that he was this close to the starlet, Cadman knew the best thing he could do for his friend was step up to the plate and help him out. Well, okay. It would not be a hardship for him to keep Rosalinda close. "And you, my dear," he told the raven-haired goddess, "will come with me. You are no longer safe back at your hotel room, but I know a place where I can take you and make sure you're out of danger."

Colten's eyes bulged. "Wait a minute," he sputtered, "earlier today, you said I had to protect her, and now you're jumping in to do it. Why's that?"

Cadman's face lit up with a wide smile that conveyed to Colten the obvious explanation of his enthusiasm—Rosalinda was stunningly beautiful.

"I can't expect you to protect both of them," Cadman said. "I wouldn't want your attention divided."

Cadman reached out his hand for Rosalinda's, "My dear, I am so sorry you had to endure that horrible incident. Please, I'll take you to a safe place, and you can clean up and rest."

Rosalinda took his hand, her lips curling into a sexy smile, as she pushed herself up from the chair. "I feel safe already, Monsieur." She gave Jacqueline a mischievous wink before looping her arm through Cadman's and walking toward the door with him. Before they reached the exit, Rosalinda paused and looked back at her friend. "Behave while you are with him." She motioned with her chin toward Colten, then left right through the door.

An awkward silence hung over the room as Jacqueline felt the heat rising in her cheeks. She could not believe Rosalinda just said that, knowing full well she would probably sleep with Cadman Benson before the day was done—but Jacqueline did not have the same nature. Her blush ran from head to toe, and she refused to look at Colten. If she had she would have noticed her flushed face matched his, which had turned a deep red.

She was not the only one discomfited by the starlet's parting words.

"Well," Colten's voice was overly bright, and he cleared his throat to bring it back to its normal pitch, "I guess," he said finally, "we're off to Pennsylvania."

Chapter Five

Once Cadman left, Colten spent some time thinking about the best way for Jacqueline to leave the Police station. Going through the main entrance wouldn't be wise, as whoever shot at them in Rosalinda's hotel room could have followed them here and be waiting outside for her. With a long-range rifle, it would be simple enough to take a shot at her while she walked out the front door. It was a difficult situation – either exit could be monitored, so walking out into the open wasn't sensible. He couldn't be sure Pierre had been acting alone.

He looked in Jacqueline's direction. She was walking back and forth around the room, waiting for the doctor who would take care of her scrapes and cuts. When his mind flashed back to her turning from that hotel window, the glass shattering around her, his heart tightened. It was a puzzling feeling since they had just met, and he told himself his discomfort was caused by the fact that someone entrusted to him had been too close to facing death.

She required a new outfit since hers was covered with blood, as was his. However, they'd have to wait until they arrived at their first destination. They would spend tonight in Philadelphia. In the morning, Cadman would provide a rental car, and they would drive to Clarion. He also promised any supplies they might need, including a government I.D. for Colten, would be waiting for them at their destination, provided by one of his aides.

Colten took a moment to admire Jacqueline as she bent over in front of him to pick up a magazine she found resting on a side table. His eyes roamed down. Although the hemline of her dress covered from the knee up, his mind filled in the gaps with an image of long, shapely legs. His gaze continued down, taking note of her calves and tiny ankles perched upon black pumps. He couldn't help but admire them.

They were great ankles.

He quickly averted his gaze when he realized that he was staring, and he wondered how he could go on without touching her for an indeterminate amount of time.

He was in trouble, and he knew it.

He rose from his seat and put his Stetson on his head, announcing he'd be right back. He needed to distract himself with something else to keep that thought at bay. Planning a safe escape route for her was as good of a plan as any. When she swiveled around to enquire where he was off to, he made an effort not to admire the quizzical expression on her face.

"I have to discuss something with the chief of police."

As he moved away and started toward the door, she sighed. Mr. Fisher wasn't one for talking much, but she couldn't help admiring his figure. His jeans were snug around him, like they were tailored just for him. They hugged his butt perfectly and rested low on his hips.

Now that she was alone, she could openly admit Colten Fisher was quite attractive.

After Colten reached a decision on how he could transport Jacqueline out from the station without anyone being the wiser, he returned to the tiny conference room. Chief Erickson would make the preparations which would ensure privacy for them to leave the police department.

Colten noticed Jacqueline sitting in a chair against the wall, absorbed by the magazine she had grabbed earlier. The sound of his footsteps drew her gaze, and her eyes drifted up and met his deep, dark-brown ones.

She looked exhausted; he decided. And could relate completely, but there would not be rest for either of them for a few more hours.

He noticed that the physician had come and gone while he was busy devising his scheme to get them out of this situation. The pieces of glass that had caused the cuts were swept away, and a single bandage covered the spot where he'd removed the biggest fragment earlier. The other lacerations were just minor scrapes and didn't need any band-aids.

"We'll be flying to Philadelphia in about an hour," he told her. He had gotten the confirmation from Cadman's aid less than fifteen minutes ago.

Jacqueline's blue eyes widened as she looked down at her stained dress. "I can't go like this," she exclaimed, gesturing to the spots of blood visible on the front of her clothing. "I need a shower and a change of clothes."

"I assure you; it's all being taken care of. Cadman sent someone to buy clothes for you and has a room reserved in Philly for us when we get there. But first, you'll have to wait just a bit longer before you can change into something new."

She huffed out a burst of impatience.

"Hey," he snapped, "I'm not any cleaner than you, and I'm not complaining."

That shut her up. Colten's shirt was stained from the blood he'd gotten from when he lay on top of her in the hotel, shielding her just in case another shot was fired through the window. "You're right," she said apologetically. Embarrassment filled her expression.

He nodded and sat down at the conference table. A stillness filled the room. Colten decided to break the silence by questioning, "What brought you to a college in the states?"

With a shrug, she remarked, "I've always wanted to explore America. Although my family could easily have paid for me to come here, I decided to make my own path and applied for an exchange program. I ended up with a lovely host family, the Davidsons's, who had three children - one of them, Grant, is challenged. It was the perfect chance to put the skills I was learning in class into practice."

Colten's throat closed; his heart seemed to stop. Could it be that she meant what he thought? It was unbelievable that a woman, particularly one who had money enough to not work, would choose to teach children who were different from others. "Are you saying," he coughed, trying to clear his throat, "that Grant was difficult to handle because of his high energy level?"

She laughed and shook her head. "Not at all," she informed him. "Grant has Down's syndrome."

Colten shifted his gaze, unsure of how to respond. It didn't matter that Clinton wasn't born with Down's syndrome; Colten knew there were other parents who shared the same experience as him. All he could focus on was the fact that it was his own child who wasn't perfect.

Jacqueline's eyes narrowed, "Are you prejudiced, Mr. Fisher?" Her voice came out, sounding like a dare.

Was he? He could not think of a reasonable response. It was unfair to dislike anyone with a disability, and yet, there it was. He was angry that Clinton's brain did not function properly. But Colten struggled with trying to love his child who didn't deserve hate. Not knowing how to conjure up any deep affection for the boy only complicated matters further.

He placed his Stetson on the table and ran a trembling hand through his hair. If he owned up to his prejudice, then it would make her realize what a horrible person he was; so instead of apologizing, he kept quiet.

Lieutenant O'Donald stepped into the room, and Colten was relieved by the interruption. He could see that Jacqueline was awaiting a response, but he had nothing to say.

"We're all set," O'Donald announced as a fellow officer rolled in a large container. It was slim enough to pass through the doors without any trouble.

O'Donald gestured towards the wooden box and offered a slight bow to Jacqueline as he said, "Your transportation awaits you, madam." He undid the latch on top of the crate, and its side dropped open with a loud thud. O'Donald grabbed two coats from inside, handing them to Colten before adding, "That was all we could find. As it's going to be quite chilly tonight when you land in Philadelphia, you can put these on without worrying about overheating or anyone spotting the blood stains on your clothes during your flight and taxi ride to the hotel."

Rising to his feet, Colten motioned for Jacqueline to join him. He held out a hand and guided her to the large wooden box.

"Ladies first," he said with a mischievous grin as he gestured for her to step inside.

Her eyes darted from his to the empty box, "Excuse me?"

"Trust me on this," he told her. "We're getting in. They'll box us up and wheel us out to a delivery vehicle. We'll be just another unit of cargo to anyone who might be watching this

41

place. Then, once the van has departed for the airport, an officer will let us out." He pointed at the crate, indicating to her that it was time for them to take their positions.

She eyed the wooden enclosure skeptically, "You want us to get in there?" He must be out of his mind.

He gave a short nod. "We'll only be in it long enough to be rolled into the truck. Once we're let out, we'll ride the rest of the way in the back of the van. No windows," he smiled at his cleverness. "No one can see in."

She frowned. "No air," she argued, taking a step back.

O'Donald tried to reassure her, "Miss Grymes, this is not airtight. You will not suffocate."

She shook her head. "Perhaps you are right, but..." her voice seemed to hitch, "once the door is closed, I assume there will be no light."

Colten's eyebrow raised. "Are you afraid of the dark, Jacqueline?" he asked her while a smirk played on his face. His eyes appeared to dare her, like he was offering a challenge.

She folded her arms across her chest, raised her nose in the air, and said, "Certainly not."

"Um-hum," Colten coughed to conceal a laugh. She was not a good liar. "I won't let the boogeyman get you," he reached out, took her hand in his, and tugged her forward. "I'll go first."

He wedged himself in, patted his lap and said, "You can sit right here."

Her eyes widened, and she felt the blush creep up her face.

"For the love of Mike," annoyance was evident on his face, "I thought you had more grit than that."

She straightened up and met his gaze with defiance. "I am not afraid," she declared, her tone suggesting that Colten's implication was highly offensive.

His eyes filled with challenge, "Prove it."

She stared for a moment before turning toward the table and snatching his Stetson from it. Head held high, she returned to him and threw the hat into a crate, where he was able to catch it with both hands. With an unwavering gaze, she declared, "I do not want you to forget this. It is the only thing I like about you."

All right, and perhaps she liked that cocky smile he sent her. But she would not admit that to anyone, not even herself.

Colten adjusted himself as she climbed in and settled on his lap. Then, the door closed and tossed them into darkness. He was feeling quite pleased with himself as he detected the movements of Lieutenant O'Donald and another officer pushing the crate down the corridor. Then Jacqueline shifted her bottom in an attempt to find a comfortable position, and Colten had to contain a groan when his groin reacted.

He decided this would be the longest ten minutes of his life.

Chapter Six

By the time Colten and Jacqueline arrived in Philly, it was well past nightfall. The officers who drove them from the airport dropped them off at the lodging Cadman's agency had arranged for them. When they entered the room, they found two sets of clothing neatly folded in opened suitcases. One was placed on the bed, while the other lay atop a chair.

"Clothes," Jacqueline breathed out the word on a relieved sigh when she noticed them. A shower and to stretch out on that bed regardless of the fact it did not look comfortable enough for a dog. She just did not care.

Hunger gnawed in her belly, and she revised her list of needs: shower, change into fresh clothes, eat, then sleep; in that order.

Colten, sifting through the garments in the case on the chair, realized with a sigh that they were his; Cadman apparently had someone break into his apartment to get them for him. He didn't like the idea that someone had been rummaging through his stuff when he wasn't home. He didn't have anything to hide; it just seemed creepy to know someone had been going through his belongings.

Colten noticed a new wallet among the clothes and opened it to find his identification cards replaced, along with a wad of cash thrown in for good measure. Nestled between the bills was a note: Don't let this one get lifted.

Colten scrunched up the paper and tossed it away as red splotches showed up on his cheeks, his embarrassment showing. He would never live the incident down. He truly intended to torture that young pickpocket slowly and painfully if he laid eyes on him again.

He shook his thoughts away and started to undo the buttons of his shirt. When he removed it, intending to replace it with a fresh one, Jacqueline let out a shocked gasp. "What do you think you're doing?" she exclaimed in a voice that was so high-pitched, it sounded like a tiny mouse had spoken.

He stopped in his tracks with his arm suspended in the air and peered at her with suspicion. Her eyes widened in alarm, and she seemed ready to flee. Once he comprehended what was going through her mind, he allowed the devil to have his tongue; for no other reason than the fact that he was exhausted and irritable and simply not in a good mood.

"Well then, Miss Grymes," he purred in a lazy drawl, "I'm just about to make love to you. Is that what you wanted to know?"

Her eyes grew as big as saucers.

With a scowl, he grabbed the fresh shirt and threw it on. "For the love of Mike!" he snorted. "I'm going for food while you take a shower and put something else on. When I get back, it'll be my turn in the bathroom."

If possible, her eyes grew larger, "You can shower in your own room!"

His eyebrows rose to emphasize his point. "Sister, this room is just as much mine as it is yours. I've got orders to stick with you like glue, and that's exactly what I'm going to do."

Her gaze quickly shifted from him to the bed and back again.

He nodded in agreement. "Yes, that's correct; there's just one bed because Cadman booked the room for Mr. and Mrs. John Drake, as a married couple. And no, I'm sorry, but I'm not enough of a gentleman to offer to sleep on the floor."

"Then I will!" she promised with heat in her voice.

He gave a little shrug. "That works for me. I like having the bed to myself. Thanks for offering." He strolled over to the doorway and opened it. Then he glanced back at Jacqueline. "Be out of that shower when I get back; I'm gonna jump in with or without you in it." He grabbed something from the stand in front of the TV and shoved it into his shirt pocket before pushing open the outside door. The door slammed closed, once he stepped through it, hard enough that Jacqueline could feel it resonating through the walls. She figured if somebody thought they were a married couple, then they'd assume there had just been a fight between lovers.

Her chest felt tight as her heart raced. How could she possibly stay the night in a motel room with someone she just met? She had no money to get a separate room.

Jacqueline hurried over to the entrance and secured the door. That should keep him out, she thought. He'd have to find his own place to sleep.

Picking up the long nightgown provided for her she entered the cramped bathroom. The walls had been painted an unappealingly pale pea-green color and there was hardly enough space to turn around in it, but she appreciated its practicality.

Spotting two new toothbrushes on the counter caused her to smile, amazed to realize how the simple things seemed to make all the difference in the world.

In a hurry, she twisted the faucet open and adjusted the temperature accordingly before peeling off her soiled dress and chucking it onto the floor, thinking that she'd get rid of it as soon as possible. Feeling the warm droplets from the shower cascade over her head, she paused to enjoy the momentary bliss before pondering about the strange man from the government who had appeared in her life earlier that day.

To say he was attractive would be an understatement. Jacqueline had felt her mouth go dry as she took him in. His sculpted chest and defined abs almost made her drool when he'd taken off his shirt earlier. She was embarrassed that she had thought he had wanted to make love to her when, in fact, all he wanted to do was change his clothes. But, despite her body's reaction, she wouldn't share the bed with him because she wasn't sure if she could resist the temptation of doing anything more than sleeping with him.

But she had locked the door, and that brought a smile to her face.

Over the years, she had a few relationships with men, but she was not Rosalinda either. She wanted the sexual act to mean something to both parties and knew she was probably grasping at straws. The men she'd known weren't looking for a permanent relationship.

After her shower, she put on the nightgown with a sense of relief that it was modest enough to feel decent. She quickly brushed her teeth and grabbed the comb from the other toiletries. As she opened the door, she was immediately engulfed with the wonderful scent emanating from the room. It came from the direction of where Colten sat at the small table, wolfing down spaghetti and meatballs.

She couldn't help but stare. How had he gotten into the room?

He glanced up at her briefly, then returned his attention to the plate in front of him. His mouth was full as he said, "There's plenty here. Help yourself."

She kept her thoughts to herself, not daring to ask how he had gained access to the room and was doing her best not to comment on his terrible manners. As far as she was concerned, he could have been crawling around on all fours eating from a bowl, the swine.

The smell of the meal made her realize how hungry she was. Her conscience chided her for being so ungrateful. After all, the man had gone out and brought them both food. He had put her need to get cleaned up before his own, and despite that, all she could do was silently criticize him? She felt ashamed of herself for being a shrew.

Honestly, when had she become so spiteful?

Steeling herself, she walked to the table. "Thank you," she said as she took a seat and grabbed a plate provided from whatever eatery Colten had ordered the food from.

He let out a low grunt after a few bites, then pushed his plate away. "I'm glad you locked the door behind me; it would give anyone trying to get in a bit of trouble," he said with a playful glint in his eye. "I made sure I had the key on me, so if you were still in the shower when I got back, I wouldn't have to break in."

Her hands stopped moving. When she glanced up at him, she noticed the knowing sparkle in his eyes that suggested he was aware of her motive for locking the door. She sheepishly replied, "I just figured it was for the best." She wouldn't admit she had purposely excluded him from entering.

His lips twitched as he said, "In the future, you'd better make sure you know where the key is before you try to deny someone entry." He tapped the pocket of his shirt.

She resisted the urge to stick out her tongue at him.

He put his plate aside and announced, "We'll be hitting the road early tomorrow to go over to Clarion first. We can check in with the Davidson's there before we drive up to Allegheny National Forest. Hopefully, they'll have information about your Mr. Digger that will save us a trip." He was doubtful, but he continued, "Cadman should have provided transportation for us that will be here by morning."

Her brows knit together, "We are driving?" Mentally, she calculated the distance. "It is well over three hundred miles away."

He nodded, "Yep, that's about right."

"A plane would be faster."

He visibly shuttered and couldn't meet her eyes as he said, "I hate flying. I used up my quota of all I can stomach for now just getting here. So yeah, we're driving."

She stared at him. Slowly, she clarified, "You are afraid to fly?" He had made fun of her for having reservations about being put into a tiny box in total darkness, yet he himself was afraid to fly?

The color rose in his cheeks, and he averted his gaze, "I didn't say that." He cleared his throat. "I said I hate it, not that I was scared. There's a difference."

She could not have contained her laughter had she tried.

He scowled.

After her glee subsided, he changed the subject by saying, "Here's what I don't understand, beyond the fact you mailed the Sancy off to some guy you're not even related to." That still boggled his mind. "But why him? If he got it, he probably thought someone handed him the moon and skipped town."

"Uncle Digger wouldn't do that. He'll keep it safe for me."

Colten rolled his eyes, "And why would he do that?" A half-million-dollar diamond would tempt anyone.

She spoke with the unwavering conviction of a child claiming Santa Claus existed: "I made sure to include a note that explains everything.

Colten shook his head at the woman's naivety. It wouldn't last long; her 'uncle' was probably miles away celebrating his new-found fortune.

He got up from his seat and declared, "I think I'll take a shower and then call it a night." As he moved toward the bathroom, he grabbed some new clothes to change into.

He quickly shut the bathroom door and leaned against it, breathing heavily. He had thought Jacqueline was attractive this morning when she opened that hotel door, but when he saw her come out from the bathroom moments ago with her wet hair, combing through it with her fingers, something inside him stirred. It was something he hadn't felt for years. After Caroline's passing, he believed his capacity to feel any attraction besides physical had vanished. But Jacqueline Medora Grymes pulled on his heartstrings as if trying to jumpstart it. He did not welcome these feelings. After loving once and experiencing immense heartache, he could not face that again. Because of this, he cruelly pushed away the emotion and told himself the only thing he felt for her was lust.

And he was in a hotel room with her, and there was only one bed. He needed to get those lustful thoughts out of his head. Fast.

But, and God save him, who would have thought a long, formless, flannel nightgown could be so sexy?

By the time he finished his shower and stepped back into the bedroom, he found Jacqueline had been hard at work. She had taken off the bedding and was stretched out on the floor on top of the comforter, which she had divided into three sections to act as some sort of cushion for her body. He tried not to feel guilty; after all, it was a large enough bed for two people. But she had chosen to sleep on the ground.

He lay on the bed, his head resting on the pillow, and released an audible groan of pleasure that she could not help but overhear. He was aware of how juvenile he sounded, yet her presence seemed to bring out the worst in him. To add to the insult, he asked, "Are you comfortable?"

"Oui," she confirmed, "I am very snug."

He reached out and flipped off the light switch, a smirk played across his lips. Even though Jacqueline's comment was light, he could tell she wouldn't give in that easily. He'd give her an hour before he decided his next move; but he had to admire her grit. She had more than he gave her credit for.

Apparently, she had more perseverance than he'd originally thought.

Around 4:30, he heard her moving around and felt the comforter being arranged on the bed. If he had been asleep instead of dozing, he would have missed her getting into bed. Her movements were so slight that she made sure there was a wide space between them - enough to fit a large truck. But he knew she was there and, in a soft voice, said "Goodnight Jacqueline."

He rolled away from her and closed his eyes.

He felt the sudden tension in her body, as though she was taken aback that he had been awake. Then a low and gentle "Goodnight, Colten," had his eyes snapping open. He knew she had not meant it to sound sexy as hell, but it had. Damn it! He would have a hard time sleeping now, with her so close. And the images that accent brought to mind would haunt him for the rest of the night.

Shit.

When slumber finally came, he envisioned a dream. Despite understanding it was just a sleep-induced mirage, the vision of Caroline felt surprisingly real. And yet, he knew the undeniable truth -- she was dead, but the apparition seemed genuine enough.

Caroline was standing in front of his grandfather's cabin, illuminated by the sun as it shone down on North Dakota's Badlands. When he came up close to her, she turned and looked at him, but stepped away when he attempted to touch her and shook her head.

"No," she told him gently. "It's time for you to let me go."

"I'll never let you go!" he said with conviction, reaching for her once more.

"It's time," she repeated. "I've been waiting for this moment, and now that it is here, I have to go." She scanned her surroundings with a sorrowful gaze. "This was your grandfather's land; now yours. People will come from far and wide to see what you create here, and I'm just sorry I won't be here to watch that happen."

"Colten," she said earnestly, "Clinton needs you. Please be a father to him."

He felt tears trying to gather behind his eyes. "I don't know how," his voice faltered as he watched her begin to fade.

"Give him your love, Colten," her figure slowly becoming more transparent with each passing breath. "Just love him and she will help show you what a wonderful boy he is." Her voice was like a gentle breeze, carrying away the last of her words.

And suddenly, Caroline was gone, just like that.

Colten jerked awake on a gasp and discovered a pair of bright blue eyes riveted on him.

"Are you all right?" she asked tentatively, reaching out a hand to touch his fingertips in an attempt to comfort.

"Yeah," he said with an unsteady laugh, embarrassed. He ran a hand over his face, trying to shake the dream away.

They lay there, staring at each other. Unconsciously, Jacqueline continued stroking his hand.

The sharp knock on the hotel door jolted them. Colten sprang from the bed as though the hounds of hell were close on his heels.

"Yeah," he called out.

"Philly Rent-A-Car," came a man's voice through the pine door. "We have a delivery for a Mr. John Drake."

Colten opened the door.

"Here you go," the man said, handing him some keys, then pointed to the Buick Special parked in the slot just outside the door. He glanced into the room, saw the woman on the bed, and blushed, "Ah, sorry for the interruption."

Colten took the keys and closed the door in the man's face.

He looked over his shoulder and saw Jacqueline was already off the bed and heading for the bathroom.

He hoped this morning wasn't a prelude to the rest of the day.

Chapter Seven

Rosalinda stretched like a cat, graceful and sleek. Rolling over in the bed, she gazed at the man beside her and smiled. "Good morning, Monsieur Benson," she leaned closer and placed a passionate kiss on his lips.

He put a hand on her shoulder and pushed lightly. "This was a mistake," he said with a gruff tone. Even though this had been something he wanted, he never intended it to actually occur.

He was still confused about how they had ended up together like this. His brain was a jumble of passionate memories.

Bringing her to his apartment from the police station had been a genius idea on his part. Not necessarily because he wanted something to happen between them. He just thought it would be the safest place for her; no one would think of looking for her there.

As the evening wore on, they sat together in his living room and had a pleasant conversation over drinks. When she finished her drink, she stood up and walked towards him with an alluring sway of her hips. When she stood before him, she leaned down and kissed him passionately with heat he'd never felt before. But the kiss was not enough for her. She whispered a sultry promise into his ear that no man could resist, and he practically came in his dress slacks.

They did not made it to his bed that first time. On the way down the hall, she'd thrown herself at him, literally locking her arms around his neck and wrapping her legs around his hips. He'd answered her embrace by pushing her back against the wall with only his trousers undone, her dress hiked up to her waist.

Christ, all mighty. He felt cheap and used, and what the hell? He loved every minute of being her sexual plaything. Nevertheless, the morning brought a sobering reality--he served as an agent of the United States and had promised to protect and serve.

He supposed he could say he had been serving her last night, but that would be sick. It was a careless way to soothe his conscience, and he had too much integrity for that. The fun was over; it was time to step back and hope to hell he would be stronger next time.

Knowing damn well he didn't have the strength to refuse her, he promised himself that he'd find a different place for her to stay before nightfall.

Rosalinda's mouth formed a small, sad pout as she asked, "I did not pleaze you?"

Cadman grimaced inwardly. Please him? She had driven him wild the previous night. Her skill in bed was unrivaled, but that was beside the point. His objective was to protect her, not screw her.

He felt her hand on his penis, and he took a sharp inhale of breath, reminding himself of his vow not to continue the affair. "Rosalinda, I can't do this," he muttered through clenched teeth.

Her emerald gaze ran down his body, finally settling on the tent created by his arousal beneath the sheets. She gave him that mischievous smile, the same one she'd given him last night that started this entire escapade.

He bolted from the bed before it was too late and headed for the shower. Pausing in mid-stride, he spun around and said, "Rosalinda, last night was amazing, but it cannot happen again."

With a casual shrug, she said, "As you wish." She plumped the pillows before easing herself onto them, and inquired, "I need to phone someone. Is that possible?"

"Who?"

"His name is Charles Lafayette. I was to meet him thiz afternoon."

Despite himself, jealousy reared its ugly head, "Is he your boyfriend?"

"No," she replied, averting her gaze. "Charles is a movie producer from my country. He asked me to consider a screenplay he has for his next venture and wishes me to take on the lead role."

"Congratulations," Cadman grunted, "I'll see what I can arrange."

She gazed at the bathroom door as it clicked shut before covering her eyes with her palms. Cadman's question had hit her right in the gut. She wasn't romantically involved with Charles – but she was aware that he felt strongly for her. He made it so obvious every time they were together. He was always kind and genuine, his heart clearly visible on his sleeve when near her.

She had a strong affection for Charles, despite the eleven-year age difference between them. The truth was, she did not think she was good enough for him. If she were honest with herself, the real reason their relationship hadn't gone anywhere was because of her own faults: she had a wild streak, loved to go out partying, and could never manage to be faithful to someone who deserved it.

With a deep breath, she threw the blankets aside. She thought about joining Cadman in the shower, it wouldn't be difficult to convince him to give in and enjoy each other again.

Sometimes though, it was best to let things go.

To take her mind off things, Rosalinda thought about Jacqueline and where she could be. Cadman was tight-lipped when it came to telling her anything about where his friend had taken Jacqueline. He told her the less she knew, the safer Jacqueline would be, so Rosalinda did not press him for answers. However, she had noticed the strong attraction between Jacqueline and the government man and wondered how long it would be before they both finally acknowledged it.

Cadman walked into the room, looking refreshed and attractive. But his sense of responsibility had taken away from the morning's pleasure. She could see the guilt in his eyes when he got out of bed, and she internally rolled her eyes. They were both consenting adults, after all, why couldn't they indulge in each other whenever they wanted?

Occasionally, she was pleasantly surprised by men. Men who treated women with respect and not just as sexual objects. However, she could never seem to stay attracted to the good ones. She felt that if she could, she would have been wise to encourage Charles' affection a long time ago. He was the epitome of politeness and chivalry, yet it was clear he had more than romance on his mind. Even though he wanted marriage before anything else, it was still evident.

The idea of locking herself down with one man felt like far too much commitment. With so many choices in the world, why should she limit herself to just one?

She shook her head to clear her mind before turning to Cadman and asking him, "How long will I be here?".

"We'll move you to another location sometime today," Cadman said nonchalantly, as if this were a normal thing that was done all the time. In reality, it was for his own protection.

"Will I be there long?"

"That depends upon how long it takes to find Pierre and lock him away."

Her eyes widened, "You believe I am in danger?"

He gave a slight nod before speaking, "It's an idea worth considering, Rosalinda. It is clear he knew Jacqueline was with you. It wouldn't be far-fetched to think he might come after you to get his hands on her."

Now she shivered. Pierre was evil, and she did not wish to be anywhere near him, "Perhaps I should return to Paree."

Cadman gave a noncommittal shrug. "If he's really set on finding you, it doesn't matter where you run," he remarked. He nodded his head towards the bathroom door. "Go have your shower and I'll see what I can do to let you make it to your meeting with Lafayette."

* * * *

It was noon when Cadman escorted Rosalinda to a house on the outskirts of New York City at high noon. Charles was already there, conversing with a woman whom Rosalinda soon discovered to be the owner of the property.

As soon as Rosalinda appeared in the doorway, Charles got to his feet. He placed the coffee mug he had been holding aside and went to her. He asked softly, "Are you all right?" lightly brushing her arm with his fingertips.

She felt her eyes begin to water as she stared at him and wondered what it was about this man that made her heart ache. Despite her instinct to allow him to play the song he seemed to be writing upon her heartstrings, she resisted; deep down, she knew it wasn't the age gap between them that held her back. Nothing about him felt fatherly to her. His balding head, with its wisps of dark-brown hair, kindled a momentary illusion he could be someone's grandfather, but she had never viewed him as such. She yearned to embrace his broad figure and draw strength from his warmth.

Determined to remain distant from him, she sidestepped his proximity and said, "Of course, Charles. Why wouldn't I be?" She deliberately ignored the hurt that was evident in his eyes by her seemingly unaffected response. It would be crueler to give him any hope when she knew she could not offer anything more. He deserved better.

Cadman said his goodbyes, exchanged pleasantries with the woman of the house, and left without a backward glance. Another woman might have been bothered by his quick exit, especially if she had spent the night in his bed, but Rosalinda was not that type of woman. She used the man to satisfy her own desires, and that was all there was to it.

Charles closed his eyes, inhaling to steady himself, and gestured towards a chair. "Please, take a seat, Rosalinda. I brought the script with me; you are just right for the part. We will be filming in Cannes—France, of course." He smiled slightly, as if he needed to clarify.

Rosalinda's eyes lingered on his mouth, finding it incredibly attractive. She had to force herself not to reach out and touch it with her fingertips or with her lips. No! She couldn't risk hurting him. He was so good and kind; the last thing she wanted was to hurt him. Taking a few steps back, she created some distance between them.

"I have not been to Cannes in years," she said wistfully, switching to their native language of French. "Did you know my family heritage is rooted in Cannes?" Jacqueline had the same connection—their shared ancestors were buried nearby. Her eyes lit up at the memories of her youth. "My family had a villa there in Cannes," she reminisced.

His eyes sparkled mysteriously as he spoke the words, "Oui. The Vallombrosa Castle." His gaze lingered on her for a few moments, and she couldn't help but feel a sudden shiver of excitement, even though she had decided to keep her distance from him.

"I believe," Charles continued softly, "it was purchased in 1858 by Richard Manca Ama, who took the title, Duke of Vallombrosa, a title created for the House of Manca. It's an exquisite structure constructed out of pink gneiss."

Rosalinda closed her eyes to conjure up images of her childhood as she remembered the Neo-Gothic Castle with its nine towers and pepper-box turrets. Her family used to frequent the villa; though it no longer belonged to them, it held a special place in her heart due to its connection to her heritage.

She looked at him over her shoulder, "You seem to know a lot about my family's history."

He gave a casual shrug, which Rosalinda found both elegant and alluring. "Really, Rosalinda," he said, "I'm researching the Castle Vallombrosa for my next movie." He pointed to the screenplay resting on the coffee table in front of them. "For this particular film," he clarified.

For someone as skilled as she was at hiding her true feelings, the sudden intake of breath and widened eyes were a real sign of her surprise. She couldn't believe she was being granted access to such a precious family treasure. "Truly?"

His smile was amused as he gestured to the script. "Yes, I'll leave it here and you can take your time in deciding," he said, though they both knew her answer already. He saw how passionate she was, and it made him love her so much more—he could see so much in her that she had yet to discover about herself. He wanted to marry her but knew it was impossible;

she was too young, with a drive to explore that was all-consuming. Despite everything he admired about her he knew, deep down, she was not ready to love him in return.

The smile she gave him caused his heart to falter.

Taking a deep breath, she responded to him, "Thank you. I will consider it and give you my answer at the end of the week."

"That will be soon enough. Once all the rolls are cast, the filming will either begin in November or in the spring of next year."

She bid him farewell and stood for a long time in the grand sitting room, without really seeing it. Yet, as Rosalinda watched Charles leave, her heart felt like it was being dragged off with him.

Chapter Eight

Jacqueline gazed at the view visible through the passenger window as Colten steered the rental car down the highway, heading for Clarion. She had no choice but to watch the scenery. Apparently, her companion either disliked chit-chat or was angry about being forced to accompany her on the ride out of Philadelphia. She tried a few times to engage in conversation, but all she got in response were disinterested male grunts.

She should have insisted he buy her a book at that gas station they stopped at in Allentown.

Letting out a deep sigh, she tried to make conversation again. She asked Colten how he knew the name of her ancestor, whose name her parents gave her at birth for a middle name. His knuckles tightened around the steering wheel, and it was clear that he wasn't going to respond. She sighed deeply and crossed her arms over her waist, feeling just as frustrated with him as she was with this predicament.

A few miles later, he surprised her when he said, "I know the current Duke of Vallombrosa."

She looked at him and stared, "You know my cousin Tony?" He was a distant cousin; how many times removed, she could not remember. Saying cousin made the relationship easier to understand.

He nodded and then asked a question of his own. "How much of his family, his immediate families," he clarified, "history do you know?"

She raised a brow. This was interesting. Colten appeared as though he would continue with this line of conversation.

"Enough to know he's the only surviving grandchild of the family and that the line will probably die out with him. I do not believe he will ever marry."

Under his breath, Colten agreed, but not loud enough for his passenger to have heard. His opinion of the man was that he was a strange duck.

"What?"

He shook his head, "Nothing. Anyway, as I was saying, what do you know of his grandparents?"

She looked confused, "Which side of the family?"

Impatiently he said, "Vallombrosa."

"Oh...kay," she rolled her eyes. "His grandfather, Antoine-Amédée-Marie-Vincent Manca Amat de Vallombrosa, Marquis de Morès et de Mon-temaggiore, was the oldest son of Riccardo, or Don Richard if you prefer, Count of San-Giorgio, Baron of Tiesi, Tisse, Ossi, second Duke of Vallombrosa, fourth Duke of Asinara and..."

He snapped, "Enough!"

She shrugged, "You asked how much I knew."

"For the love of Mike."

He ran a hand through his hair in his frustration, "Okay, let's narrow the history lesson down. What do you know of their time in the western frontier?"

She took a moment to search her memory. "It was the early 1880s when Tony's grandfather, Antoine, decided to try his luck in the American West. Somewhere in North Dakota, he founded a town and named it after his wife, Medora." She leaned in closer as if speaking in confidence. "I'm from the other side of the family - Medora's mother was a Grymes, from America, but their blood is not so strong in my line anymore."

She waved that away, knowing he would probably explode if she went down that road of heritage, "It is a romantic story, and tragic, too."

Quietly he told her, "My grandfather worked for them."

Ladylike or not, her jaw dropped. "Really?"

He nodded, "During their time in North Dakota. He mentions them often."

"Mentioned," she corrected his grammar.

He gave her a questioning look before quickly moving his eyes back to the road ahead.

"You said mentions. Mentioned would be past tense."

He let out a short laugh and said, "Is that the teacher in you speaking? Sorry to let you down, but I did use the right grammar. Grandpa's still alive." At least Colten hoped he was. Damn, he wanted that vacation to see for himself how Howard was getting along.

Jacqueline stared at him for half a mile before she could find her tongue, "But... he would be..."

"Ancient," he said with a grin that made her heart skip a beat. She couldn't deny it—the man had an attractive smile. "He was seventeen years old back then and is turning ninety-six this month. Yet incredibly, he just keeps on going."

It amazed her that she was having this conversation, "It would be so interesting to speak with him about them." More than that, it was mesmerizing. History becomes real when you hear it through the voice of someone who experienced it, and she treasured her family's legacy. She had been researching her genealogy for a long time. It piqued her interest more when she discovered the relations between her Grymes and Vallombrosa ancestors with significant figures.

Jacqueline's mind swam with new information when she learned not long ago about Medora's maternal grandmother. Her name was Susanna, also known as Suzette, Bosque Grymes. She had been the third wife of William C. C. Claiborne, the first American Governor of Louisiana, and also his widow. To further add to the intrigue, her grandfather, John Randolph Grymes, had served as United States Attorney for Louisiana and acted as Andrew Jackson's personal counsel during the Battle of New Orleans.

Medora was named after her maternal aunt, who had been the second wife of Samuel Ward—the Washington lobbyist whose sister composed The Battle Hymn of the Republic. Sam's first wife had been Emily Astor, whom Jacqueline was very familiar with. She wondered why she hadn't given the Sancy diamond back to the Astors instead of mailing it off to Digger. In hindsight, the decision seemed foolish, but sometimes people make bad decisions in stressful moments.

Colten looked at her curiously, "You like history?"

She shrugged, "Mostly family history, but yes, I enjoy learning about the past. It's important to remember the people who lived and died; to honor them by not repeating their mistakes."

"Are you a philosopher, Miss Grymes?" he teased.

She laughed and shook her head, "Now, tell me about my ancestor's time in North Dakota."

So, he did. As the miles went by, he recounted the stories his grandfather shared about the Marquis de Morès and his failed business ventures in Medora, North Dakota. "But now," Colten concluded, "there is a man with his own ambition for the town of Medora. He wants to rebuild it and turn it into a tourist destination. There is more than just de Morès' legacy—once upon a time, Theodore Roosevelt lived there, too. It is a known fact Roosevelt said, 'I would not have been President had it not been for my experience in North Dakota'."

"Perhaps one day I will visit the town of Medora," Jacqueline said and realized she wanted to see it. It would be enjoyable to walk on the same ground as her ancestors and feel what they might have felt, to be so far away from their family and friends.

The prospect of Jacqueline coming to Medora made him feel things he had no desire to admit. "You know," he said, as the car slowed for an exit sign indicating 'Clarion 10 miles', "de Morès built a 26-room hunting lodge overlooking the town. After Medora's passing in 1921, it was given to Louis, Tony's father. He donated it to the state of North Dakota in 1936 with the condition that they keep it open as a museum."

Her eyes widened, "It is still there?"

He nodded, "Yep. It's in great condition, too, since the Civilian Conservation Corps restored it from 1937 to 1941."

"Colten, must we go to Clarion? The diamond can wait. I want to see the chateau!"

The way her accent spoke his name always seemed to make his heart skip, but he ruthlessly pushed the feeling away. Instead, he raised a brow and frowned at her. As much as he liked the idea of her being in his domain, they had a duty, and that meant recovering the diamond first.

He forced himself to sound annoyed as he said, "I can't believe you'd even suggest such a thing! That diamond is..."

"Colten, it was only a joke!" Her gentle voice brought out a red tinge to his cheekbones that she was finding endearing.

He coughed. "I knew that" he asserted.

She grinned at him, making the blush deepen further.

* * * *

The Davidson's split-level home was on a quiet residential street of Victorian townhouses. "Nice place," Colten said, stepping from the car and moving to her side to open the door for her.

"Yes, it is. It is elegant."

Colten shook his head at the horse-shit-green paint job covering the house. The color of the paint was not flattering, he thought. But kept his opinion to himself.

He and Jacqueline made their way up the sidewalk towards the front door. Before they reached it, an abnormal but still fast running boy emerged from within, and he barreled toward Jacqueline before Colten had the opportunity to process what was happening.

The shape of his eyes, coupled with the space between his upper and lower lids, were key features among those living with Down syndrome. It didn't require a lightning bolt for Colten to work out this was Grant Davidson.

"Miss Jackie," Grant gushed slowly, his words slightly off because of his somewhat protruding and oversized tongue, "I saw you! I saw you... in the car! I told mom... you were here."

Jacqueline bent down to his level and gave him a gentle hug. "I have missed you, my dear friend," she said and kissed him on the cheek.

Colten noticed the boy wiping away the kiss she had given him, then patting his chest over his heart. "Guess he didn't like that," he said, but watched with interest as Jacqueline welcomed the boy with openness and understanding, acting like nothing was unusual about him.

Grant smiled up at him, "I like... Miss Jack-ie's kisses. I put them... in my heart where... I can keep them... forever."

Colten stared, a funny ache forming in his own heart at the clear and honest answer.

"Grant, this is my friend, Mr. Fisher. He brought me here to see you. Wasn't that nice of him?"

Grant regarded Colten with complete adoration. Anyone who would bring Miss Jackie to him had his undying devotion, but Colten felt more than a little uncomfortable to suddenly be the kid's soul focus.

"Ah... hi," Colten said with uncertainty. Then, not knowing what else to do, he stuck out his hand like he would when meeting an adult.

Grant wasn't having any of that. He suddenly grabbed Colten by the legs and held on tight. "Thank you,... Mr. Fish... er!" He gazed up at Colten, "Are you... Miss Jackie's boy... friend?"

The adults' eyes collided with shock and embarrassment. "No!" they said in unison.

Grant grinned.

"Come... in!" the boy said, taking each of their hands, he pulled them toward the house where a woman was waiting in the door's opening.

"Welcome, Jacqueline," Linda Davidson beamed.

Grant looked at his mother. "This is Mr. Fish... er," he leaned toward his mother to whisper, but his voice carried regardless. "He is not Miss... Jackie's boy,... friend."

Linda's lips twitched as she witnessed Jacqueline blush. The stranger's skin over his cheekbones took on a reddish hue. "Oh?" she looked down at her son. "Should we let him in the house, anyway?"

To Colten's amazement, Grant looked as though he was seriously considering the matter. "Okay," the boy said and walked into the house.

Linda ushered them upstairs to the living room. "Would you like anything? Coffee?" Linda asked, motioning them to have a seat on one of the reclining chairs near the sofa.

"Thank you, oui. I would like that," Jacqueline looked to Colten to see if he would like some as well.

"Sure, that would be great. Thanks."

As Linda went into the kitchen to prepare a pot, Grant brought Jacqueline a sketch pad and handed it to her, "I have more... pictures, Miss... Jackie."

Jacqueline took the pad. "Do you?" she smiled up at him. "Come, sit next to me and show me."

The boy beamed and complied, "I drew this... one yestur... day." He flipped the book to the last used page. "I was... thinking of you... and God... brought you... to me. I should... have drew... it sooner!" He grinned up at her.

Tears formed in Jacqueline's eyes as she gazed at the image on the page, "Grant, it is beautiful." But really, it was more than beauty - far beyond what mere words could express.

Colten mentally shook his head. He could not see the sketch from where he sat, but he doubted he could have pretended to like something a kid like that had drawn. But he would try, so he cleared his throat and asked, "What is it?"

Jacqueline looked up, her eyes still wet with unshed tears, and studied Colten. It made her angry to see that he thought the drawing would be of poor quality, all because of Grant's disabilities. People were so quick to judge someone who had a disability, as if they didn't deserve to live in the world.

She felt Grant move off the couch to show Colten the drawing, but she stopped him, "Wait, Grant." She looked at Colten, "Have you ever spent time with someone who struggles physically or mentally?"

The challenge in her voice irritated him. His request to see the drawing had been an innocent one, yet here he was being interrogated. Her expression made him feel like some sort of beast. "Yes," he replied sharply through clenched teeth, feeling as if he could grind them down to the gums any minute.

Her laugh, a skeptical one if he ever heard one, went up his spine and grated on his nerves, "Obviously, not enough time."

Colten grasped at the chair's armrests, wishing he could lash out at her. Her words were true, and they resonated with him in a way he couldn't ignore. "My son," he said slowly, deliberately, "has autism."

Jacqueline's body jerked as though he physically punched her. The seconds passed by; they stared at one another without either knowing what to say.

"Grant," Jacqueline said at last, softly, taking her eyes off Colten to look at the child, "I think you can show Mr. Fisher the drawing now."

The boy, innocent as any other child of eight, hadn't a clue there was tension between the adults. He beamed as he walked to Colten and handed him the sketchpad.

Colten barely looked at the offer before quickly looking back at Jacqueline in an effort to keep his composure. When he did finally drag his eyes down to the drawing, he was taken aback. Rather than seeing simple doodles, there was a stunning pencil sketch of Jacqueline sitting in a meadow, with shades of black and white blended together to create an image. Whatever the image of her was looking toward it held her gaze, aimed off into what looked like a haze—maybe it was a mist or maybe it could be a horse and rider. Whatever it was, Grant had created a convincing illusion that almost seemed real enough for

Colten to reach out and try to touch. The likeness of Jacqueline was uncanny.

He tore his eyes away before he became lost in the drawing and found the flesh and blood person looking at him as though he were on display under a microscope.

Softly she told him, "Never underestimate someone different from you or me."

He got up and walked out the door.

Linda Davidson returned to the room, handed Jacqueline a coffee cup, and set the other one on the table next to the now-abandoned chair. "I believe my Grant has shocked your Mr. Fisher."

Absently, Jacqueline nodded her head. Colten had a son. That fact kept playing over in her mind. If he had a son, obviously, he had a wife. Her heart thundered in her ears. The connection she felt for him had been strong and now it felt as though her world shattered, which was ridiculous because they had only just met. They were strangers, not lovers but she felt the ache in her heart and pushed it away. They would never be lovers because she would never sleep with another woman's husband.

But what of the son? To her, Colten's angry reply was a clear indication he had yet to come to terms with the situation. He was stuck on outdated ideas about people who were handicapped. Many of them could do the same things as their able-bodied counterparts: working, cooking, living a fulfilling life. It was individuals like Colten - isolating those with disabilities from everyone else - that perpetuated this narrow-minded view of the world. Jacqueline believed that if disabled kids were accepted in regular public schools, it would help others understand them better and create a sense of community.

It seemed an impossible dream because, sadly, even the blacks continued to fight for their place in this world. Jacqueline couldn't comprehend why something as superficial as skin color mattered so much. People were equal in her eyes; they should be judged and treated based on who they were and not what they looked like.

Knowing it was only a dream that people could one day respect each other, she sighed and answered Linda's statement, "Oui, I think Mr. Fisher has had a shock, but I believe he needed a good jolt." She glanced at Grant. "Let me see your other sketches," and she began slowly flipping through the other works that were quality enough to be showcased.

Chapter Nine

Colten traveled through the streets of Clarion, unsure of how long or far he'd gone. It was difficult to get lost in such a small town, but he wished he could disappear. If a hole suddenly opened in the ground, Colten could remove himself from his own self-loathing. Coming to terms with being wrong was like going through hell.

When his wife died during childbirth, the grief nearly consumed him. He drank himself into a two-month long stupor to numb the pain. His parents had to take his newborn son from the hospital; Colten was in no shape to bring him home. Caroline's family hadn't wanted Clinton at all.

Once he sobered up, having no clue what to do with a newborn, his mother stepped in. Because his parents had taken care of the boy for the first months of his life, Colten saw no reason to remove his son from his parent's home. Besides, by Clinton's first birthday, Colten had already been off to Washington, his application to the Secret Service approved. He made the trip back to North Dakota as often as allowed, spending time with his son. In the early years, he tried to swallow his anger; blaming Clinton for Caroline's death wasn't right. Colten knew that, but the underlying need to blame someone was there. The truth of it was; Caroline's heart had been weak. She might have lived longer if she had not gotten pregnant, but she wanted children, and so had he. Selfishness never turned out right in the long run. Had he been stronger, insisted they remain childless, Caroline might still be on this earth.

He settled onto a bench in the park he wandered into. Taking off his hat, he ran his fingers through his hair before placing it back on his head. He stared at the deserted playground without really seeing it. Or perhaps he did because his thoughts turned to Clinton.

The boy had been three years old when Colten's father phoned him in Washington with the news. Closing his eyes, holding back the tears of self-disgust, he remembered his reaction when he was told his child had autism.

Colten did something then, which surprised him, but it came from the depths of his heart as he vowed to himself to become a better father to Clinton. The boy deserved love, not blame and rejection. When this assignment was over, Colten would head to North Dakota and be the parent he should have been from the beginning.

Two hours passed before Colten made his way back to the Davidson's home. He said little once he entered the house, except to ask Grant to show him his room and other drawings he had, which were plentiful. Grant's primary passion in life was art.

As evening neared, Colten and Jacqueline accepted Linda's invitation to a homemade supper of mashed potatoes, green salad, and sizzling stakes grilled on the patio. Although Colten took part in the conversation, Jacqueline could sense his reluctance to do so. He seemed withdrawn, and she wished she knew how to help him through whatever dilemma he was facing. Which was ridiculous since he was not hers to comfort.

After they cleared the dishes, Jacqueline brought up why they were there without giving away details, "Have you seen Uncle Digger recently?"

Gary Davidson, Linda's husband, sat back in the chair he occupied, finished the beer he had been drinking, and smiled, "Digger? Jackie, you must be joking. It's not the end of the month. You know he holds up there until then. It's like clock-work. He'll show up when he's ready and not a moment be-fore."

Colten leaned back in the wicker chair and said, "Jacqueline told me a little about him. We thought we'd make the trip to his place and visit."

Gary shrugged, "He might like that. Not many people take the time to see him since the only way to get to his place is on horseback." He shook his head and chuckled, "He's a complete recluse, that brother of mine. But he sure took a shine to Jackie. Must be their mutual love of horses." He winked at Jacqueline. "You impressed him that time we made the trip up there, your first summer here. Impressed me, too for that matter, but I wasn't raised near horses like you were."

When he turned his gaze on her, Colten's stare was full of questions and held no small amount of surprise.

"My family," she told Colten, "breeds Arabians. I am afraid I caused my mother's hair to gray early. From the moment I could walk, I was always with the horses." She suddenly laughed, a sound like a wind chime blowing in the wind and a sound Colten found enticing. "When I was six," she told the group, "I wanted to be a trick rider. When my mother saw me standing on the back of my horse as it trotted around the arena, I believe she came close to having a heart attack."

Colten could almost picture Jacqueline being daredevil enough as a child to do just that. A lady who had the guts to stick a loaded gun into a man's belly would undoubtedly have the courage to attempt just about anything.

He looked at his watch. It was getting late, and they needed to go. "Thanks for the meal, Linda," he said, rising. "But it's time we call it a night."

"Anytime," Linda began, but stopped to look at Jacqueline, "I just remembered something. Excuse me, I'll be right back."

It did not take long for her to return. She carried a box and handed it to Jacqueline, "I believe these are yours. I found them in the back of the closet, in your old room."

Jacqueline looked into the open box and smiled. "My riding clothes!" she laughed. Surprised and pleased to have them. "I was not sure how I would manage on horseback in a dress." Whoever provided her with the small wardrobe at the hotel room last night did not include trousers.

Once back in the vehicle Jacqueline settled into her seat and shut her eyes, feeling exhausted. "At least we'll have separate rooms tonight," she mentioned to Colten as he slid into the driver's seat. She sighed in relief at the prospect of laying out in a cozy bed and getting a good night's rest.

"No."

Her eyes flew open, "What?" She turned her head and stared at him.

He eased the car into the street, "One room."

She shook her head, "You cannot be serious! We are miles away from Pierre. I am not in any danger here."

"We don't know that, and I promised Cadman I would protect you."

Ridiculous, she thought, and that had her saying, "Does your wife approve of your sleeping in motel rooms with other women?" She was sorry for it. Sorry to have caused his mood to sour once more. But damn it, finding out he had a son had to mean he was married. The direct hit she had taken to her heart devastated her, regardless of the fact it was ludicrous, this attraction she had for this man she just met.

His body tensed. His hands tightened on the steering wheel. A muscle ticked in his jaw as he clamped it down, telling himself not to snap out. But it didn't work because when his mouth opened, his words were ice, "Caroline's dead. It's been seven years since she cared what I do."

Jacqueline had no response to that. One moment she opened her mouth to say something, anything, to comfort, then she would close it, because what could she say? The man had deep scars far below the surface.

He pulled the car into the parking lot of a nicer place than the dive they stayed in last night. That, at least, was something to be thankful for. He parked, exited the vehicle, retrieved their bags from the backseat, and strolled up the walk toward the motel's office at an angry clip. For once, he did not bother to play the gentleman and open her door.

She sat there, stunned and feeling horrible for having responded to his irritation with her own.

Suddenly her door was thrown open. A yelp formed on her lips as her body jumped. But when she saw Colten standing there, looking grim, she managed to push the sound back down her throat.

"Are you coming?" he inquired in an angry hiss.

She did not dare refuse.

The motel room was indeed more beautiful than the one from the previous night, with luxurious plush carpet the color of creamed wheat. Within the space was a dresser drawer for clothing if one would spend over one night and wanted to unpack during their stay. There were two nightstands on either side of the bed, and a small television on a stand at the foot of the bed. There was also a small table with two chairs next to it.

Resting in the center of that table was a complimentary bottle of wine.

Jacqueline had to smile at that. Obviously, the wine had been placed there while they were being checked in. It was cradled comfortably in a bucket of ice, and she was glad it was because right now, she could use something to calm her nerves.

Then she glanced at the queen-size bed and felt heat rising, warming her face. It occurred to her what the desk clerk might imagine Colten and she would do in this room, and she thought she might drink the entire bottle so she could fall asleep quickly.

"I'll sleep on the floor this time," he said, as though reading her thoughts.

Regardless of her personal embarrassment, she heard herself say, "You don't have to. We could both use a good night's rest, and believe me, I do not think this floor is any more comfortable than the one in the last place."

He studied her for a moment, glanced at the bed, and then met those blue, blue eyes head-on, "I don't think that would be a good idea."

She wasn't naïve, but something reflecting in his eyes sliced through her heart. She wanted to comfort. The sorrow in them he hadn't been able to hide from her fast enough almost made her cry. Gently, she reached out and touched his arm, "Colten...."

"Don't pity me," his voice boomed, and she jumped. Tearing her hand away, he strolled toward the bathroom.

"I do not pity you!" she exclaimed, and it was the gospel truth. He frustrated and confused her, but she certainly did not pity him. He managed to bring her own temper out, and she let it shoot from her mouth, "Why would I do that when you obviously have enough disappointment in yourself?"

He spun back, eyes flashing flames that nearly singed. God! They had not known each other more than twenty-eight hours, and yet she hit a bullseye with the first shot. Ever since meeting Grant Davidson, he'd been cursing himself for selfishly leaving Clinton and not giving his son a chance. The time he spent with Grant nearly buckled him. The child was loving and giving and so animated it caused him a chuckle or two just watching him.

Unknowingly, Grant had already slipped into his heart. But anger at Jacqueline for pointing out his shortcomings had him turning away, removing his cowboy hat, and launching it toward the bed. With a shaking hand, he combed fingers through his collar-length, sun-kissed, medium-brown hair and fought for calm.

"Look," he said after a moment, "I'm sorry. I shouldn't have snapped at you." He glanced at her. She was still standing in the center of the room regarding him, which he couldn't blame her for being leery. It wasn't as though he'd sounded friendly when he'd gritted out that sorry excuse for an apology.

She licked her lips, unsure now. She felt if she said anything, he would probably lash out. He was coiled tight, his body taut. What she wanted to do was to wrap her arms around him and hold him close. Instead, she walked to the black and white television and turned it on. Slowly, the tube came to life, and there was James Drury, in his starring role as The Virginian, acting out a scene in the make-believe world of Shiloh Ranch, Medicine Bow, Wyoming.

Sensing his eyes on her, she moved to the table where the wine rested. Without a word, she uncorked the bottle, poured each of them a glass, and held one out to him.

"Perhaps this will help."

He folded his arms over his chest, "Trying to get me drunk so you can have your way with me?"

She would not let him bait her into an argument. He'd had a shock today, seeing Grant's level of artistic ability, despite having Down syndrome. Whatever was between Colten and his son, it had given him a jolt. And right now, she sensed he needed a listening ear. Perhaps he was too proud to admit it to himself, but she refused to acknowledge his insinuation.

Because he did not reach for the glass, she took a sip of it herself and tried not to grimace. It certainly was not the rich and flavorful French wines she was accustomed to. Probably American, she thought uncharitably. She glanced at the label and knew she was snobbish when it came to her country's ability to create masterpieces from grapes.

Without a word, she sat down at the table and turned her attention to the television drama playing out. A moment passed with only the voices of the actors on-screen filling the otherwise silent room.

Colten moved forward, took the glass of wine from her hand, and took more than the sip she had. Picking up the bottle, he refilled the glass then sat in the adjoining chair. "Quarter horses are better," he said.

Her eyes snapped to his, "Excuse me?" Where on earth had that statement come from?

He leaned back in the chair, raised his leg, and crossed his heel over the knee of his other leg, "Your family breeds Arabians. The quarter horse is the best horse there is."

She stared at him. All right, if he wanted to change the subject and argue over horses, she would let him for now. With a shake of her head, she disagreed, "Arabians are more elegant and graceful."

He nodded. He would give Jacqueline that. But from where he came from, the stockier quarter horse had better footing, "But Arabians are known for being hot-tempered and spirited."

She laughed. That gentle chime wrapped around Colten's heart, "Are you afraid of a spirited horse, Mr. Fisher?"

He studied her. Perhaps a conversation about horses wasn't the best idea. He found himself reaching out to touch her cheek, trailing a finger down her face and lingering at her lips. "It depends," he murmured, "if the horse is female."

She closed her eyes, a sigh escaping through her lips. At that moment, Colten moved in and kissed her; a sweet, slow, lingering kiss that had moisture gathering behind her eyes. There had never been a man in her life who had such complex emotions, nor had anyone ever kissed her like this. It was as though a butterfly had landed, its silky wings softly rubbing her flesh. It made her shiver and, yes, brought forth the want to do more than sleep in that bed with him, regardless of them being practically strangers.

Colten eased back on a shaky laugh and ran his hand through his hair, "That wasn't a good idea either." Why he was drawn to her in this way, he could not answer. But he was, and that meant trouble with a capital T. Perhaps he should request a separate room, but then he wouldn't be keeping watch for any danger that might lurk for her beyond the walls. But, he wondered, who would protect her from the danger of him?

Her eyes opened; those soft blue eyes, now hazed over with passion, tore a groan from him. Knowing what was right and what was wrong would not play out in this. He knew it. Perhaps she did, too, because she was still looking at him as though she expected more. He had not had a woman in quite some time, and not one that seemed to crawl under his skin in ways Caroline never had.

He stood, pulled her up with him, and crushed his lips to hers in a devouring storm of crashing waves and lightning heat.

Jacqueline gasped his name as he moved them toward the bed. Her mind told her no, but her body disagreed with the command. If that made her a woman of no morals, so be it. She didn't care. The only desire she had was to feel his skin next to hers.

Her knees hit the bed, and she went down. He followed without breaking away, and their hands tore at buttons and skimmed across the flesh being revealed as they stripped away the layers. They were of one mind, one thought.

This had to be, and it had to be now.

Her hands reached up, ran through his thick mass of hair, usually covered most of the time by his Stetson, and anchored his mouth to hers.

Clothing was tossed hastily in every direction, in their eagerness to have nothing between them. When there was only flesh against flesh, their hands explored as though trying to memorize the other, cherishing the feel and textures they discovered.

"Colten..." she sighed when he nuzzled her throat. He did not know if it was a protest, sigh, or acceptance, though he didn't really care. He had one goal. Just one.

His hand moved down to the junction between her legs, cupping her, massaging, and she almost jettisoned straight up at the sensations he caused with his stroking fingers. "My God!" she cried. A chain of words he could only assume were French flowed through her lips as moisture formed on his hand.

He crushed his mouth to hers as he entered her. That soft, velvety heat nearly undid him. My God, she had said, and oh yes, she'd nailed it right on the head. He couldn't seem to get enough of her. All too soon, she was keening, her body arching as she convulsed around him. It undid him. He thrust once, twice, and on the third reentry, he erupted.

When the last of the tremors subsided, he rolled off her but brought her close, tucking her to his side with a tenderness he hadn't known he had.

Her hand came up to rest on his chest. He covered it with his, refusing to think beyond this moment and let sleep take him.

Chapter Ten

It was past nine the next morning when they woke. Colten had planned on starting the trip to the National Forest much earlier than that. But Jacqueline needed her sleep. He had been a selfish bastard last night, using Jacqueline three more times to sate his desire for her.

He told himself it was only lust he felt for her and nothing else. He was not looking for a long-term relationship with her nor anyone else. He had that once, and once was enough.

He looked at her as she slept, admiring the features of her face and lingering on her lips. Why did they remind him of someone? He couldn't recall who it was, but he knew her beauty and kind heart could wreak havoc on him if he let himself get too close. He would keep his distance. What happened last night was sex and nothing more.

He glanced at his watch, resting on the nightstand where he placed it at some point during the night. He calculated and made the decision before he changed his mind. Rolling off the bed, he reached for his pants. He was just sliding them over his hips when she said, "Good morning."

He grunted. He was not about to give Jacqueline any reason to hope for a future with him. Women liked declarations of love and commitment in the morning after sex. He did not have those to offer, nor would he lie. He grabbed his shirt, put it on, and began tucking it into the waistband of his jeans, "Why don't you go take a shower? I have something I need to do. When I get back, we'll find a place to eat and then head out." He walked toward the door and ignored the look of hurt he saw in her eyes when he skimmed over her face.

Closing the door behind him, he made his way down the stairs to the front desk. The little old man manning the station greeted him with an overly cheery good morning.

"Got a phone I can use?" Colten asked.

The guy adjusted his glasses before they slipped off his nose, "Well, now, will it be local or long distance?"

"Long distance."

"Over there," he said, jerking his head toward a phone booth in the lobby's corner. "Need any change?"

"Yeah," Colten pulled out his wallet, handed the guy some bills, and received the change in a mountain of coins. Scooping it up, he settled into the booth. Picking up the receiver, he dialed the operator. He gave the woman the number he wanted to connect to, slid the proper amount of coinage into the slot, and waited for the connection to be made.

After what seemed like forever but was not long at all, a sleepy voice picked-up, "Doctor Fisher's residence. This had better be an emergency. It's not even eight o'clock in the damn morning."

"Thaddeus," Colten smiled into the phone. His twelve-year-old brother would be in horrific trouble if their mother knew how he just answered the phone. Especially had it been an emergency call from the Bismarck Hospital for their dad. "Kid, you got a stick up your butt?"

"Colt?!" his brother whooped. "Where are you? We got the word you couldn't come home." He lowered his voice conspiringly, "Are you undercover?"

Colten rolled his eyes. Only Thaddeus would dare ask the question. "Are mom and dad home?" he asked instead.

"Well, hell, Colt. Where do you think they are? They happen to be sleeping. Dad had a late shift at the hospital. I guess some poor guy had an accident on Main, about eleven last night. And dad spent four hours stitching him back up. Mom, well, you know mom. She...,"

"Thaddeus!" he boomed, cutting his brother's ramblings off. "Just get one of them on the phone."

"You don't have to go ape on me," Thaddeus grumbled just before Colten heard the receiver dropped, literally, onto the table it was near.

He had to plunk more change into the coin slot while he waited. If Thaddeus didn't make it quick, he would need to get more coins to complete the call before it began.

"Hello? Colten Marshal Fisher, is this really you, or is my youngest playing a joke on me?"

Colten chuckled. "It's me, mom," he confirmed. God, it was great to hear his mother's voice. He made the conversation quick. He didn't have that much time nor change left. Just before he hung up, he asked the main question on his mind. "How's Clinton, mom?" and heard his mother gasp. He had never asked about his son since specialists diagnosed him with autism, and yes, it made him a horrible human being, but Colten was sorry for the past and wanted to redeem himself. He was ready to move forward. Once this was over, Jacqueline safe, and Pierre locked behind bars, he was going home to be a father to the child he abandoned.

God help him.

When he hung up the phone, he was feeling pretty good about himself. He had made the first step toward mending bridges.

Before going back to the motel room, he stopped by the desk once more to ask where a good place to eat breakfast was and, after receiving the information, whistled a merry tune on his way up the steps, to the second floor, to room 205.

Inserting the key, he turned the lock, opened the door, and got a fist in the face.

"What the hell?!" he exclaimed, his hand flying to his mouth and came away with blood on the fingertips.

"Fils de salope!" Jacqueline hissed, shaking her hand. Hitting his face, though satisfying on a personal level, had hurt like hell. But it did not stop her continued rant. French phrases that would have had Colten's cheekbones turning red with embarrassment if he understood what she was saying shot from her mouth as she shouted at him.

When she picked up the half-empty wine bottle from the night before, the intent clear enough in her eyes, Colten leaped forward and grabbed it before she could launch it.

"Settle down!" he yelled, barely avoiding her knee coming up, aiming directly at his crotch. "God all mighty!" he put the bottle back on the table, grabbed her arms with both hands, and spun her around, pinning her against the wall.

"Let go of me!"

"Not until you tell me what in the hell is wrong with you."

She struggled against his grip, unable to move from his grasp. Fury coursed through her veins. How could he have made love to her like she was the most valuable thing in the world last night, then act as if nothing had happened between them the next day?

"What in the hell is wrong with you?" he repeated, his voice sharp. He almost shook her but refrained from doing so.

She made an unladylike snort, "If you do not know, then you are stupid."

He spun her back around to face him, "Then, I'm stupid. Because I don't have a clue as to why you punched me."

Damn the moisture she felt gathering behind her eyes. It was the one female emotion she hated, the ready tears that could come to the surface when they were not wanted.

His hands came up to cup her face. A thumb brushed away a tear that escaped her lashes while his heart squeezed tight. He realized he did not like seeing her cry, especially when, deep down, Colten suspected he caused them. "Don't cry," he whispered.

She tried to jerk free, but he held her tight. "Talk to me, honey," he heard himself say. "I can't help if you don't tell me what's wrong."

Her eyes narrowed. "What is wrong?!" her voice hitched, her accent becoming stronger and more pronounced in her upset. "You made love to me last night, and this morning you treat me as though I were a whore! A slut you paid to sleep with you last night!"

His eyes widened. "I did no such thing!" and yet his mind was nasty enough to tell him, "Oh yes. You did." Loved her and left her without having the decency to respond to her words of good morning.

She attempted to free herself once again, and once again, he held her firm. "Oh?" she said. "And earlier, you did not walk out the door as though you did not expect me to be here when you came back, or without a simple good morning?"

"Well, excuse me," he snarled, refusing to give in to the guilt, "I will not say things I don't mean. If you expected me to get all mushy and tell you flowery words, you're going to be waiting a long, long time. Last night was sex," he ignored her body's jerked response, "nothing more than that."

She raised her foot, brought it straight down his tibia, and dug her heel into his foot.

He yelped, released her, and danced around the room on one foot as he nursed the injured area with one hand, "Holy Jesus Christ!"

Smiling with satisfaction, she told him with a voice boding no-nonsense, "Do not touch me again, Mr. Fisher." She wiped the moisture from her eyes. Anger did wonders to close tear ducts. "Since last night meant nothing, neither do you," she spun and walked toward the bathroom. "I cannot wait until this is over, and I will not be forced to be in your company any longer."

"That makes two of us, sister!" he yelled as the door closed with a solid thud.

He hobbled to the bed, sat down, and brought his heel onto his knee to better rub the wound. God, the woman knew how to hurt a man. Maybe he deserved her anger, but damn it, that last move of hers had hurt like hell, and then some.

He would probably have a black and blue mark for weeks.

Chapter Eleven

They arrived on the outskirts of Allegheny National Forest in a little under two hours. Before leaving Clarion they ate brunch in a nice ma-and-pa diner that served pancakes, scrambled eggs, and mugs of coffee that never seemed to go empty. It was a homey atmosphere, reminding customers of their growing-up years with a house full of noisy siblings and mom at the stove, cooking up a meal for her brood while dad sat at the table and read the newspaper. Except in this diner, it was pa behind the scenes, whipping up the batter, and ma in a light blue waitress uniform, with a small white apron attached to it, hustling from table to table, taking orders and refilling the coffee. The couple seemed competent and determined. Their eight-year-old daughter was the star of the day when she walked into the diner with a stray kitten dangling from her arms and asked her frazzled mother, "Can I keep him?" as the woman was trying to take an order from a group of six.

The mother, Angela Stevens, sighed and shook her head, "No, Tabitha. Not that one either."

"You never let me keep them!" the girl wailed.

Taking a deep breath, and appearing to silently count to ten, Mrs. Stevens told the child they had to stop somewhere. It seemed the child brought home every stray animal she found, whether it was a dog, cat, squirrel, mouse, or anything else in between.

Defeated, the child hung her head and turned to go. But she was not quite finished yet. Determined to find a home for the cat, she marched up to the booth Jacqueline and Colten shared, oblivious to the tension between the two adults, and said, "Excuse me, ma'am." She looked directly into Jacqueline's eyes, pleading with such a crestfallen face Jacqueline's heart squeezed a fraction as the child asked, "Would you like a kitten?"

Colten, the man of many words, said, "No."

Undaunted, the child turned her sad hound-dog look on him, "He wouldn't be any trouble, mister."

Colten felt himself softening as she sucked him into those huge, amber-colored eyes of hers. He had one fleeting thought, which was to feel sorry for the poor sucker she fell in love with when she was older. That expression and killer eyes would be the death of any man. Fortunately, she was quite a few years away from maturity. She hadn't perfected the fledgling gaze yet, or Colten knew he would have probably been a goner. "Sorry, kid. We have no place for a cat."

He thought that would be the end of the conversation, but the child squared her shoulders, as though she were a salesperson ready to hawk the goods and began the sales pitch. "Don't like cat's mister? Not a problem. I've got all sorts of animals you can have...."

"Tabitha!"

Her mother's voice was like the crack of a whip. It caused the child to jerk to a halt as though the parent had struck her.

"I'm sorry," Mrs. Steven's apologized to the couple, and with a stern look to her daughter, said, "Out. Now. Put the fleabag back where you got it."

"It's not a fleabag! It's a Himalayan."

The mother closed her eyes, visibly fighting for calm.

Jacqueline felt sorry for the mother and admiration for the child. The girl was undoubtedly an advocate for animals. "Little one, the kitten is beautiful, and if it were possible, I would dearly love to take it with me," she silenced Colten with a look. "However, I am not from this country, and when my stay here is over, I will return to France. Your poor kitten could not come with me."

The girl's shoulders slumped again, but her eyes slid toward Colten with enough sorrow in them to melt a glacier and he knew a skilled advocate in the making when he saw one. It impressed him enough to say, "You know, I might know someone who'd like a cat." He leaned back into the booth and marveled at the words that had just come out of his mouth - he couldn't believe what he was about to do. But the idea popped into his mind, and he was determined to see it through. Looking at Mrs. Stevens, he asked, "Mind if I use your phone?"

Angela Stevens was wringing her hands, "You don't have to do that."

Colten waved the comment aside and slid from the booth. He wove his way toward the wall where a payphone hung and dialed a number he had only obtained the night before. Within minutes, with the cat in hand, he and Jacqueline were back in the car and backtracking to the Davidson's.

Jacqueline watched from the car as Colten handed the wiggling kitten over to Grant. She just couldn't figure him out; earlier she wanted to throttle him, but now all she wanted was to embrace and thank him. Before Tabitha had arrived at their booth in the diner, they had not been speaking. However, when the little girl rushed up to them, Colten surprised Jacqueline by offering the kitten to Grant.

She closed her eyes, rubbed at them with the heels of her hands, and told herself the burning in them was because she was tired. Last night had been like no other in a man's arms. Not that she had much experience in that area of life. She could count on three fingers the number of times she was with a man sexually, and Colten Fisher was the third. She was not looking for any relationship before their unexpected introduction, but from the moment she opened that door on Rosalinda's hotel room and came face to face with the man currently speaking to Grant and gently stroking a kitten, she had been smitten.

She never believed in love at first sight until it happened to her. But she knew deep down it was foolish to feel that way when the man was not interested in her for anything other than sex.

* * * *

There was little conversation during the drive to the National Forest. Jacqueline occupied her time paging through the McCall's and Life magazines she picked up at the gas station they fueled up at before leaving Clarion. Why she purchased the Life publication, she wasn't sure. It was not for the cover story of the stock market worries, but it amused her to see the full-page color Snow Crop ad that read; Helps you romance vegetables. People were strange, and that was a fact.

Paging through McCall's only caused her mood to sour. With articles covering the marriage of June Allyson and Dick Powell, and Yves Montand's "Dictionary of Love" article, she gave up and set the publication aside. Even the damn novel this month was titled The Day of the Wedding which, because she'd been daydreaming in the back of her mind of marrying Colten Fisher, was not a welcome story.

She jerked in her seat as a gasp escaped her lips at the thought. The groom in question, — er, the man in question, glanced over at her and raised a brow. "What? Isn't this the right ranger station?" he inquired. It appalled her to know how immersed in her ridiculous thoughts she had been. She had not realized they had arrived at their destination, and the car was stopped in front of the building complex where the ranger dwelled when he was on duty.

Glancing around, she nodded, "Oui, this is the correct place." This time she did not wait for Colten to open her door but climbed out and headed up the cobblestones leading to the office. When the door opened, and a ranger stepped out, she forced a bright smile on her lips and called out in greeting, "Hello Peter!"

The ranger shielded his eyes against the sun. For one fleeting second, those eyes seemed to widen with stunned surprise before he controlled the emotion and stepped off the porch, "Well now, if it isn't Miss Grymes. What brings you out this way?" He moved toward her with a extended hand, caught sight of Colten, and seemed to stumble a bit.

Taking the offered hand, Jacqueline gave it a quick squeeze, "I was visiting the Davidson's and thought I would like to see Digger. Have you seen him recently?"

Ranger Peter glanced at Colten. A nervous glint flashed in his eye, which put Colten on alert. Something did not seem right.

"Digger?" Peter cleared his throat. "I saw him a few days ago. He came to pick up his mail. I thought he would head into civilization, but something changed his mind. As far as I know, he went back to his place."

"We'll need two horses," Colten said, jerking his chin toward the corral just visible behind the complex.

Peter glanced at Colten, "Um... sure, I guess."

Jacqueline smiled and introduced the two men, "If you do not mind, Peter, I will use your bathroom to change into my riding clothes." At his nod, she retrieved her clothing and went into the building.

Colten admired Jacqueline's swaying hips as she walked up the path, despite his resolve to put distance between them. Last night had been a mistake. That's what he told himself, although he could not deny the fact he had felt a sudden sense of loss when she told little Tabitha Stevens she would go back to France soon.

Forcing himself to focus on something else, he turned to the ranger. There was just something about the man that didn't sit well, but he could not quite put his finger on what that something was. Maybe it was the way the guy looked at Jacqueline. A glint of something. As though he received an unexpected present and already knew what was inside.

"I'll help you with the horses," Peter's voice snapped Colten from his thoughts, and with a nod, they walked to the corral together.

By the time Jacqueline emerged from the building, they'd tacked the horses and loaded saddlebags with supplies. Canteens holding water were dangling from the saddle horn. Digger lived deep, almost in the heart of the National Forest. It would take at least two hours to reach his cabin. They would undoubtedly need water along the way, considering the ninety-degree day. The saddlebags were stuffed with supplies for Digger, as they decided to bring the man items he might need.

Colten glanced at Jacqueline and tried not to salivate over himself. Who would have thought a pair of jeans could look like that? They molded her long legs and curves in such a way, a man could drop to his knees and beg for her attention. The ache in his leg reminded him well enough, he would not touch her again.

Rather than beg, he cleared his throat and sprang onto the horse's back, with the ease and grace of one accustomed to doing so. It pleased him to no end that the horses were the quarter breed he preferred.

When Jacqueline did not appear as though she would climb into the saddle any time soon, he looked down at her and frowned. She was standing next to the horse he borrowed for her, stroking its neck and carrying on a conversation with it.

What in the hell? "I thought you said you knew how to ride a horse," he snapped.

She regarded him a moment with a raised brow, "I always speak with a horse before riding it. We are strangers. If I expect it to do its best for me, I think we should know each other."

He scowled, "Well, Christ, why didn't you say so? I would have picked up some tea and crumpets for the social."

"There is no need for sarcasm."

"Just mount the damn horse and let's go."

With a sigh, she apologized to the horse he was on, "Please forgive him, he is a cranky man."

"For the love of...." he began, but she suddenly vaulted onto her mount without using the stirrups, gathered the reins, and took off like a shot. His mouth stayed open as he watched her cute derriere moving away from him.

It took him a second to realize she was doing just that, moving away from him, at an alarming speed, without a backwards glance. If he didn't get his own fanny in gear, she would be out of sight in seconds. The damn trees were thicker than flies on shit. He preferred the wide-open spaces of home, but that was beside the point. He kicked the horse, and they were off at a breakneck run.

Ranger Peter Warford kept his gaze on the retreating couple and felt ecstatic as hell. Spinning on the heels of his boots, he all but ran up the cobblestones, leaped over the last three steps leading to the porch, and raced inside to the room he used as a study. Scanning out the windows to assure himself no one else had driven into the parking area, he sat down at his two-way radio, turned the dial to the correct frequency, and clicked on the mike and said, "Hey, you there?" The static seemed to go on forever. Impatiently, he tried again to make contact. He had almost given up when a voice came back at him.

"You are never to contact me on this unit!" the voice snarled.

Peter grimaced but did not apologize, "Yeah? Well, you'll never guess who just showed up on my doorstep."

Chapter Twelve

Pierre Bellefeuille put the two-way radio microphone down and grinned, an evil, calculating grin. The little bitch thought she could get away from him, did she? She had traveled far in the attempt to elude. Pierre admired her attempt to hide from him, but it was not going to work.

He had not been confident he would find Jacqueline after losing her at the police station and was contemplating a visit to Rosalinda. He knew where that bitch was. He had eyes and ears all over this city. It would have been a simple matter to enter the premises and make her tell him where Jacqueline had taken off to. He would have enjoyed making her scream while obtaining the information from her. Perhaps, once he was through with his stepsister, he would still pay the actress a visit and teach her a lesson on why she should not have helped Jacqueline hide from him.

It would well be worth the wait; he was sure of it.

He stood up from the table where the two-way radio sat; turned and walked to the closet of the run-down room he managed to rent with no one asking questions. God, he hated this filthy place. He preferred the finer things in life: fast cars, expensive clothes, and anything else that struck his fancy. He had been so close to being set up in the big leagues had it not been for dear old stepsister spoiling everything.

Where had she put the diamond?

He intentionally missed the clear shot he fired at her as she stood by the window of Rosalinda's hotel room, knowing it would be a mistake to kill her before he had gotten the diamond back. However, the pleasure he had gotten as he imagined her terror when the bullet whizzed past her head caused his cock to stir. There was nothing like torture to heighten his arousal. He would use her before he killed her, he vowed. How slowly or quickly he made the pain last would come to him as the act happened. Perhaps he would cut off her fingers, one by one. That would show her for having taken the Sancy from him.

Pierre sat down at the rickety table, in what the landlord of this hideous place called a dining room, to study the map of America he picked up that morning. Trailing his finger from New York to Pennsylvania, he calculated the distance to Allegheny National Forest. The thought of being surrounded by all that woodland, and who knew what wildlife, made him shutter. He despised nature. Give him the opera, an orchestra, or a ballroom gathering, and he was at home in those elements. Being surrounded by classical music always soothed his soul, although arguably, he did not have one to calm.

Securing transportation for the five-hour trip would be tricky, but doable. It paid to have a network of friends who excelled at petty theft. He would contact one of those experts, and within a matter of hours, he would drive down the road in whatever vehicle provided to him.

It was nice to know Peter had not forgotten he owed him a favor. Back in Pierre's early days, when he was ten, and his parents brought him to America, he would walk the darkened alleyways at night because they drew him like a light pulled in a moth. It was there he had gotten his first taste for blood. Happening upon a street gang surrounding two young boys from another clan, he watched in fascinated horror as they beat one of the kids to death.

The other one fled, although Pierre had watched in what direction the kid ran.

When the police sirens were heard coming down the street to investigate the crime, Pierre moved off to the location where the escapee lay curled up and weeping like a baby.

"You will owe me one day," Pierre told the boy. "If you do not promise me that, I will let the others know where you are hiding, and they can finish the job of sending you to hell."

Regardless that Peter, over time, turned away from running with gangs and made a career for himself, he never forgot Pierre's promise. It was a streak of luck that Peter's chosen profession would land him right where Pierre's stepsister ran off to.

Pierre would get back that diamond no matter what. He already had a buyer for it lined up in Asia, and the man was impatient, anxious to have the Sancy.

With a sigh, Pierre began gathering the few pieces of clothing he had with him. If all went well, he could reach that forest by tomorrow night or early the next day, and then he would deal with Jacqueline.

He wondered if his stepsister would be happy to see him.

Chapter Thirteen

Mrs. Richard Crowe was standing in her foyer with her hands over her ears, trying to block out the deafening music emanating from her Zenith Console record player. She had been enjoying Elvis Presley singing his popular tune "Good Luck Charm" when suddenly Little Eva's "The Loco-Motion" blasted through the house at an ear-splitting volume, followed by Chubby Checker's "The Twist". That was it; she had had enough. She called Cadman Benson and told him to "remove that woman from my house!"—referring to Rosalinda who had spontaneously thrown a party at Mrs. Crowe's estate after she left for dinner.

But Mrs. Crowe had not called Cadman when she at first walked into her house and discovered the gigantic party going on within its walls. She'd been rendered speechless, flabbergasted to discover among the wall-to-wall people celebrities, like Sean Connery, Natalie Wood, Shani Wallis, and the Duke himself, John Wayne. Once the shock wore off, and the hour grew later and later, it was time to end the merrymaking.

Mrs. Crowe attempted to reason with Rosalinda and asked her to put an end to the festivities; it was well after two o'clock in the morning. But all she got for her effort from the woman was a pat on the cheek and a very intoxicated French actress telling her, "Va te faire enculer"—which Mrs. Crowe didn't understand because she did not know French. Turning towards Charles Lafayette, who had been shadowing the actress all night, she inquired: "What did she say?"

Charles cleared his throat, looked a little uncomfortable with the translation but shrugged his shoulders and answered the woman's question honestly with, "Go fuck yourself."

Eyes rounding, and on a gasp, Mrs. Crowe stammered, "How dare you speak to me in such a vulgar manner!"

"Mrs. Crowe," the film producer said quietly, "you requested a translation; I provided it for you."

Enraged by the woman's words, she headed straight for her telephone as if going to battle and dialed Cadman Benson. When he arrived, she shouted in his ear over the loud music so that he heard every word—demanding that Rosalinda leave "This instant!"

With a long sigh, Cadman strolled into the living room, unplugged the Zenith Console, and told everyone, "Get out. Party over." He blinked twice when John Wayne staggered by on his way to the door. And when Natalie Wood stopped next to him, as she thanked Rosalinda for the lovely evening, he managed not to drool.

As though she just noticed he was there, Rosalinda beamed a lopsided grin at him. "Cadman!" she slurred, took a step forward, and almost tipped over. If not for Charles's hand reaching out to steady her, she would have gone down face-first.

"Rosalinda," Cadman heaved an exasperated sigh and said, "you are supposed to be lying low, so Pierre won't find you."

Rosalinda giggled, then in a low purr told him, "We have already laid low." She gave him a sensual look as she slid her hand down the front of his shirt and would have grabbed his crotch had he not stopped her hand in its downward journey. Cadman knew she was alluding to their one night together, and damn it, it made him feel like a schoolboy caught in the act.

Especially when he felt Charles regarding him, as though he suddenly became enemy number one.

He ran his fingers through his hair in exasperation as he glared at her, "Rosalinda, what am I going to do with you?"

Oh crap, he thought as he watched a sly smile spread across her lips, that was the wrong question. Rosalinda licked her lips provocatively and said, "I can think of a few ideaz," and her eyes glanced down to where he had stopped her hand from going.

The look he turned on Charles was one of helplessness.

Without a second thought, Charles spoke, "She will be safe with me. I will take her to my home."

Cadman's brows drew together, "You mean, hotel. You live in France too."

Charles heaved a deep sigh and, speaking as if Cadman was a child, explained, "I have homes in Paris and Cannes, and two more in the US - one of which is here in New York City. I will take her there tonight." He immediately saw that Cadman was about to argue and added, "I can guarantee her safety; I have enough money to hire an army if you think it is necessary." As he spoke, Charles absentmindedly rubbed Rosalinda's back with slow, small circles.

Rosalinda's eyes fluttered shut and her breathing steadied as her head rolled against Charles's shoulder. "Chuck," she slurred sleepily, "you are too good for me."

Gently, Charles brushed his lips across her cheek, "Perhaps, but Rosalinda.... I love..."

Even in her drunken state, she could not bear to hear his declaration. "No!" she shook her head hard and almost caused herself to throw up from the spinning dizziness it brought on. Despite her resolve to keep Charles at a distance, she leaned back into him and closed her eyes. She told herself she only did so because she needed someone to hang onto at the moment. "I want to go home," her voice sounded like a child who was too tired to know what they wanted.

Placing one of his hands tenderly on her raven-black hair, he stroked it soothingly. "Soon," he said kindly.

"She's not going back to France until Pierre is behind bars," Cadman declared.

Charles's eyes narrowed, "Is that because she is in genuine danger or because of your feelings for her?"

Cadman opened his mouth, closed it, and then opened it again. "I'm not going to bother answering that," he finally said.

"No matter. And now," Charles led Rosalinda toward the front door, "I will take her home to my villa."

"Going to take advantage of her is more like it."

Charles stopped abruptly and stared daggers at Cadman with enough heat to scorch steel. "Mr. Benson, I respect Rosalinda. I would never, as you say, 'take advantage of her'. Some men are weak," he raked Cadman with his eyes and left no doubt what he thought of this American government man. "They see a beautiful woman, and at the slightest invitation from that woman, they use her. Then toss her away without remorse."

Cadman met Charles's gaze with a with a scowl. "I didn't toss her away!" He looked at Rosalinda, wanting her to say something in his defense. After all, it had been she who had initiated everything. Well, he had not been about to deny what she had thrown at him. However, it appeared as though Rosalinda would not be speaking up in his defense anytime soon. She had fallen asleep on her feet. Only Charles's broad chest and muscular arms were keeping her upright. As a defense, he added, "I do care about her."

Charles could not comprehend why some men thought that sleeping with a woman was the same as caring for her. For Charles, actions spoke louder than words. He loved Rosalinda deeply, even though he knew she might never return his feelings. Regardless, he would always treat her with respect.

He gently lifted Rosalinda into his arms, cradling her as one would a small child. To anyone who did not know she was indeed a grown woman, they might think she was a young girl. She was petite when standing; the top of her head came to the bottom of his chin. And she probably did not weigh over ninety pounds.

Charles paid the driver of his Crown Imperial Limousine well and expected him to be ready the moment he was prepared to travel. The man did not fail in his duty this night. He observed his employer walking down the steps, opening the door, and ignoring the woman who was being carried in Charles's arms, even though it was unusual. His employer did not make a habit of being alone with women.

Settling Rosalinda onto the backseat, he draped an arm around her and pulled her snug against his chest and allowed her to sleep. As the limo drove through the city to his estate, he told himself he was foolish for loving her.

Chapter Fourteen

Whatever preconceived notion Colten had about Digger Davidson, Gary's much older brother, was replaced upon meeting the man. Digger was slim of build, sported a stubbly beard and mustache, and had a crooked stance. It reminded him of some old guy who just came in from a month-long trail drive. Colten half-expected the man to smell worse than cow dung because of his appearance, though was pleasantly surprised to discover there was no foul odor preceding the man.

They arrived well after three in the afternoon, riding into the small clearing of Digger's old cabin with grateful hearts. The place was a small two-room shack with no modern comforts that Colten recognized well; it was not much different than his own place back in Medora.

The day started off bright and sunny, but the sky started darkening as the hours on the trail passed. By the time they could see the clearing Jacqueline pointed out belonged to Digger, the banking clouds gave up their moisture in a downpour that soaked the ground and drenched them with no mercy.

It certainly put a damper on Colten's plan to retrieve the Sancy, if Digger had it, and be back to civilization by five, six at the latest. They were stuck here until the rain stopped, since the wet forest floor would be dangerous to traverse in such little light. They had to wait until the weather cleared.

It was now after midnight, and Colten still did not know if Digger had the diamond. It seemed the man could not remember receiving a package from Jacqueline. Colten would have scoffed at that, except Digger did not appear to be playacting.

Could the man indeed be that absent-minded? Colten questioned why Jacqueline had trusted the scatter-brained man with a half-million-dollar diamond.

To top off the whole crazy-old-man thing, Digger had a pet raccoon who had the run of the place. It would scamper all over the house, climbing tables, hopping up on counters and more. Now and then, Digger would chuckle at the critter, shake his head, and say, "Mr. George, you know you ain't suppos' to be up there!"

Colten doubted Mr. George knew anything, other than he had gotten lucky enough to have a human feeding him and keeping him fat.

Colten's sigh was heavy. He glanced at his watch, looked again at the two people sitting at the table, heads bent together. Digger was showing Jacqueline a photo album and reminiscing about days gone by.

For God's sake, who in the hell cared? It was after midnight. They should have been looking for the diamond, not chatting together like two old hens. He had been sitting on this understuffed couch that felt as though it had rocks in it, flipping through magazines from last year, for at least three hours, and had grown bored long before that. He thought it was a step up in his endurance to sit here, letting the two of them chatter together. But enough was enough.

"So," he said as he stood and stretched, "hasn't this been a swell time? But shouldn't we be looking for a package?" He gave Jacqueline a pointed look.

Two heads moved in unison, both pairs of eyes landing on him. One set of those eyes looked at him as though he were being rude. The other set looked at him as though it was the first time they had seen him.

"Colten, we have time to look for the package. There is no reason to rush." Thunder cracked outside, seeming to emphasize the statement.

The sound Colten made was a half laugh combined with disbelief, "We've been here for over nine hours, sweetheart!"

Digger's eyes darted back and forth between the two of them, confusion evident in every line of his face, and he asked, "Miss Jackie, who is that man?"

Colten nearly choked. The man was more absentminded than a loony bird. It was apparent the Sancy diamond was lost forever. Unless an archaeologist dug it up, three hundred years from now. "I can't believe you would send it to him," he rubbed a hand over his face and wanted to pull out his hair.

Digger's confusion appeared to deepen, "Did you send me something, Miss Jackie?"

Jacqueline smiled softly at the man she adopted as an uncle, a gesture of affection. She had brought the topic up several times since they arrived, but it was as though he had no recollection of the package. That was Digger for you; it often took him a while to process something. Jacqueline would sometimes wonder if he was only pretending not to remember, just teasing her. When she asked Grant about it once, he simply shrugged and replied with, "My brother's gotta do what he's got to do."

Whatever the heck that meant.

Smiling brightly, as though this were the first time she asked, she brought up why they were there, "A few weeks ago, Uncle Digger, I sent you a small package. And I asked you to keep it safe for me. Ranger Peter mentioned you stopped by for your mail. Then, instead of catching a ride down to Clarion, the way you normally do, you came back here." She looked into his eyes, hopefully. "Do you remember the package?"

Unconsciously, she was nodding her head as though willing him to say yes.

His head started bobbing as he mimicked her.

Colten's eyes brightened. Finally, they were going to get somewhere.

"Do you remember the package?" Jacqueline repeated and used her hands to show him the size of the box she sent.

Digger's face squished together as his eyes squinted, his brows narrowed in thought. "Hmm," then suddenly, he brightened and snapped his fingers together. "The paperweight!" His face beamed. "Oh, sure, I remember. I don't have much use for it, thank you kindly, Miss Jackie."

Colten's body tensed. He closed his eyes and thought, just wait for it. He probably tossed it away.

"What did you do with the- er... paperweight?" Jacqueline asked.

"Well, now, shoot," he looked around the room, as though considering places it could be. Then he glanced at Mr. George, currently balancing himself on the back of a chair, on its way toward a bookshelf. "Mr. George really took a liking to it." With a twinkle in his eye, he smiled at Colten and said, "He likes shiny things."

Colten made a sound between a half laugh and a snarl. Jacqueline had to admit; it was the worst sound she had ever heard. But it mimicked the sinking feeling she had in the pit of her stomach. "Uncle Digger, you did not let Mr. George have the item, did you?"

Digger gave her an indignant look, "Miss Jackie, I did no such thing." There was a collective sigh of relief from his company. "I read your note. You told me it was important for me to keep it safe for you. Oh, you have such nice handwriting."

He brought his hand up in the air, as though holding a pencil, and began writing on the air, "All those nice swirls and such. Gosh dang, where did you learn how to be so artistic like...."

"The paperweight!" Colten shouted, annoyed by the tangent the old man had driven down.

Digger blinked, "Do I know you, young man?"

Colten sat down, overcome, and put his face in his hands. "Unbelievable," he mumbled.

Jacqueline pushed her bottom lip out and blew out a breath, as though trying to move a piece of hair off her face, in her own exasperation. "Uncle Digger," she kept her voice as calm as she could, "that is Colten Fisher, remember? I introduced you to him when we arrived."

Digger's eyes brightened. "Oh, yes!" he grinned. "Your husband!"

"We're not married!" two voices shouted at once.

Digger jerked back in his seat.

Colten threw his hands up in defeat, "God, I might as well go to bed." He looked around the small room, lit up with a dozen candles. He would not get any sleep at all tonight. Other than Digger's cot against the north wall, and this thing he was sitting on that could jokingly be called a sofa, there was not anywhere he could lay his head. Unless he was a total cad and tell Jacqueline she could sleep on the dirt floor. Tempted as he was, he would not do it. He would let her sleep on this lumpy couch, but she would owe him—big time.

Jacqueline took a deep breath and tried one last time. Her own eyes were feeling as though they had sawdust in them, "Uncle Digger, where is the item I sent you?"

"The paperweight?"

"Yes."

"Well, for heaven's sake, Miss Jackie, why didn't you just ask me for it?" he motioned toward Colten. "That young man's been sitting on it, practically all day."

Colten's head shot up. He looked at Digger for three seconds before jumping up, turned around, and grabbed the cushion off the couch. He stared, and stared, and stared some more when he saw the gemstone cradled in a crease in the folds that looked as though it was made for it.

Slowly, reverently, he reached down and picked the diamond up. Once in his hand, a chuckle, suspiciously sounding like a giggle, began coming out of this throat and through his lips. He had been sitting on a half-million-dollar diamond and mistaken it for a worthless rock digging into his ass.

Jacqueline whooped, hugged Digger, and rushed forward to view the elusive gem. Without thinking, she threw her arms around Colten and kissed him soundly on the lips. "I told you!" she laughed. "I told you it would be safe!"

Colten was not feeling tired now. He felt wide awake and rejuvenated. He reeled Jacqueline back in when she would have stepped away and followed her kiss with one much deeper. One that caused her to momentarily forget she vowed never to allow his touch again. It was so easy to fit her body into his, as though it was made to be there. By their own accord, her arms wrapped around his neck and kept him firmly in place as the kiss continued.

A clearing of a throat, and a few deep coughs, got through the heat building between them. "Miss Jackie? I'm going to bed. You and your husband can bed down in the barn. You know the way and where things are."

Colten and Jacqueline pulled their lips apart long enough to reply, halfheartedly, "We're not married," before joining lips to continue their intimate conversation.

They came up for air when Digger grumbled from his bed, "Blow out the candles, will ya?"

Jacqueline stepped away, frustrated with herself for so easily succumbing to her longing to be close to him. Now she had to spend one more night with him. Alone and already, her body hummed with anticipation.

She would not let herself have what she craved. She declared it with every fiber of her being.

"We will have to make a run for it," she told Colten as she blew out the candle nearest her. He followed suit with the candle on his side of the room, without saying a word.

It was a mad dash to the barn. As thick as molasses, slippery mud pulled at their shoes as they sprinted and slid across the yard. The rain pounded unmercifully, re-soaking the clothing the couple had dried out hours earlier. They hit the barn door laughing like a couple of school children.

The soft knickers of the horses settled in the stalls greeted them. The odor of straw and hay was welcoming. It reminded each of them of childhood memories. No matter if they had grown up in different countries, barns and horses all smelled the same. Some people despised it, but to them, it was a welcoming perfume.

As their laughter subsided, tension began. They needed to get out of their wet clothes. Colten was game, but after this morning, he would not risk her punching him in the face again, nor would he touch her and risk his other leg receiving the same treatment she had given the left one.

It still hurt like a bitch, thank you very much.

The cool air was reaching him now, and it was bone-chilling. He had no qualms about taking off his wet garments, and so without a care he discarded his hat onto a post and began unbuttoning his shirt. He threw it over a wooden pole, followed by his jeans and underwear. He watched her eyes go wide and said, "Don't be insane," it was easy to see her thoughts. "I'm being sensible and getting out of these wet things. I have no intention of trying to make love to you."

"Good!" she declared. Colten was being rational. She knew he was right, but damn, damn, and triple damn. Her body responded at seeing him in the nude. His sculpted chest tapered into narrow hips and caused her throat to go dry. She almost walked back into the rain to cool herself off.

He was strolling around the barn in search of a blanket, unaware of her eyes involuntarily admiring his naked form. When he spied a saddle blanket hanging on a hook near a stall door, he was not about to complain about its small size; it was enough to wrap around his waist. "You'll want to get those clothes off before you catch a cold," he told her, without an ounce of inflection in his voice. He began looking around for something she could use to cover herself with.

She knew he was right. "There are blankets in the loft," she told him, and stepped behind a small nook that would afford her some privacy.

With a sound of annoyance—she couldn't have told him that bit of information before he wrapped this stiff and scratching saddle blanket around himself? He climbed the ladder leading to the hayloft, lit the lantern he found there and tossed one of several blankets laying in the corner down to her. "Hang up your clothes, and get up here," he said crossly.

"I am not having sex with you!" she declared once again. There was no mistaking the resolve in her voice.

"Honestly, sweetheart, I don't care. I'm cold, I know you're cold; I can hear your teeth chattering all the way up here. We'll share body heat, and that's all." Damn it.

It did not take Jacqueline long to consider her options. There weren't any. She would have to share body heat with Colten or freeze. Going back to the cabin was not an alternative since she was now as naked as the day she was born.

On a sigh, she took the lantern off its peg and climbed the ladder.

Not an easy feat. One hand was trying to hold the blanket in place, and the other held the lantern. But Jacqueline managed it, one rung at a time.

Colten used his time to push hay together, covering it with a few layers of blankets. He was lying on his back, with his hands tucked under his head when she reached the loft. He glanced at her once before closing his eyes.

Turning the wick down until it went out and placing it on a peg on the wall, she settled in, making sure there was as much distance between them as possible. She closed her eyes and willed herself to sleep.

"Jacqueline," it was a sigh, "we will not keep warm if you stay in Canada."

In spite of herself, her lips quirked. "I am not in Canada," she replied smartly.

"Might as well be," he rolled over, met those blue eyes of hers, and felt his heart skip a beat. What was it about Jacqueline Grymes that tugged at his heart in ways Caroline never had?

"I admit," Colten said as he looked at her, "I'm a mite confused. One minute you were hot, and then bam, colder than ice." He touched a finger to her lips to silence her. "Right now, that isn't important. We need to keep warm, and sharing our body heat is the wisest thing to do. I'll keep my hands to myself." His body wanted to cut out his tongue for offering that bit of gallantry.

She studied him for a moment. Eyes were the windows to the soul, someone once said. Perhaps it was true, because what she saw in his eyes, visible by the moonlight coming through the glass window on one of the loft's walls, was the truth. He would not pressure her. And at that moment, she fell in love with him.

Unwrapping the blanket as he lifted his, she snuggled in next to him and fell asleep within moments. It took longer than that for him to do the same.

Chapter Fifteen

Laying in the loft above the barn, with Jacqueline pressed up against him, Colten was in no hurry to start the day. No point since there was a drizzle of rain hitting against the roof of the barn, letting him know they would not leave Diggers' place soon. And once the rain finally stopped, it would be who knew how long before the forest floor would be dry enough to allow safe passage.

He sighed. He might as well accept that.

Moving as stealthily as he could, Colten eased away from Jacqueline far enough for him to look at her. She was curled up next to him with her head resting on one arm, sleeping soundly as though the sound of the rain soothed her into a deep slumber. It surprised him she could sleep like that, but perhaps she was still exhausted from the other night when they had done more than shared body heat.

Guilt tried to raise its ugly head. Never in his years with the Secret Service had he acted in any way that would call into question his integrity, but he certainly had blown that when he chose to have sex with a woman entrusted to him for her protection. He would not think about whatever consequences there could be because of that indiscretion. The worst thing that might happen would be to get kicked out of the Secret Service, and that would just send him back to North Dakota permanently.

That thought didn't worry him in the least since he'd been thinking about getting out of this line of work, anyway. But until then, he still had a job to do. Return the diamond and keep

Jacqueline safe from Pierre until the authorities apprehended him, and he was locked up behind bars.

As Colten contemplated finding a place that would keep Jacqueline hidden from view, it slowly dawned on him, they were already in a secluded area, and he grinned. Perhaps the rain wasn't an inconvenience after all. They could stay here for a while once the sun came out. Maybe a couple of days at the very least, and then Colten would ride down to the ranger station, contact Cadman, and find out if there was any news on Pierre's capture.

With that plan settled in his mind, he glanced back down at Jacqueline and wondered what she would think of having to stay here with no comforts. Apparently, she came from wealth and probably was never forced to sleep in these conditions before. And yet, something told him it would not matter to her. She'd been comfortable enough to want to ride up here to get that diamond, already aware of the conditions Digger lived in, and she had not complained about it. Nor had she objected to spending the night sleeping in the hay, which caused Colten to admire her grit.

"You are thinking too loudly, Colten," he heard Jacqueline say in a sleepy voice that caused her slight accent to wrap around him and tug at his heart.

He wished she would stop doing that. Especially when she said his name.

"I was wondering if I dared climb down the ladder and find out if Digger has anything resembling breakfast, but then I considered he probably won't remember who I am and shoot me."

Jacqueline chuckled.

"Do you think I'm joking?"

"He would not do that."

"Ha. As absent-minded as he is, he'd probably think I was a grizzly bear."

Her laughter did things to his heart he did not want to acknowledge. The way her face lit up and her eyes twinkled when she laughed would be a memory he took with him long after they parted ways.

Not liking the idea of never seeing her again and not wanting to question why it would bother him, he told her, "I think I'll head on down that ladder. I'll throw on my pants, then bring your clothes up to you so you can dress." It was that or give in to the temptation of rolling her onto her back and making love to her. Which was what his southern buddy was screaming at him to do since it had woken up at first light and kept growing harder the longer Colten lay here feeling her flesh against his. Since he made that mistake once, he would not do it again no matter how much his cock wanted to.

"Mind looking somewhere else while I do that?" he asked. He had never been ashamed of his body, but he did not want to get up while his penis was standing at attention.

When she complied, rolling away from him, he felt a twinge of disappointment that she had not hinted at wanting him to stay curled up next to her. Well, she told him she would not allow him access to her body again, and apparently; she was going to stick with that resolve.

Without another word, he climbed down the ladder to accomplish his mission of putting on his jeans and bringing her clothing to her.

She was sitting up with one blanket wrapped around herself, covering those enticing breasts from his view when he handed her pants and shirt to her.

"Thank you," she told him, taking her clothing from him.

Colten gave her a quick nod, then climbed back down from the loft and opened the barn door. Glancing up at the small amount of sky he could see through the dense trees, he determined the sun was going to win the war soon, and the drizzle would stop, probably within the hour.

Placing his Stetson firmly on his head, he walked the short distance to the front door of Digger's cabin.

Perhaps he should have knocked to let the old man know someone was there, but he didn't. Stepping into the small space, which was a combination of living room, bedroom, and kitchen, Colten's eyes widened when the barrel of a shotgun greeted him.

"If you're fixing on robbing me, I ain't got nothing you want."

Colten stared at the crazy old man, then just reached out with his hand, and slowly moved the barrel away from himself. He was taking a chance the idiot wouldn't shoot him, but he'd had enough of this loony bird game, "Put the damn gun away before you shoot someone. And besides, Jacqueline's going to be along any minute, and she sure as hell doesn't need to see you waving that thing around."

Digger's eyes brightened, "Miss Jackie?"

Colten shook his head, "Let's not do this dance. I need coffee before I can function, let alone deal with your absentmindedness."

There might have been amusement behind Digger's eyes for a brief moment before he said, "I don't know if I want to give a stranger any of my coffee."

A growl formed in Colten's throat, "We met last night, and you damn well know it. I came here with Jacqueline to retrieve that diamond she sent you."

Digger snapped his fingers together, "Miss Jackie's husband! Sure, I remember."

Colten would not bother correcting him. The man would forget within five minutes, anyway. "Coffee," he said.

Digger pointed toward the small ancient stove near one corner of the room, "Help ya self, Cole. And if you're wanting breakfast, I've got fresh eggs from the chicken coop and bacon I can cut up for ya."

Grunting his thanks, Colten poured himself a mug of coffee and sat down at the table when Digger pointed him to it.

Jacqueline entered the cabin at about the time Digger was setting a plate of bacon and eggs down in front of Colten. She stopped inside the door, closed her eyes for a moment, and inhaled. "That smells fantastic," she commented as the aroma of bacon touched her nostrils.

"Set yourself down, Miss Jackie. I'll make you up some breakfast too."

Thanking him, she took a seat across from Colten at the small table.

"I think we'll stay here for a few days," Colten told her between bites of scrambled eggs.

Startled, Jacqueline stared at him, "I thought you were in a hurry to return the diamond."

For a moment, Colten moved his hand to the pocket of his jeans where the jewel rested, wanting to assure himself it was still tucked away safely. Once he confirmed it was indeed where it should be, he told Jacqueline, "Taking it back only solves one issue. There is still the matter of Pierre. He won't give up searching for you. I don't believe you could be any farther off his radar than your being in the middle of a forest."

Digger set the plate of scrambled eggs and bacon he prepared for Jacqueline on the table in front of her. He did not comment on Colten's statement, but there seemed to be approval in his eyes when he glanced Colten's way.

Jacqueline could see the wisdom behind Colten's decision; however, a few things did not make the idea appealing to her, which she brought up by saying, "We did not bring extra clothing. I cannot imagine having to wear these for who knows how long." She already felt grimy, desperately wanting a bath and the use of her toothbrush, which was another item on her list of missing necessities.

"Sponge baths will keep us clean, and I think we can launder our clothing every other day," he glanced up at Digger. "Do you have a water source nearby?"

The man walked over to a tiny counter, picked up a pitcher of water, and set it down in front of Colten. "Here's some water for you, Mr. Cole. You can have as much as you'd like. There's more in the well, and if that dries up, there's a creek behind the house."

Colten had not wanted a drink of water, but because the man managed to tell him where the water source was, he did not make an issue out of Digger's misunderstanding him.

But he did grin at Jacqueline. "Ever take a bath in a creek?" Colten asked her and almost laughed at the shocked look on her face.

"Certainly not," Jacqueline scoffed.

Grinning, Colten said, "You'll love it. Very refreshing."

She shook her head.

With a shrug, he told her, "You might change your mind by tomorrow."

She shook her head again.

Smiling, knowing she would probably cave once she could no longer stand not being clean, he stood up and stretched, "While you finish your breakfast, I'll check on the horses."

"That's a nice husband you've got, Miss Jackie," Digger said when Colten walked out the door.

Jacqueline closed her eyes and wished Digger would stop that, "He is not my husband, Uncle Digger. I explained that to you last night. He is a Secret Service agent."

Digger shrugged, picked up Colten's dirty dishes, and moved them to the small sink he would later fill with water after it was heated on his stove.

"Is there anything I can help you with, Uncle Digger?" she asked him, finishing the breakfast he provided.

"Not that I can think of," he told her, moving to his bed. Reaching under it, he pulled out a small box and brought it to her. "I have some items in here you might want."

Jacqueline opened the lid of the box, then laughed with delight when she saw an assortment of new toothbrushes, samples of toothpaste, and several bars of small soaps one could find at almost any motel. "Where on earth did these come from?" she asked.

"Every time I go to the dentist, they give me a new brush and a sample of toothpaste. Don't know why. There's nothing wrong with the one I use. But I take 'em anyway because I like free stuff."

"And I'm glad you do!" She stood up and hugged him. "I hope you don't mind us staying for a few days."

"Any visit from you is welcome, Miss Jackie. You stay for as long as you like."

Thanking him again, Jacqueline moved to the small sink, toothbrush, and toothpaste in hand, and readied herself for the day the best she could.

* * * *

By one, the sun had managed to drive away all but a few lingering clouds, flooding the ground with its warm rays and turning the drizzle-covered surface into a dry haven.

Jacqueline helped Digger prepare a late lunch. A simple fair of biscuits and gravy. After that, Digger brought out a box of books from a small closet and gave it to Jacqueline.

"Maybe there is something in there that will help you pass the time," Digger said, nodding to the box filled with paperback novels.

Regardless of the assortment being limited and she wasn't a fan of science fiction, she appreciated having the books.

Choosing The Man Who Fell to Earth by Walter Tevis, Jacqueline stepped outside to sit on the porch to begin the story about an alien who came to Earth seeking a way to ferry his people here from his home planet, which was suffering a severe drought.

Colten was keeping himself busy at Digger's woodpile, chopping wood. The steady thwack, thwack sound the ax made as it broke apart the wood was distracting enough for Jacqueline to lose interest in the novel in her hand.

He had removed his shirt so it would not become drenched with the sweat his body formed doing the hard labor, and she decided she would much rather watch Colten work than read any day of the week. The way his muscles rippled with every movement and his biceps strained caused her mouth to go dry. The memory of what it had been like to be held by him during the night, with her cheek pressed against that chiseled chest, caused her face to blush. If she were honest with herself, she would admit it had taken all her will not to beg him to make love to her last night. But she made that mistake once, and where had it gotten her?

Not that she would expect him to suddenly fall madly in love with her. It would be absurd to consider the possibility. People said love at first sight did not exist, however, she would tell them they were wrong because she'd already fallen for Colten and knew that fact made her a complete fool.

Deciding he might appreciate a glass of water, she moved into the cabin, poured him one from the pitcher Digger kept in an antique icebox, kept cool with a supply of ice he stored in a root cellar. Taking it back outside, she walked the short distance to where he was working up a sweat. "It looks as though you have done that before," she commented, stopping close enough to converse yet remaining at a safe distance.

Colten took one more swing with his ax, splitting the log in two and resting the blade on the ground. With a swipe of his hand, he wiped away the sweat dripping down his face and then gave her his full attention. "I have. I did it often for my grandfather before my parent's moved him into town to live with them." He did not add that he'd taken over his grandfather's old homestead for a while until he married Caroline.

Jacqueline held up the glass of water, "I thought perhaps you might like something to drink."

Her thoughtfulness touched him, "Yeah, thanks." Taking the glass from her, he moved it across his forehead before taking a swallow, then two, then downed the contents. He'd needed that more than he thought.

"It looks as though you've chopped enough wood to last Digger quite a while. I'm sure he appreciates it."

"I might as well make myself useful. He needs a stockpile for the winter months."

"That he does."

Colten looked around the area, "Where'd he go off to, anyway? I haven't seen him for a while."

"He told me he was going fishing for tonight's dinner."

Picking the ax back up, Colten carried it to the place next to the cabin where he found it. "Hope he remembers the way back."

Jacqueline chuckled, "I think he remembers better than he wants me to believe."

The declaration caused Colten to smile, "Glad to know I'm not the only one suspicious of that act he puts on." He watched Mr. George moving across the cabin's porch and shook his head. Digger's pet came and went whenever he pleased.

"I think I'm going to head down to that creek I saw not far from here and take a quick dip," he told Jacqueline. "Now that the sun decided to show us who's boss, it's hot, and I just worked up a sweat. I'm going to wash the stickiness off." He handed her back the now empty container of water she had brought to him. "Thanks again for the water."

As she excepted the tin mug, she felt her own sweat slide down her back and was almost willing to sell her soul to feel cool, even for a little while. Did she dare? Never in her life had she considered doing such a thing, but she was considering it now.

"I think I will grab a couple of Digger's lightweight blankets to use as towels and join you."

It surprised Colten since this morning she indicated that wouldn't happen. But who was he to refuse her company when he liked the look of her body?

Soon enough they were standing at the edge of the shallow creek where it fed into a small pond. The pond would serve their purpose better than the creek, and Colten searched for a place along its bank that would allow easy entry. Once he found one, he stripped down and waded in.

The water was a refreshing cold, and without hesitation, he sank under for a moment. When he resurfaced, he saw Jacqueline standing on the shore, still fully clothed.

"I thought you were going to get wet," he told her. The pond wasn't too deep; he had managed to walk a ways out before the water rose up to his waist. Now he stood there, feeling the coolness of the water against his skin, looking at her as she stared back at him.

She wanted to, but she wasn't sure she wanted to take off her clothing, "Maybe I could roll up my pants and wade in."

He rolled his eyes, "Now you're being silly. The water's great. You can put your clothes next to mine." When he saw the hesitation in her eyes, he told her, "Look, you ain't got nothing I haven't seen before, and there is no point trying to be modest when we've already did the tango. Not to mention we slept next to each other flesh-to-flesh last night."

Jacqueline knew he was right, but still... "Turn around."

With another roll of his eyes and a shake of his head, he turned his back to her. He was tempted to peek when he heard her entering the water but refrained from doing so. Until he heard her cry out.

Spinning around quickly, he was confused for one moment when he did not see her. Anywhere. But when her head suddenly reappeared above the surface, he laughed, "I thought for a moment you were..."

He watched her go back under. "Jacqueline!" he yelled, heading toward the spot where he last saw her. He had not anticipated a drop-off nor questioned if she could swim.

When she came back up, he was close enough to grab her before she went under again. He could still feel the bottom of the pond where he stood and could not fathom where the deep hole was that kept sucking her in.

"Are you alright?" he asked, pulling her against him. Dang it to hell. His heart was drumming with the knowledge she could have drowned.

She blinked at him, unable to understand why he looked frazzled, "I am not sure why you would not think I was-."

"I heard you cry out and saw you go under! Are you alright?" he asked again.

When understanding dawned, she pressed her lips together to prevent herself from laughing but did not succeed from stopping it. It burst out of her as he continued to hold her, looking concerned.

His scowl removed the worry from his face quickly, "Are you telling me you didn't fall into a drop-off?"

She shook her head, "I cried out because this water is freezing, then I decided to submerge myself right away. I thought it was better to get used to it as quickly as possible, and why do you seem angry at me?"

He was not angry. In truth, he had been scared shitless. What if she would have drowned? There would be no tomorrow with her, and although he was not at a point where he could admit it to himself, she was rapidly getting under his skin; he could acknowledge he never wanted to see harm come to her.

His eyes went to her lips, and damn her, he wanted to feel her mouth on his.

127

Not asking permission, he lowered his head and took what he desired. To know the taste of her as his body conveyed what his heart could not say. That he was glad she had not drowned and was okay because he did not want to lose her.

God, the man knew how to kiss, Jacqueline thought as he assaulted her mouth. If she weren't standing in a pool of water already, she would have become one as she felt herself melt against him. Flesh against flesh and God help her, she wanted more, and by the feel of the hardness pressing against her stomach, so did he.

"There you are, miss Jackie!"

The entwined couple broke apart as though a whale suddenly surfaced between them.

As though she had just got caught by her father doing something wrong, Jacqueline gazed wide-eyed toward the bank where Digger stood holding up a string of fish.

"I sure did have good luck, miss Jackie! We're going to feast tonight!" He seemed not to notice he was talking to two people standing naked in a pond as he continued, "I'll just take these on up to the cabin and get them cleaned up."

Colten could feel Jacqueline's embarrassment as though it were a tangible thing, and he did the best he could to shield her from the old man's eyes by moving in front of her. "Thanks, Digger. We'll be along shortly," he said.

Giving a nod, Digger walked off in the cabin's direction.

"I'll grab that bar of soap we brought with us," Colten said, turning to Jacqueline. "I'll wash your back if you wash mine." He grinned, more than willing to take up where they left off.

"I can manage," she told him, swimming away. She needed to stop allowing Colten Fisher to kiss her because rational thought went right out the window when he did.

Chapter Sixteen

That night, when evening fell and night creatures stirred, Jacqueline knew she would face another night with Colten alone in the loft of Digger's barn, and wondered if she could keep her resolve not to give in to her body's desire to make love to him again.

Thankfully, she would have her clothing as an added layer between them tonight, and with no rain this time dampening the air, there would be no need to share body heat.

Honestly, she was a tad disappointed not to have that excuse to feel his flesh against hers, but acknowledged it was for the best. She did not need any kindling to spark her body into longing for him.

Yes, they were adults, but there was no commitment from him and besides, having sex with Colten could lead to complications she hadn't considered until now. Like pregnancy. They had not used protection in that hotel room, nor was there a local pharmacy where condoms were easily obtained. The birth control pills the Planned Parenthood Federation of America developed had only recently become publicly available, and she had yet to ask her doctor to write her a prescription.

Nor did she believe in abortion, so abstaining until some contraceptive was available was her only option.

Bidding Digger goodnight, she and Colten crossed the short distance to the barn. Once the door was closed, Colten said, "We can make up separate areas to sleep if you would feel more at ease, but I have a feeling the temperature might drop later tonight. It would be wise to be together rather than separately, but that's up to you. And I'll give you fair warning. Either way, I'm not sleeping with my pants on. I want to be comfortable, and they are constrictive."

He undid his belt, dropped his pants but left his underwear on, and hung the jeans over a railing after assuring himself once again the diamond was still in the pocket. He felt keeping it there was the safest place right now. Had he left it with Digger, the old man would likely forget what it was and toss it out.

Jacqueline could not fault him for wanting to be comfortable as he slept. She understood the wisdom of it. "I will be up shortly," she told him, stepping behind the nook she had been using as a dressing screen.

He shook his head, not able to understand her modesty in front of him with all that had transpired between them. "I'll meet you topside," he told her and climbed the ladder.

When Jacqueline's slender form came into view, Colten was lying on the bed of hay covered with blankets. He did not believe he had ever seen a sexier sight than her walking toward him in nothing more than her underwear and the button-down shirt.

She said nothing as she lay down next to him. For now, there was no need for pulling a blanket over themselves. It was warm and stuffy in the loft, but later, as the temperature dropped, they would make use of the covers.

"Can I ask you something?" Colten said after they had been lying there for close to a half-hour.

Jacqueline, having been resting with her back toward him, slowly rolled over to face him regardless of it being too dark to see his features. "Sure."

"Why did you want to become a teacher for students who are..." He stopped himself before he said something offensive to her. "Children with disabilities?"

She smiled to herself, knowing he was trying to grow as a person. "I attended a private girl's school in Paris. Teaching never crossed my mind until I began my ninth year. We, the school, had a new student join us that year. I noticed there was something different about her, and almost all my classmates shunned her. She would throw tantrums, have outbursts, and required a lot of extra help from the teachers. It broke my heart when others teased her. One day, I asked one of my teachers why Beth struggled. I was told it was because Beth was re-tarded. A term I had never heard before, and I loathe it to this day."

Colten reached out, stroked her hair lightly, and could agree the word sounded horrible, and the fact it was a label given to his son made it that much more difficult to hear.

"And?" he prompted when it did not appear she would say anything more.

"I began researching the subject, trying to find ways to help Beth. My teachers did not mind me using her as my test subject since it set them free from dealing with her. They did not know what to do for her, and sadly, there was not a lot of information on the subject. But I wanted to know everything I could. It was slow, but by the time we graduated, she could control her out-bursts better."

Colten wondered if Clinton had outbursts like Beth and hated himself for not knowing even that much about his son. "Maybe one day you will write a book about it."

She chuckled. "I think I will leave that to the professionals. However, I will certainly benefit from their research."

When he said no more, she closed her eyes and tried to sleep while Colten remained awake a while longer, wondering if he should ask her for some recommended reading material regarding autism. Perhaps it would be a way for him to understand his son.

By three o'clock, Colten finally succumbed to slumber, and as he and Jacqueline slept, they were unaware of Mr. George entering the barn, tugging on the pants Colten draped over the railing until the denim fell on top of him. After a five-minute struggle, the raccoon got itself out from under the weight and was inquisitive enough to find the pocket Colten had placed the Sancy diamond in.

Mr. George, if he could smile, would have. He indeed enjoyed shiny things and did not feel the least bit of guilt as he took the diamond through the barn door with him.

In the morning, the sun's translucent beams found their way through the cracks in the walls to rest upon the couple entwined in the hay. Being sound asleep as they were, they had not heard the visitors ride into the yard early in the morning. It was not until Colten felt something poking him in his side that his sleep-laden eyes opened as he tried to push the annoying object away. The sight that greeted him turned his blood to ice.

The barrel of a pistol was three inches from his face.

Forcing himself to move his eyes off the weapon of death, he looked at the man holding it. Ranger Peter's face was grinning back at him with a gleam in his eye that told Colten he was a dead man if he even flinched. "A friend of mine wants to see you," he said, motioning for Colten to get up. He jerked his chin toward Jacqueline. "Especially her."

The voice penetrated Jacqueline's brain enough to wake her. As she opened her own eyes, fear gripped her, and a scream tore from her throat.

Inside the cabin, the man tying Digger to a chair heard the sound, and an evil grin spread across his lips. "Ah," he said, and not particularly to Digger, "I do believe my dear sister is awake."

Ten minutes later, the cabin door opened, and Peter announced, "Looky who I found." He shoved Colten through the door with enough force Colten almost lost his balance. "Try it," he said when Colten spun toward him. "I won't mind putting a bullet in you. You tried giving me trouble back there when we were coming down that ladder, so I'm not in no mood to put up with any more bullshit."

Rigid with anger, Colten glared back at him but was thrilled to see the man's eye was swelling where he had kicked him while he climbed down the ladder. Unfortunately, he'd almost lost his balance, and Peter managed to avoid most of the impact. After that, once on the ground floor of the barn, Peter kept the upper hand by keeping an arm wrapped around Jacqueline and the gun aimed directly at her temple.

Fear of Jacqueline being shot was the only reason Colten had not tried to overpower the man once on solid ground.

"Well now," came a voice from the shadows, and Jacqueline froze in horror, "If it isn't my dear sister and might I add, how lovely it is to see you." His gaze caressed her body, stopping at the junction between her legs which was barely covered by the cotton underwear, and it caused Jacqueline to feel as though he'd violated her physically.

Jacqueline spit at him. "Vous fils de sal-ope...."

133

Pierre shook his head slowly. "Now, now, Jacqueline. I could speak of your mother in the same manner. Please, let us not be spiteful. You gave me a merry chase, and for that, I have something for you." He walked forward and backhanded her with enough force, it threw her body into the wall. Blood sprang from her lip where the blow had landed. The dizziness had her knees buckling. She slid down the wall and landed on the floor; she was not unconscious, but wished she were. The pain raging through her body caused her stomach to pitch.

Heedless to the gun, blinding rage overtook Colten as he leaped at Pierre, "You fucking son-of-a-bitch!" His heart drummed in his ears. Seeing Jacqueline crumpled on the floor, dazed, caused the wall he'd built around his heart to crumble, and he knew the other night had not been just sex for him.

Peter cold-cocked him with his pistol, inches before he could reach Pierre. Colten's eyes rolled back in his head, and he crumpled to the floor in a heap.

"Well done, Peter," Pierre said, walking to Colten and kicking him in the ribs with enough force to break one. When he came to, he would be in a lot of pain, but that did not concern Pierre in the least. "Tie him up with the old guy." Then he turned to Jacqueline. "So, my dear, where did you hide the diamond?"

"Go to hell, Pierre," she spat.

Pierre raised a brow. Glancing at the man already tied and gagged, then at the one Peter was struggling to secure, he said, "Your choice, Jacqueline. Which one do you want to die? I am in no mood for your games!" His body vibrated with his anger. What should have been an easy enough trip to this god-forsaken forest had turned into a disaster within miles of leaving New York in the stolen car. It had gotten a flat tire, there'd been no spare, and he'd had to walk quite a distance, in the rain, before securing one from a rest stop while its owner was using the facilities.

That delay alone caused his blood to boil, but after reaching the ranger station and having to delay the trip to this cabin longer because of the continued rain added to his temper. Peter was lucky that Pierre needed him to guide him to this secluded spot, otherwise, he would have killed him then and there for no other reason than being able to take his displeasure out on someone.

Silently, Jacqueline shook with horror. She knew it had not been an idle threat. Was the Sancy worth the life of anyone? Wasn't it only carbon under it all? "I will show you, but you must promise not to harm them."

Pierre cocked his head. Did she truly believe he would spare anyone?

Pulling herself up on shaky knees, she glared. "I mean it, Pierre. I am the only one who knows where it is," she lied. "I will not take you to it if you harm them anymore."

He chuckled. "My, my. I had forgotten your temper." He shrugged. "They are of no concern to me." His eyes blazed with heat as he continued to view her long legs and the V between her legs and felt his arousal growing as he contemplated what would come after he had the diamond.

With a glance at Peter, he asked, "Are you through there?"

Giving the rope bindings one last tug, Peter nodded. "Yep. They aren't going anywhere. That's for sure."

Pierre's grin was wicked. "Good," he approved, ready to end at least one life to satisfy his need to appease his anger. Pulling out his own gun, he shot Peter between the eyes. The man had kept his promise to pay him back one day for having kept his hiding place secret from the gang looking for him, but Pierre had never agreed to not killing him by his own hand.

Peter's blood-splattered on the men tied in the chairs and his body, as it fell, almost landed in Digger's lap.

The muffled sound Digger made through the gag stuffed in his mouth sounded suspiciously like, "Holy shit!"

Before Jacqueline could push the scream, the sudden violence invoked past her lips, Pierre grabbed her arm and pushed his face within an inch of hers. "Now, where is my diamond?" he hissed in a voice that sent chills up her spine.

Shaking but forcing her voice to remain calm, she told him, "In the barn."

He skimmed his pistol down her jaw, slowly sliding it down her neck until he came to where her breasts hid from his view beneath the button-down shirt. "I have always wanted you, Jacqueline." Quickly he moved to the side, deflecting the knee she tried to send into his groin. "Ah, ah, ah, dear sister. You play nice." He spun her back out of the cabin door.

Digger watched them go, then frantically worked on the knots holding his arms behind his back. Mercifully, he got the gag out of his mouth by using the corner of the table to pry it off. Pierre had not secured that very well. The son-of-a-bitch. "Damn it, wake up, Colten!" He got his chair to move closer to the unconscious man by wiggling that way and pushing with his feet against the floor. Once there, he used his head to hit Colten on the shoulder. "Wake up, God damn it!"

Colten moaned.

"That's right," Digger's voice was urgent. "Get those eyes open." He head-butted Colten's shoulder a second time while continuing to try loosening his own bounds.

Colten's eyes opened, blinked, and he groaned again. He felt as though someone had run him over by a dump truck. His head hurt like a son-of-a-bitch, and whenever he took a breath, it was painful.

"Come on, come on!" anxiously, Digger tried moving his chair, so they were back-to-back. Feeling with his fingers, he found the knots on Colten's wrists. "Jacqueline's in trouble! Wake up!"

Colten's head snapped up. The dizziness caused by the sudden movement almost sent him back to unconsciousness. Jacqueline. His eyes traveled the room. "Where is she?"

"Shit-head took her to the barn!"

"Where's good old Ranger Peter?"

"Well, now, if you'd look at the floor to your right, you'll see Peter."

Colten did just that and grimaced. "What the hell happened?"

"I would have to say Jacqueline's stepbrother doesn't want to share the diamond."

Something clicked in Colten's mind, and he said, "How is it you don't sound very scatter-brained? You get hit on the head, and sense got knocked into you?"

Digger broke into a round of laughter. It wheezed out of him. He was chuckling so hard he was having a hard time working at the knots. "Confession time, but you'd better not tell Jacqueline. The truth is, I'm not absentminded. I retired from the FBI, pert-near ten years ago. I've seen too much and like my privacy. Being empty-headed keeps people away, 'cause they think I'm crazy. But not Jacqueline. She's the kindest person I know. She likes to dote on me, and I kind of like it." He was glad Colten could not see his face. He knew he was

137

blushing. "So, I keep the act up whenever she's around, and my brother indulges me. He's kept his mouth shut about the ruse, bless him."

Colten felt the knots loosen on his wrists. Just a little more, and... his hands fell apart. What felt like pins and needles took over as blood rushed into them. He went to get to his feet and almost fell to his knees as the pain in his side doubled him over, and he tried to breathe. He felt like his rib was cracked. Or broken. Not much difference, because either gave excruciating pain. "Mother of God and Jesus H. Christ," he hissed, clenching his teeth against the pain.

Turning, he worked the knots holding Digger's wrists. Once the older man was free, Colten started for the door, holding his bruised side in an attempt to stop the raging pain.

"Hold up," Digger shook his hands, dealing with his own pins and needles.

But Colten was not waiting. He went out the door as his heart hammered in his chest, nearly choking him because of his fear for Jacqueline.

He pushed the thought away.

She'd be all right.

He had to believe that.

* * * *

"Where is the Diamond, Jacqueline?" Pierre demanded as she dug through the pockets of Colten's jeans.

"It is in here!" she exclaimed frantically. She knew Colten had kept it in the left pocket since they found it and was always assuring himself it was still there. She'd watched him check and double-check last night, before hanging them on the rail, but she did not question why she'd found them lying on the ground when she led Pierre into the barn.

Frustration tore a sob from her throat.

Pierre moved forward, grabbed her, and spun her around to face him. "I am not playing games! I want that diamond! Now!" He shook her, causing her head to snap back and forth like a rag doll.

"Get. Your. Hands. Off. Of. Her." The order was full of menace.

Pierre spun toward the voice, fired his gun, and missed. The shot had been wild, and Colten did not provide a stand-still target. He came in low, dove for Pierre's legs, and took him down, but the pain from his rib prevented him from fighting the man effectively and nearly caused him to blackout.

Laying there, trying to breathe, made him an open target for Pierre's wrath. The man grabbed a large rock and slammed it into Colten's left eye without hesitation.

Blood splattered. Colten's howl of pain caused the hair on the nape of Jacqueline's neck to rise.

Pierre stepped away from the man withering in pain on the dirt floor and scattered hay as though he were unaware of Colten's trauma. Breathing hard, he turned toward Jacqueline with a smile so evil; it sent her heart thumping in her ears. "Well, my dear. It appears your lover isn't much of a hero." He cocked his gun, aimed it at Colten. Without thinking, Jacqueline jumped onto his back and pummeled his head with her fists.

Pierre reached around, dislodged her, and threw her to the ground in the opposite corner from where Colten lay. "You little bitch!" He stalked toward her. "I'm going to kill you!" He kicked her in the head, stomach, and thigh. He did not care where his foot landed. He was in a blinding rage. "I should have killed you a long time ago!" Somewhere along the way, he lost his gun, but he did not need it. Oh no, he would rather squeeze the air from her lungs and watch the life leave her eyes as he strangled her.

He reached down, pulled her up by the neck.

Fighting for air, Jacqueline made a useless attempt to dislodge his hands from her throat. Black spots began forming behind her eyes. She knew she had little time left. Just when she thought she would succumb to death, Pierre's hands loosened; his head flew forward narrowly missing her face. His eyes rolled up in his head, then his body slithered to the ground. And there was Colten, face covered with blood, holding a shovel he had used to hit the back of Pierre's head with.

Colten's body wavered for only a second before his knees buckled, and he crumpled to the floor.

"Colten!" she rushed to him, forgetting her own bruises. "My God, my God..." she looked around, frantic for something to stanch the blood coming from his damaged eye socket. Seeing nothing, she removed her own shirt and pressed it against the injury.

Digger rushed into the barn, a gun in his hand. Taking in the situation, he first checked on Pierre. Damn if the man wasn't still alive. Unconscious, but alive.

Taking no chances, he found some rope and quickly tied the bastard up before moving to where Jacqueline cradled Colten's head in her lap, pressing her shirt against his eye.

Without a word, Digger lifted the shirt away from Colten's eye and could not help the bile that rose in his throat when he saw the extensive damage that had been done to the younger man. Gently, he told Jacqueline, "I've got a shortwave radio in my cabin. I'll get help up here, Miss Jackie." With that, he ran out of the barn.

Jacqueline looked down at Colten. He was still breathing, but he was unconscious. The pain had to be unbearable. The damage to his eye socket and possibly his eye caused her heart to squeeze tight.

Her stomach lurched.

Gently, she brought her hand to his hair, smoothing it away from his face. "Je t'aime," she whispered, bending forward, and touched his lips with hers, regardless of the blood on his face. With a shaky hand, she wiped the scarlet liquid from her lips. "I love you, Colten." She admitted on a sob and prayed help would arrive before it was too late.

Chapter Seventeen

She hated hospitals. The aroma of rubbing alcohol, ammonia, and death had a way of bringing back memories of when her father passed away. Her mind flooded with images, remembering those last days of her father's life in ICU.

Colten would not die, she told herself. He had made it here, and by God, he would not die here!

It had taken what felt like hours for help to arrive at Digger's cabin. Longer still for the ambulance to transport Colten to Clarion Memorial Hospital. He had lost a lot of blood; it shocked the Doctors to have found a heartbeat when the paramedics wheeled him in.

They rushed him to surgery, and she heard nothing regarding his condition since the surgical room doors closed.

That was over five hours ago.

Doctors had examined her, pushing and prodding as they checked every inch of her battered body. She would be black and blue for weeks, but she did not care. All the aches she felt were dull compared to what Colten had endured.

Bringing the heel of her hand to her mouth, she stifled the sob and turned her head to rest her cheek on the stiff hospital pillow of the bed she was assigned. She felt it was all her fault. Had she just let Pierre keep the diamond and not taken it from him in the first place, none of this would have happened. Colten was on the brink of death, and the guilt of it was threatening to consume her.

"Please," she whispered, directing the anguished plea toward heaven. "Please, God...." A tear escaped, slowly trailing down her face and onto the pillow. "Please let Colten live."

A knock on the door brought her head around to see Cadman Benson leaning against the door frame. He looked haggard, as though someone had awakened him in the middle of the night and was now functioning on only five minutes of sleep.

"Hi," he said, putting his hands into the pockets of his jeans he entered the room. "The Clarion police called me. I got here as soon as I could."

She said nothing as he pulled a chair up and sat down. "How are you doing?"

She shook her head. Her condition did not matter. "Have you spoken to the doctors?" she asked anxiously, her French accent more pronounced in her distress. "Is Colten out of surgery? Is he..." she trailed off on a choked sob.

Cadman never knew how to comfort a woman in distress. All he could think to do was reach out and pat her hand and felt like a fool. "I just finished speaking with the head nurse. She said the doctors will wrap things up in another hour or two. When it's over, she'll have the head surgeon report to me. I'll make sure you're allowed to hear what he has to say."

"It is my fault!" she exclaimed, her emotions pouring out.

Cadman shook his head. "Bullshit. This was Pierre Bellefeuille's doing. He's to blame, and he'll have years behind bars to reflect on it."

Jacqueline's laugh was hysterical. "That is not enough." Not nearly enough for everything he had done.

Cadman shrugged. "Probably, but it's a matter for the justice system now. Knowing how things work, I figure he'll be transported back to France to finish out his life sentence."

"He needs to be sent to hell!" She exclaimed, her voice holding a combination of anger and dismay. Then she covered her eyes and shed tears she did not realize she still had.

Cadman cleared his throat. "Yeah," he mumbled, too low for her to hear. "Yeah, he does."

And they waited together, silently praying for Colten to pull through.

Another knock sounded. This time, standing at the door, was the Davidson family, including Digger.

"May we come in?" Linda asked, her voice soft and hesitant.

At Jacqueline's nod, Cadman stood as the group entered the room, and they made introductions.

Linda moved forward, took Jacqueline's hand in hers. "We wanted to be with you..." her voice trailed off. What was there to say?

The two oldest Davidson children came forward to hand Jacqueline a vase of assorted roses. "You're going to be okay," they told her with confidence.

Jacqueline tried to find a smile but failed miserably.

Grant came forward with his own offering.

A framed sketch he had done that morning. When Jacqueline saw it, fresh tears began running down her face as she gazed at Colten's image, staring up at her.

"I... didn't... mean to... make you... cry... Miss Jackie," Grant's voice broke, distressed that his gift had not caused the smile he desired.

"It is all right, Grant. It's... perfect." Jacqueline swallowed and managed a small smile for the child.

Linda took the framed drawing and placed it on the hospital tray next to the bed.

Digger came forward. "I... found," he cleared his throat, moved his right hand out of his pocket. Opening his fist, he revealed the Sancy resting in the palm of his hand. "Mr. George had it."

Jacqueline shook her head. "I do not wish to see that thing ever again."

Cadman's eyes almost bulged out of his skull, seeing the one-of-a-kind diamond being treated as though it were a worthless rock. "I'll take that," he said, reaching out.

Digger hesitated for an instant, but when he saw Jacqueline's nod, he handed it to Cadman.

After that, there was not much conversation, as the group waited for news on Colten's health.

An hour later, there was another knock on Jacqueline's door. This time when she looked up, hoping to see the surgeon, she saw an older couple instead, probably in their 50s, standing in the doorway. Their faces showed sorrow; deep lines of distress were etched there, and Jacqueline's brows drew together with confusion. She did not know who these people were. She assumed that whatever trauma someone in their family was experiencing had confused them into making a wrong turn into her room.

Cadman, leaning against a wall, speaking in low tones to Digger and Gary Davidson, pushed off the wall, moved forward, and extended his hand to the gentleman. "Donald," his voice was somber. He nodded to the woman. "Barbra. You made good time."

The woman reached out, grasped Cadman's arm in a grip that felt like a vice. "Is there any word? Is there any word on my son's condition?"

Jacqueline's eyes widened. Oh God, these must be Colten's parents. Surely, they would begin pointing fingers at her, condemning her for her part in this tragedy.

Cadman shook his head. "Not yet, but I expect something soon."

"I'll give it five minutes," Donald Fisher said, "Then I'm going into surgery to find out what the hell's going on with my boy."

Cadman nodded. Doctor Donald Fisher was one determined man. And one who could get answers much quicker than even he could.

Barbra noticed Jacqueline lying in bed for the first time. Her eyes widened, and then compassion filled those red-from-crying depths. "Oh, you poor dear," she rushed forward. "You must be the woman my son was protecting when..." she faltered, took a deep breath for calm. "Are you all right?" Then she laughed. Not gaily, but with an apology. "Of course, you're not. I'm sorry." As though she had known Jacqueline for years, she reached out a soothing hand and ran it down the younger woman's hair.

Despite herself, Jacqueline reached up and took the woman's hand in hers. Their eyes met, and at that moment, Jacqueline felt acceptance, and something else. A bond. They both loved the man, who was, at this very moment, fighting for his life. When Barbara bent down and wrapped her arms around her, they held each other tight.

Another knock sounded. Ten pairs of eyes turned to the doorway to find the surgeon standing there. He looked ready to drop.

After introductions, the man got to the point everyone wanted to hear. "He's a strong fighter," he began. "I'll give him that. Thankfully, he's O positive. We were able to get enough blood into him." He grimaced, remembering how many pints they had needed. "We'll keep him in ICU for a few weeks; watch for infection. The next forty-eight hours are critical. That's all I can say. It's up to him to heal, but with the determination his body gave to stay with us, I'd say he will pull through."

A short celebration began, but Doctor Harrison cut it off. "The broken rib punctured a lung. We've put a chest tube in for drainage and to help inflate the lung. It's going to take several days for his chest to expand and we'll monitor that as well. We hope we won't have to go back in, but that all depends upon the healing process. If all goes well, it's going to take six to eight weeks to fully recover."

He gave a weary sigh and knew they were waiting for farther information. "The impact to the left side of his face fractured his cheekbone, eye-socket..." He trailed off. No reason to go into all the details of what a mess that had been. "We were hoping to save his eye but," he shook his head. "Fragments of bone severed the muscles that support the eye and cut nerves. There was no way to save the eye."

Silence. No one spoke for a few moments, and then Jacqueline said, "But he will be all right?"

Doctor Harrison nodded. "I believe so, yes, as long as complications do not arise, such as an infection. It's going to be a long hall, but as I said earlier, he's a fighter."

She could not have prevented the sniffle as fresh tears, this time tears of joy, clouded her vision. Through the cloudy liquid, she met Barbra Fisher's eyes, and slowly, both women's mouths curved into beaming smiles.

* * * *

He'd gone to hell. He knew it was hell because heaven was reported to be peaceful and tranquil, and, well, heavenly. But hell was a place of pain and suffering. And Lord God have mercy; his face and chest were one raving mass of hurt.

No. Hurt was too tame of a word, although agony might touch the tip of the iceberg of describing how he was feeling. His face throbbed like a son-of-a-bitch as he made the climb farther into consciousness.

"God," he choked, his tongue feeling as though a thick layer of old leather had replaced it. He tried to find saliva. But it felt as though the Sierra Desert had more moisture in it than his mouth did.

He tried opening his eyes. The left one wasn't cooperating, so he made do with his right. It took a while to focus. Once his vision cleared, the single eye widened when he saw his mother sitting in a chair, chin resting on her chest, as though she had fallen asleep there. Confused, he managed a gritty, "Mom?"

At the sound, her body jerked awake. She looked up, and when she saw his good eye open, looking at her, her smile burst like sunlight, pushing away the darkness.

"Colten! Oh, baby!" She jumped up and leaned down to hug him close, mindful of all the bandages I. V's and the tube inserted into his chest cavity to help drain air from the space surrounding his lungs. The hug she gave him wasn't nearly as gripping as she would have liked to have given him, but this would do.

Colten grimaced, finding it difficult to breathe. "Mom don't call me baby. Thaddeus is your baby."

Her eyes misted. "I know who my children are, and if I want to call one of them baby, I will. Including your forty-four-year-old brother."

A slight smile curved his lips. His brother, James, probably loved that, he thought with affection as one of his older sibling's images came to mind.

"How do you feel?" she asked, running a hand down his arm.

"Like shit run over. Can I have some water, mom?"

She reached for the glass resting on the metal tray next to the bed, poured a glass full from the provided pitcher, and held it to his lips. Where he would have tossed it back in one swallow, she allowed only a few sips; always the doctor's wife, she knew better than to give a man too much at once.

"I have to get the doctor," she said, turning, but before she could step away, he took her hand, stopping her.

"What are you doing here, mom?" Where was he, anyway? He glanced around the room. Obviously, a hospital, but he could not remember a thing past....

He almost bolted out of bed. Sudden nausea sent him back on to the pillow. Sweat beaded his upper lip and forehead as he fought the queasiness and the pain. Once under control, he managed to say one word, "Jacqueline..."

Barbara smiled. "She's fine, honey. They released her from the hospital a few days ago."

The relief that she was okay felt almost tangible. Colten's body relaxed back into the bed. Details would come later. For now, it satisfied him to know she was safe. "How long have I been here?"

She looked uncomfortable. "Really, Colten. I need to get the doctor. Your father, too."

His mother seemed nervous; clue number one that something was up. His mother was always calm. "Mom...."

She sighed. "Eight days. You've been here for eight days."

He could only stare. "Eight... days," he repeated, as though the words were a foreign language. "You've been here that long?"

She nodded.

"Who's taking care of Clinton?"

She raised a brow. Something had changed in her son, she thought. He phoned out of the blue recently to talk about his son, and now he was wondering about his safety. It swelled her heart to know he was coming around. His son, eccentric in many ways, was still a great kid. "Oh, your father and I put him out on the curb. And told him to fend for himself while we were gone."

She said it so deadpan; it took him a moment, but his lip made a slow climb upward before she walked out the door to find the doctor and her husband.

She hoped her son's humor would last once he knew his face wouldn't ever be quite the same.

Colten reached for the glass of water his mother had set back on the tray and fought against the pain in his chest. He was exhausted by the time he had it in his hand, but he was stubborn enough to bring the glass to his lips just as his mother returned. Not taking the chance, she would take it away from him, he tipped it up and drank it in four gulps. It was not an easy feat, because of the amount of gauze covering the left side of his face, but defying his mother almost seemed worth the disapproving look she shot him.

His stomach lurched at having something thrown into it after days without being filled. The only reason he kept it down was with a will of iron because he could see her looking at him, with her arms crossed over her chest; prepared to gloat and give him one of her famous, I told you so, speeches if he puked.

When he was certain his stomach would not eject the liquid and make a mockery out of him, he gave his mother a grin that reminded her of all those times when he had been a little boy and he gave her that same smirk that told her well enough, he'd been up to no good.

"Are you proud of yourself?" she asked.

"Well, I'm not thirsty anymore, if you're wondering."

Barbara shook her head, tried not to laugh, but could not contain her chuckle.

Once the doctor arrived, along with Colten's father, the man explained the damage his body had suffered. "Your lung is making progress. We're monitoring it closely and are confident the tube in your chest will come out sometime next week."

And then he delivered the news about his eye and that information did not go down nearly as smoothly as the water had.

Chapter Eighteen

They would not let him see his face. It was too soon, Doctor Harrison claimed, to remove the bandages which made Colten irate.

His father got in his face and told him to settle down. Donald Fisher did not upset easily, but Colten's attitude had pushed the right button, and there was concern that if Colten did not quiet down, he would be in danger of causing farther damage to his healing lung and ribs.

But Colten did not care if his father was mad or not. After all, it was not his face that had changed forever. For Colten, losing an eye was just one more blow in a long list of emotional upheavals. Between Caroline's death, and Clinton's diagnosis, he felt as though he had been battered with wounds that would not heal, and time couldn't erase. And now he was half-blind. And they acted as though it was no big deal.

Screw them!

"Out!" he shouted, thrashing around so violently that Doctor Harrison ordered a sedative. Despite his recent accident, it still took his father and Doctor Harrison to hold him down while the nurse injected the sedative into the I.V. Once the medicine reached his vein, his body slowly relaxed and his head fell back to rest on the pillow. "Damn it," he said in a voice slightly slurred. "God damn it." His eye closed, and within minutes he was asleep.

The group breathed a sigh of relief.

"Oh God," Barbra cried, wrapping her arms around Donald's waist, her forehead on his chest. "What are we going to do?"

Donald stroked her hair. "He'll be all right, Barbs," he assured her and hoped he was telling the truth. "He's been through so much..." his own voice hitched. Out of all his children, all ten of them, it seemed Colten was the one who had the least attractive hand in this game called life.

Doctor Harrison ran a hand through his hair and felt as though he had just grown four more gray ones. "He's in shock," he murmured, then realized he was trying to explain the situation to a peer. "Sorry," he said, shrugging helplessly.

Donald glanced at him. "Everyone reacts differently to trauma. Colten, well.... He's always been one to blow-up first, then comes around in time." He grimaced. It had taken his son seven years to desire a relationship with Clinton. He hoped it would not take that long for Colten to accept this new situation.

His eyes traveled to his son's sleeping form and sighed. "We'll just have to wait and see what happens when he wakes up." He hoped to God Colten did not plummet into a depression so severe he couldn't climb back out.

Colten's parents continued taking turns at his bedside, keeping a watchful eye for when he regained consciousness.

During Barbara's afternoon shift, she felt a presence behind her and turned. Her eyes widened when she saw Jacqueline hovering in the doorway, looking unsure if she was welcome.

Barbra offered a smile, stood, and extended her hand. "Come in," her brows knitted together. "Shouldn't you be resting?" Despite the high-necked collar dress Jacqueline was wearing, Barbra could see the bruising around the younger woman's neck. Its black coloring had faded to a pea-green and still had a long way to go before it disappeared completely.

"If I rest any more, I will go crazy," Jacqueline said, stepping closer to the bed. Without realizing what she was doing, her hand moved out to touch Colten's hair, stroking it. Jacqueline studied the man, examining the wrapping covering half his face. Her eyes lingering on his lips, remembering their texture and feel on hers. Desperately, she wanted to lean down and touch her mouth to his. However, with his mother standing only a few feet away, Jacqueline held back on the desire to touch her lips to his, unsure what the woman's reaction would be. But had she looked, she would have seen approval in the woman's eyes.

Barbra saw all she needed to know as she watched Jacqueline with her son. It made her smile and gave her hope.

"He woke up this morning," Barbra told her.

Jacqueline's head snapped up. She looked at Colten's mother. "That is wonderful news!" She wished she had been there, but convincing the Davidson's she was well enough to be out and about had not been easy. She wanted to be with Colten. To hold his hand and give comfort, not only for him, but to assure herself he was indeed alive and was going to be alright.

Barbra hesitated for only a moment before telling Jacqueline about Colten's reaction to the news his eye was gone, and his facial damage was extensive.

Jacqueline closed her eyes, took a deep breath, and looked back down at the man she loved. It no longer shocked her to admit her feelings for him. She just did not know how she would convince him he needed her.

"May I sit with him for a while?"

With a smile on her lips, Barbra nodded. "I could use a cup of coffee. I'll just go down to the cafeteria." She walked out the door, stopping just outside to turn back and watch the woman stroking her son's hair. The girl wore her heart on her sleeve, Barbra thought, and hoped her son would hang on to this one.

Jacqueline stood for a long time, merely enjoying the texture of Colten's thick carpet of dark brown hair. He needed a haircut, she thought, then smiled to herself. He could wear it however he liked, as long as he was alive.

Colten's unbandaged eye fluttered, then opened. He stared at her, though his vision was not clear, and he thought he might be hallucinating. His body felt as though he was floating on a cloud, and he could not seem to think clearly.

Had someone given him a drug? He couldn't remember. Was he in the hospital? Or only dreaming?

"Good afternoon," she said.

He stared at her. Was she real or an illusion?

She gave into impulse, bent forward, kissed him, and smiled.

Real, he thought, but perhaps that too was a delusion. "Thought you'd be on your way back to France by now," he told the apparition. The real Jacqueline would have no reason to be here, although he could admit it would be nice if she were. He had so much he wanted to say to her.

When they were in that barn, and he'd known the danger she was in, it caused his adrenalin to kick in. It was the only explanation of how he could have knocked Pierre out with a shovel when he himself was suffering.

But love was a powerful force and yes, damn it. He loved her despite not having known her for very long. Something about her called out to his soul and he could not deny its pull.

She pulled back from him and frowned. "France? Why would I go there?"

He shrugged. "It's your home, and you're safe now. It's where you belong."

She stared at him, shook her head. "I...."

"Anyway, best of luck to you." He tried to clear his head. If this was the real Jacqueline, he sure in hell would not be telling her to leave when he wanted her to stay.

Her frown got much, much deeper. "Colten, I am not going back to France."

"Yeah? Why not? There isn't- anything for you- here-" Except me, his mind said, but the thought only came out as a groan as he tried to focus.

"Colten-" What was there to say? She brushed at the tears threatening to surface, cleared her throat and tried to ignore the pain in her heart. Obviously, he did not want her here.

Having no words, she turned away from him to walk out the door but stopped momentarily to look at him one last time. "Speedy recovery, Colten."

He closed his eye, cursed, and shook his head, attempting to clear it. His head spun from the movement, but he could feel the cloud lifting. "Jacqueline," he sighed and to her ears, it sounded as though she bored him.

Squaring her shoulders, she told him, "I'm sorry for everything, and I wish you all the best in the world," as she walked away.

"Now just- a damn- minute," he said, cursing the I.V.'s, and his weakened state. The brain fog was almost gone enough for him to understand this was not a dream. She was real and about to leave him. "Don't you dare walk out that door!" He could shout above a whisper, but not loud enough for her to hear through the door that closed behind her.

Outside the door, Jacqueline allowed her tears free rein. It was ridiculous to feel this heartbroken over a man she had known only a short time and yet, during their brief time together, she felt a connection with him she had never felt with anyone else.

She passed Cadman Benson without seeing him as she all but ran down the corridor. She could not blame Colten for not wanting her there. Who would wish to spend time with the person responsible for them having been on the brink of death? Even if it had not been her hand to have delivered the damage.

Turning a corner, she ran straight into Barbra Fisher. The older woman took one look at Jacqueline's face and said, "Oh dear." Taking her hand in hers, she told her, "Come with me," and left not an ounce of doubt in her tone that implied Jacqueline had a choice.

On the second floor of the hospital, walking into Colten's room and closing the door, Cadman said, "Well now, that was interesting. "I just passed Jacqueline Grymes, and she was crying."

"Shut up." Colten told him. He was so frustrated, he could spit.

Cadman raised a brow. "Just stating a fact. No reason to get your knickers in a knot." He moved closer to the bed. "You look like hell."

Despite everything, Colten's mouth quirked upward. "I wouldn't know. They won't give me a mirror."

Cadman looked around the room, looking for one. When he saw none, he shrugged. "Doesn't matter. You're mostly hidden under all that cloth, anyway. Besides, you never were that good looking."

Colten's chuckle started low. He still felt like hell that Jacqueline would not give him a chance to explain. But it was good to feel his humor coming back.

"The President sends his regards," Cadman said, pulling up a chair next to the bed and straddling it. "He mentioned something about your taking a vacation longer than allowed. But he'll forgive you, under the circumstances."

Colten sighed. "Well, you can tell JFK to...."

"Careful. This is the President of the United States we're talking about. Your commander and chief."

"Not anymore. I'm resigning, effective now."

Cadman's eyes widened. "Now Colt, there's no reason for you to do that. You can still function with one eye..."

Colten waved a hand to silence him. "It's something I would have done, anyway. I just want to go home."

Cadman shook his head. "Damn it, Colt. You're good at your job."

Colten's right brow rose. He was lying in a hospital bed because the bad guy had gotten the drop on him. In his book, that hadn't been being good at his job. "It has nothing to do with this," he claimed, gesturing to his face. "I just want to go back home and be a father to my son."

Cadman glanced at the closed door, then back. "Does Jacqueline Grymes fit into any of this?"

His heart squeezed. "I, um, might have just blown that," he said and told Cadman what transpired moments ago.

"Damn drugs," Cadman said, and Colten could not have agreed more.

His mother walked in, looking grim. "Colten Marshal Fisher, I want to speak to you."

Cadman blew out his breath and looked Colten in the eye. "I think you're in trouble." He was glad at that moment the woman was not his mother. He could almost imagine smoke coming out of her ears. Everyone knew; if your mother used your middle name, you were toast.

Getting up, he told Colten, "I'll talk to you later." He nodded his head at Barbra. "Mrs. Fisher." He acknowledged her and headed for the door. As he retreated, he heard Colten mumble, "Coward." He grinned as he closed the door, wishing he could be a fly on the wall to witness Barbra Fisher giving her son hell.

Barbra marched to her son's bed like a general. "Colten, I just ran into Jacqueline Grymes, downstairs. She's in tears. Did you know she blames herself for your being here?"

"That's ridiculous," he cursed the fact he could not get up.

"I told her exactly that. And still she's devastated, you would blame her for your being here."

"What the hell?! I never said that." His mind raced. Had he?

"And," his mother's voice rose with that word. "She claims you slept with her. Colten, how could you?"

He flushed with embarrassment, from the top of his head, all the way to his toes. "I..." he opened his mouth, closed it. The glare his mother was giving him made him feel as though he were an adolescent. Not a grown man, who had already been married once, and had a seven-year-old son. The devil made him say, "It wasn't a hardship, mom. She's pretty."

"Colten!" her eyes rounded.

He winced but did not apologize. "Look, mom. I'd just woken up. I wasn't thinking-"

"No kidding."

God, his mother had a way of making him feel like a pile of crap. "Look, I tried to explain, but she walked out before I could shake off the lingering effects of whatever drug they forced into me. It's not as if I could just go running after her. I have to wait until she comes back."

She shook her head. "That's the problem, Colten. She's not coming back. She's leaving Clarion tonight."

Chapter Nineteen

July 20th, 1962

Colten's first breath of fresh air almost made him drunk. It had been eight weeks since he had been outside of the walls of that hospital.

He almost did a little jig the moment he was wheeled him out the front door to the vehicle his parents rented to take him to the airport and home. The celebration would have to wait, though. His rib was almost mended. However, a wrong move would cause more than a little discomfort.

The collapse lung healed, although he continued to do the breathing exercises prescribed by the doctor and would finish what was left of the medication to help fight off infection. Other than that, he could breathe deep without feeling as though he would die.

Hospital rules forced him to sit in a wheelchair, like some invalid, as the nurse wheeled him out from the room he'd occupied for two months. That had grated, but he accepted it. He would have done anything to get himself the hell out of here.

When the doors of the hospital opened, the sunlight was almost too bright in its intensity. It forced Colten to raise his hand to shade his eye. But the feel of the sun's rays on him, for the first time in months, felt like heaven. The sun on his face spoke of promise. There would not be clouds hanging over his head anymore. He would see to that. There was only one thing he needed to take care of. Once that was done, he would build a new life for himself and vowed everything would work out.

His parents stood beside the rental car. His mother, beaming, and his father holding the backseat door open for him would be a good memory that would last him his lifetime.

Colten stood up from the wheelchair and knew he didn't want to set foot in another care facility for a long, long while.

"You look great, baby," his mother said, cupping his face in her hands, and kissed his right cheek. "Now, hold still while I take your picture." With that, she pulled her Kodak two-tone gray and silver Brownie Fiesta camera from the car and snapped a photo of him scowling at her.

Colten readjusted the patch over his left eye. "Mom..." he groaned.

She laughed. "I just needed a photo of you leaving the hospital for my scrapbook."

Colten's good eye rolled. "Mom, you've taken my picture every day I've been recovering."

Donald cleared his throat. "Give it up, son. You know how your mother is. Snapping pictures is her mission in life."

Sure, he knew his mother was addicted to picture-taking, but it did not mean he liked it.

"Come on," Donald motioned to the car, "Time to go. Bet you can't wait to get back to Bismarck."

Bismarck. Colten had never considered the capital of North Dakota his home.

He folded himself into the back seat of the car and waited for his parents to get in.

They were on their way to the airport when he told them, "I'm not going to Bismarck."

His father glanced at him in the rearview mirror. His mother looked at him over her shoulder. "Well, dear. We know you're eager to get to Medora...."

He shook his head. "I'm not going to North Dakota."

His mother's brows drew together. "But why? Everything you want is back home."

"No, it's not."

"Colten," Barbra tried to sound firm, "You just got out of the hospital. Where on earth are you planning to go? We've told Clinton you were coming home, and it's all he's been talking about." Literally, Barbra mused. Whenever they phoned Margaret, their oldest daughter, who was taking care of both Clinton and Thaddeus, all Clinton would say was, Dad, dad, dad. My dad's coming home! Repeatedly.

"Yeah, I know. Clinton does the same thing to me when I've spoken to him. He hasn't made the connection that I'm the guy he's talking about." But he would, Colten vowed.

"Then why on earth are you going off to..." she frowned. "Where did you say you're going?"

He took a deep breath. Happy as a clam that his rib did not hurt him because of it, and both his lungs expanded to accommodate the fresh air. "To begin with, New York City." He leaned back in the seat. "I'm going to find Jacqueline, and if she's not there, I'm going to France."

His mother sputtered. "But, Colten, you cannot be serious!" Her voice was almost shrill, making the two men wince.

"I thought you liked Jacqueline," Colten said.

"Of course, I do!"

"Then, what's the problem?"

His father shot Barbra a look that silenced her. "No problem, Colten. Your mother is concerned about the fact you just

163

got out of the hospital. You're still a ways from being one hundred percent. We just don't understand. You told us you'd spoken with that actress friend of hers, and she said she didn't know where Jacqueline was."

"I think she's a liar." Actually, he knew she was. Those two women were the best of friends. No way in hell would Jacqueline keep Rosalinda in the dark about her whereabouts. As far as Colten was concerned, she was hiding something. She had been insistent that he returned to North Dakota and let things fall into place.

"Colten," his mother again, "why don't you come home with us? You're still recovering. I don't think you should take an unnecessary trip."

Colten leaned back in the seat. "Mom, it will take a plane less time to arrive in New York City than to get to North Dakota. Once I arrive in the Big Apple, if I'm feeling tired, I can just go to my place." He shifted. "I still have an apartment there. Besides, I need to arrange for someone to pack the place up for me."

"But... Colten," his mother all but whined, making Colten cock a brow. His mother never whined like a child, not getting her way.

Donald sighed. "Barbs, you need to let Colten do what he needs to do."

She opened her mouth to protest, but the look her husband shot her had her snapping it shut. She folded her arms across her chest and stared out the window. If her son would just listen to her, but no; he was determined to go. Fine, let him. Served him right if what he wanted took longer than necessary to find.

* * * *

Colten found Rosalinda Vallombrosa still in residence at Charles Lafayette's mansion on the outskirts of New York City. He had gotten her whereabouts from Cadman, which saved him time although he was surprised the actress was still in the United States.

Colten had been waiting in the study off the foyer for almost half an hour and decided if the starlet did not show her face in the next five minutes, he would track her down and shake Jacqueline's whereabouts out of her if need be.

No, he decided, he was not even going to wait that much longer.

He stood up from the thick leathered chair with the intent on doing a room by room search for her when the actress suddenly appeared in the doorway.

"It's about time," he growled.

Rosalinda stopped in mid-step, regarding him. "I like the eye patch. It makes you look mysterious, and... yummy." She followed the statement with a purr low in her throat as she continued forward, with the grace of a feline who was strutting for the attention of a male whose scent she just picked up.

"Where's Jacqueline?"

Her lips turned into a pout. "You asked me before. My answer iz the same."

He shook his head. "I don't believe you."

She shrugged, moved forward, raised a hand, touched his left cheek, and trailed a fingernail down the short scar, left behind from the reconstruction of the cheekbone. "What doez it matter? You are here." She moved in closer. Her voice became a seductress song. "I am here." She pressed in; raised her face to his. She had thought him handsome before, but now she

165

wanted to eat him alive. The scar and patch enhanced his looks, she thought.

Colten looked down at her. The top of her head did not make it to his chin and if he wanted to kiss her, all he would need to do was lean forward, bend at the waist, and she would be his. There was no denying her breathtaking beauty. A man would have to be dead not to have some sexual temptation.

His head dipped just a little and he watched her eyes go hot and flutter closed as his lips came within a hair's breadth of hers. But he stopped before contact and asked, "Where's Jacqueline?"

Her eyes snapped open. Taking a step back so she would not have to crane her neck to look at him, she studied him with surprise, and what seemed like admiration. From the time she had been fifteen Rosalinda had been manipulating men—married, devoted, single, or otherwise—into giving her whatever she wanted. But this time she sensed she would lose this conquest.

She turned away without a word and walked to the French balcony doors. Through their glass she stood for a moment `admiring the freshly cut lawns, and petunias in what she figured were every vibrant color of the flower they could possibly be found. The talented gardeners had not planted them in straight rows but had artfully designed the logo for Charles's production company; a circle outlined in purple, the depiction of the world housed within, and the center of that, was a vibrant red rose. She often wondered why he had chosen the design, and perhaps one day she would ask him.

She closed her eyes as she thought of Charles and wondered why she kept pushing him away, refusing to consider why she had not gone back to France when the news arrived that Pierre was safely behind bars, and she was free to do as she pleased.

She told herself she just wanted to visit America for now, and it had nothing to do with Charles.

She shook her head and willed herself not to dwell on the matter. Charles was a wonderful friend. He could not possibly love her. All the men she knew only wanted one thing from her and because that one thing was mutual, she never minded the one-night relationships, but with Charles? No, she could never commit to one man, even though he treated her with respect. As though she was more to him than a sexual play toy, and he allowed her to stay here without questioning when she would leave, as though he were content to have her close to him.

Rosalinda glanced at Colten Fisher and felt a spark of envy towards her closest friend. Even if he wasn't aware of it, his voice rose an octave whenever he spoke Jacqueline's name, tinged with tenderness. Regardless of what Jacqueline believed, this man had no animosity towards her for the hurt he had endured.

Turning, she asked, "Why are you here? Do your doctors know you are traveling, instead of resting?"

"I'm not a cripple, and you are avoiding my question." He moved toward her with purpose. "I want to know where Jacqueline is. If I have to go to France to find her, I'll do it. Because damn it, things aren't settled between us...."

"And what is between you?" she raised a brow in question.

Colten ran a hand through his hair and blew out a breath. "Damned if I know," he admitted. But he did know he would go mad if he could not see her soon.

She cocked her head, considered. "Mister Fisher, I have promised Jacqueline, I would not tell you where she was," she waved a hand to cut off his protest, "however, I encourage you to go home."

He threw his hands in the air with annoyance. "Damn it! Everyone keeps telling me to go home instead of telling me where she is!"

Her lips twitched, but she firmed them before he noticed. "Colten, are you aware, Tony Vallombrosa, is currently visiting the United States?"

Colten blinked. How had Tony gotten into this conversation? "He does that from time to time." He shrugged.

"Oui," she moved gracefully to the leather chair he had been occupying earlier and sat down. Smoothing her knee-length skirt, she said, "He is currently in a place his grandfather built a hotel in the 1880s."

Confusion knitted his brow. Why in God's name were they talking about Tony Vallombrosa and the once named Metropolitan? -Now called the Roughrider's Hotel, located in his hometown of Medora.

She sat back in the chair. "Mr. Benson mentioned you knew him."

Colten's sigh was heavy. "Rosalinda," impatience was thick. "I really don't care where Tony is...."

"I am not his only relation who knows the location he is visiting."

Colten heard the implication in her voice, and for a moment, he could not comprehend what she was telling him.

Everything you want is back home. His mother's insistence he return to North Dakota no longer seemed out of character. But damn it, why couldn't women just come out with it instead of being cryptic?

His heart seemed to lurch with the idea that Jacqueline was, right now, as he wasted time here, exactly where he wanted her to be. "You're telling me she's in Medora, North Dakota?" he clarified.

Rosalinda's smile was impishly innocent. "Colten, I have not mentioned her." She shrugged. "Besides, North Dakota, this town my cousin Tony is visiting, happens to be your home. Why would it appear strange if you show up there?"

He strolled forward, reached out, and, taking her by the shoulders, lifted her out of the chair and kissed her. "Thanks," he said, setting her back down, then walked out the door.

Rosalinda's satisfied smile followed his exit.

* * * *

As much as Colten wanted to drive directly to the airport, he had not lied to his parents. He did need to arrange for his apartment to be packed up. With that as his last order of business, he instructed the taxi to take him to his apartment.

When the cab stopped in front of his soon to be former address, he got out and thanked the driver, then headed for the landlord's office, on the first floor of the building. He did not have his keys with him. It wouldn't take long for the property owner to give him a new set or let him into the apartment.

As he headed up the steps, two teenage boys came down them. Not paying attention, as some kids didn't, one bumped into him.

Well, Colten could not put the entire blame on the kid, since it happened on his left side. He still had trouble with depth perception with that side of his body. So, he said, "Sorry," as he turned to the boy to get a better view and had a moment to think, he had seen that kid before.

The teen grunted and kept on going. One step at a time, without a care in the world except to continue to complain to his friend about the shitty day he'd had at the youth center. And didn't that Mister Maxwell think he was a badass, the candyass. That's what Mister Maxwell was, nothing more than a wimp.

When recognition dawned, Colten almost couldn't get the, "Hey, kid!" out of his mouth fast enough, and he knew, if the boy took off this time, he wouldn't have a chance in hell to catch him because of his rib still being on the mend and he was not up to full strength.

Miracles of miracles, the boy stopped and turned toward him, just as a car pulled up in front of the building, and Cadman Benson stepped out from it.

"Kiss off, man," the teen sneered.

"I want to talk to you," Colten said, going back down the steps.

The boy shook his head. "No way, man. Bet you're a narc." But as Colten grew nearer, the boy frowned. Then a cocky grin broke out across his face. "Well now, if it isn't Mr. Secret Service." His face bunched up as he zeroed in on the patch covering Colten's eye and the still raw and angry bruising of the left side of his face. "Oh man, what happened to you?"

"Life's been a bitch," Colten stopped a few feet away, with Cadman still standing on the curb, observing the interchange, as though some performance were happening.

The kid whistled. "I'd say someone messed you up real bad."

"You'd be right. So, where's my wallet?"

The kid's eyes widened. "Wallet? Man, I ain't got your wallet."

Cadman's ears perked up, and he chuckled. "Colten, this is the kid who picked your pocket?" He hooted. The kid was a skinny little runt who could not possibly weigh more than a hundred pounds.

Colten shot Cadman a withering glare before looking back at the kid. "I believe you. It's long gone by now. But I remember what I told you I would do to you if I ever caught you lifting wallets again. And that was just before you lifted mine."

The kid snorted. "You ain't look like you could hurt a fly." With that, he shot off down the sidewalk, his laughter trailing behind.

Cadman sighed. "Guess that leaves it up to me," he griped, knowing Colten was in no shape to pursue.

The kid gave a merry chase. Cadman gave him that. But he caught the little hellion at the end of the third block. Grabbing hold of the collar of the kid's shirt, he spun him around and got a swift kick to the shin. With a curse, Cadman let his hold loosen for a fraction of a second, which allowed the kid to jerk free and disappear around the corner.

Nursing his leg, cursing the kid, Cadman made it back to Colten and hissed, "Slippery bastard."

Colten grinned. "Got your wallet."

"Of course, I've got my wallet! What in the hell does that have to do...?"

Colten shook his head. "No. He got your wallet."

"The hell he did!" Cadman's hand reached for his back pocket and came away empty. "I'm going to cut off his balls."

Laughing, Colten said, "Let me know when the ceremony is. I'd like to crash the party."

Chapter Twenty

Jacqueline was not fooling herself. She knew why she allowed Colten's mother to talk her into coming to this place, although discovering her distant relation was visiting the area also aided in her decision. She had not seen Tony for several years. That alone was not what swayed her to finally say yes to Barbra Fisher's invitation. Her curiosity had. She wanted to see the land that caused Colten's eyes to light up with pride and passion when he spoke of the area, and now that she had viewed the lands, which were an alien contour to the rest of North Dakota, she knew she would have a hard time leaving it behind.

The locals said that if the Badlands liked you, they would ensnare your heart. Obviously, the area was fond of her because she had fallen in love wholeheartedly with the hills and buttes, splashed with color, that surrounded her. She itched to explore it on horseback but held back. Knowing she did not want to tour it with anyone other than the person who held her heart.

Pushing the melancholy away, she took a walk through the town, though it would not take long. The combined total area of the place was not much more than .35 square miles. With a population of 130 people, give or take. There were not any sidewalks, so she walked in the streets made of dirt.

The house where she was staying while in Medora belonged to Colten's parents, who did not live in it, but used it in the summer as a vacation home whenever they desired to come here. However, they were allowing her to stay there by herself while they remained in Bismarck.

She stepped off the porch and headed toward the center of town. In the short distance, she could see a few people standing in the center of the street; appearing as though they were conversing about the building before them, which was the Roughrider's Motel.

Two of the men were shaking their heads, as though they were contemplating something, and could not reach a decision. Jacqueline recognized the men as she drew closer, having met two of them recently. The third man she had known all her life. It was her distant cousin, Tony Vallombrosa, the relation she had in common with Rosalinda.

The first man was Harold Schafer, a North Dakota native, and self-made millionaire. He had once been a traveling salesman for Fargo Glass and Paint. Over time, Harold began packaging and selling a product he called Gold Seal Floor Wax. Then, a few years later, he introduced Glass Wax to the public and by 1948, his products had gone national. But he did not stop there. He continued his successful line of products by adding Snowy Bleach. And, just a few years earlier, in 1961, Mr. Schafer invented Mr. Bubble. A bubble bath product marketed for children and made affordable to consumers. It, and the other goods, quickly became the number one selling products in the world.

One would think a man who found success would slow down and retire. But not Harold. He was fifty years old and full of life. He had always loved the Badlands, and envisioned what this little town of Medora could do for North Dakota's tourism. He was making restoring this sleepy village a mission in his successful career. If what Harold wanted to accomplish with Medora succeeded, it would once again prove; he was an innovative businessman and marketing genius.

Harold was speaking with Russell Reid, a man dedicated to the development of North Dakota's state parks, and historic preservation of the states' past.

It was Reid who had acquired for North Dakota seventeen thousand acres of de Morès' holdings in the badlands. Which, in 1949, became Theodore Roosevelt National Memorial Park. Because of his friendship with Louis Manca-Amat, the past Duke de Vallombrosa, the de Morès heir gave the State the Chateau, along with its original furnishings, in 1936, with the stipulation the State would retain it as a museum, in honor of his parents. Louis also gave the State the packing plant site where his father once planned to slaughter, and process cattle close to the range. Unfortunately, de Morès' venture failed, and the facilities closed in 1886. All that remained now of what de Morès' had dreamed would one day be the largest meat-packing plant in the world, was the chimney. On March 17th, 1907, a fire destroyed the building.

Although the Vallombrosa family had only lived at the Chateau during the summer, and early fall, of 1883 to 1886, the building remained in the family for an additional 50 years, under the management of caretakers until 1923, when it served as a summer resort. The Historical Society restored the building from 1937 to 1941 and on August 7th, 1941, it opened to the public.

Jacqueline glanced down the street, as the men continued to talk about the hotel, and could see the Ferris Store about two blocks away. Mr. Schafer also purchased this building, along with the property still held by the de Vallombrosa family and was having it rebuilt. That little store had its own historical value. Teddy Roosevelt had slept in the attic above the store. He and Joe Ferris, the man who guided Roosevelt on his quest to shoot a buffalo when he arrived in the area in 1883, had become lifelong friends.

Reaching her destination, Jacqueline joined the men looking at the weather-worn building, discussing its future. She had heard that, after Mr. Schafer purchased the motel, he had taken its title to Reid as a gift. When the legislators refused to give Reid the money to restore the building, the cause of refurbishing the place was a loss.

Harold gestured toward the seventy-eight-year-old building and asked Reid, "What are we going to do with it?" The place was badly in need of repairs. There was still a bar and restaurant operating within. And sleeping rooms were on the upper level. It was amazing the place had not been condemned, yet.

"There's a lot of history here, Harold," Reid's voice was full of the passion he had for preserving the past.

True enough, Jacqueline thought, and not because her relatives founded the town. And not only because a United States President once walked its streets. But James Foley Jr., the unofficial Poet Laureate of North Dakota, who had written the North Dakota State Hymn, had grown up here, in the very house Medora's mother had commissioned to be built. A place where she and her husband could stay when they visited their daughter.

Foley's father had been the manager of the de Morès property for thirty-five years. Eventually, the de Morès' transferred ownership of the Von Hoffman house to the Foley family.

Tony was now the 4th Duke of Vallombrosa, and 6th Duke of Asinara, having obtained the titles not only through his father's line, but also through his mother, Marie-Thérèse du Bourg de Bozas, who was the daughter of Madame Bourg de Bozas.

Unfortunately, Tony's parents, who were married in 1917, divorced four years later.

Louis, Tony's father, never remarried although rumors in April of 1922 abounded with speculation that he would make the American actress Pearl White his new duchess as they were often seen together.

The current Duke of Vallombrosa was rugged appearing but a pleasant man, now in his middle 40s. He looked at Jacqueline and smiled in greeting. He was staying in the motel in question, which she found amusing because the man practically lived in a palace in France and could afford luxurious Hotels to stay in, but he'd chosen this one.

Possibly because his grandfather had built it, but she would never know for sure what prompted his stay there.

"It is a long way from France, to Medora," Tony commented when he saw her. His hand went up to smooth his bushy hair away from his noble forehead before replacing the cowboy hat he had been wearing. No one would ever mistake him for a Duke and a man of wealth. Yet, he had nine different titles after his name. He preferred western clothing, though he would never pass for a cowboy. Today, his jeans sported a belt and suspenders both. His left wrist sported an Accutron watch. On the right, he wore a Hermes brand wristwatch from Paris. His face was not remarkable, his height average.

The only reason people gave him attention around the area was due to him being the Marquis de Morès grandson.

Jacqueline smiled back. "Hello, Antoine." Regardless of him being considered eccentric by many, she liked him. He had been sheltered from the real world most of his life and was the last surviving grandchild of the Vallombrosa/Hoffman family line. The only granddaughter, Thais, died at the tender age of nineteen, in a horseback riding accident in Switzerland. Thais' mother, Athenais, daughter of Medora and de Morès, now lived in France and was pushing seventy-nine years of age.

If a family could have one word to describe it, tragic could easily sum up the de Morès line. Where others might one day look upon this little, nothing of a town, and think the Marquise and Medora's quest to build a meat-packing plant in the heart of the Badlands romantic, Jacqueline looked at the fact; nothing they ever tried succeeded. After the couple left the town of Medora, for the last time, the Marquis became anti-Semitic and blamed Jews for most of his business losses. In 1896, he was murdered in North Africa by his escort, while crossing the Sahara, where he planned to join the French, and Arabs, in the Khalifa's holy war, against the Jews, and the English.

"Yes," she answered Tony's earlier statement. "It is a very long way from France. Will you be staying long?"

"Not long. No." He spoke perfect English, without a trace of an accent. Jacqueline had to wonder how he managed it. She had never been able to completely rid herself of her own. Whenever she started talking, someone in town would comment on it.

"I believe we have a mutual acquaintance from here. His name is Colten Fisher." She had not meant to mention Colten. Her longing to see him was an ache in her heart. Every day she had spoken with Barbra on the phone while Colten was recovering in the hospital, wanting to know his progress, and wanting to be there. But Barbra convinced her to remain absent from Colten until he was well enough to travel.

When Jacqueline asked Barbra why that was the woman laughed and told her, "I'm using you as motivation for him to get better quicker. Just trust me on this. That boy of mine will come looking for you."

And so Jacqueline listened and wished she had not, because missing Colten was an ache in her heart.

Tony's head bobbed and a faint smile curved his lips. "Ah, yes. I like Mr. Colten. Very much so. I visited with his grandfather yesterday. He knew my grandparents. Is that not amazing?"

"Yes, it is," she agreed. She had not met Howard Fisher, Colten's grandfather, yet. But she wanted to.

"It has been a long time since I saw you last," Tony said.

"Too long," Jacqueline gave him a hug. "How is your aunt, Athenais?"

"She is doing well for a woman her age."

Jacqueline heard Reid say from behind her; as his conversation with Harold Schafer continued, "You could fix it up, Harold."

"Me?!" Harold half gasped; half laughed. The cost of such an undertaking would be sizable.

Reid nodded. "Look around you, Harold. North Dakota needs this town."

Reid was not talking him into anything he had not already considered, but the financial hit to his bank account would be sizable. "Maybe Tony would like to donate to the cause," Harold suggested. There was a faint lifting of his lips because he already knew what the answer would be. Tony was self-centered, and certainly not charitable. A total opposite of Harold. Schafer was known for his generous spirit.

Tony's eyes widened. "Me?" he all but sputtered. It did not matter to him that his grandfather had commissioned George Fitzgerald to build the hotel in 1884 with the anticipation of a boom in Medora, because of the packing plant; and the stage-coach line, and several other businesses de Morès had started. Tony would not lift a finger to preserve it.

Jacqueline brushed her hand along his arm in a soothing gesture. "Your grandfather would approve," she tried to encourage him.

Tony almost choked at the thought.

With a sigh, Jacqueline changed the subject as the other two men continued their talk of restoration. "How have you been?" she asked, knowing it had been difficult for him when his father passed away a few years earlier.

He shrugged.

"What brings you to North Dakota?"

"Mr. Schafer was kind enough to send me an invitation. And a ticket, so I could visit. I have not been here since my father passed away. But this is a wonderful pleasure trip, and I am fortunate Mr. Schafer was kind enough to reach out to me and pay for my expenses." Tony leaned close to her. "I do not have money, Jacqueline. I do not know how else I would have managed to get here."

Over Tony's shoulder, she saw Harold roll his eyes; having heard Tony's claim of having no money and covered her laugh with a cough. Tony had plenty of money. More than Schafer, who had millions. Sadly, however, Tony did not understand how to earn funds. Or how to spend them or use them. All of his wealth was held in a trust fund controlled by lawyers and Tony had never taken an interest in how his bills were paid.

Later, Jacqueline would learn that all of Tony's travel, meals, and even spending money had been provided by Schafer's Gold Seal Company. Harold had thought Tony would be a valuable resource in the history of the Marquis, Medora, and their family. In that department, Tony had been as useful as a dirt road leading nowhere and Colten's father was the valued resource.

"I'll call my brother-in-law," Jacqueline heard Harold say to Reid. "Mark could oversee the project." And with those words, another historical event would begin, the rebuilding of an entire town.

About half an hour later, the small group broke up, each of them going their separate ways. Tony turned down Jacqueline's invitation to dinner that evening, saying he had a party to attend. As it turned out, he was having a grand time being the guest of several people in Bismarck during his visit.

Jacqueline suspected they invited him for no other reason than he was the Marquis de Morès' grandson. Knowing Tony as she did, Jacqueline assumed that was exactly how he managed to get the invite. He liked riding on the shirttails of his grandfather.

As she turned to walk back to the Fisher's Medora residence, her thoughts turned once again to Colten. Thinking of him caused an ache in her heart. She missed him more than she would have thought possible, having known him for such a short time.

She regretted her hasty decision to leave Clarion. She had honestly believed Colten hated her for having brought him into her stupid mess. She had gone back to France as soon as she could book a flight. In France, despite the excitement of Paris, she had been so down-cast, her brother told her to go back to America.

So, she had. She spent time with Rosalinda at Charles Lafayette's New York estate. Even her best friend had grown weary of her depressed state and told her to go away.

And so, she had, after phoning Colten's mother at the hospital, to check on his progress. It was Barbra who had suggested Jacqueline travel to the Badlands.

"It's so peaceful there," Barbra told her. "It's a good place to rest the mind and allow God's direction to flow." And before she knew it, Jacqueline found herself, moved into the Fisher's Medora residence, and anticipating Colten's arrival. Regardless of the fact she made everyone promise not to tell him where she was until she was ready to face him, she knew deep down; they would let him know without breaking their promise to her.

But it was time to face him, to confront her feelings for him. And ask forgiveness from him if need be. It was not just her future she needed to consider anymore.

Unconsciously, she pressed her hand to her stomach, wondering if she did not owe Colten at least this. She wondered how she would broach the subject when the time came when he finally made his way home. Would he reject her? Or would he feel as though she were trying to trap him once again into something he wanted no part of.

She would never do that to him again, but she was frightened at what her future would be if he shunned her.

* * * *

As the sun set and the heat of the day lingered in the home, Jacqueline made her way to the porch. She took a seat on the swing strung up from the rafters and felt blessed by the gentle breeze that came with dusk; it was a welcome respite from the sticky air inside.

She brought a book out with her to read, and a pillow for back support while she stretched out her legs. For a while, she rested quietly and viewed the landscape. Just across the street was the St. Mary's Catholic Church. It and the Von Hoffman house were the only two remaining brick buildings in the town. Unlike most everything else in the town, Madame de Morès commissioned the church for the community in the summer of 1884, not her husband. She used her own independent income of ninety thousand dollars a year from her stock portfolio, a gift from her father.

The sun was slowly sinking into the west. The colors the fading sun brought forth on the nearby buttes were like a kaleidoscope of bursting colors. She knew at that moment, as she watched the colors dancing over the buttes, this was a view she would never grow tired of.

On a sigh, she picked up the book from where it rested on her lap and began scanning the pages. Almost forty-five minutes later, she heard a car approaching. Well, in this quiet town, that was probably no more than six blocks square, the car's engine could be heard the moment it turned onto the first dirt road into town.

As the minutes passed and she continued to read, she sensed the vehicle stop in the street in front of the house she was occupying and heard the engine turn off and a door slamming shut. When her eyes moved up from the page to see who had parked on the road, her heart lurched.

The book fell from her hand to drop carelessly onto the porch.

Colten stood there for a moment, taking her in before walking around the front of the car and strolling up the boardwalk toward her. He did it in such a slow, leisurely manner, she wanted to shout for him to hurry. But her voice would not come. For the life of her, she could not speak.

The eye patch gave him a sexy appeal she had never known she liked.

His collar-length hair was in disarray. The top three buttons of his shirt were open, exposing that broad, muscled chest. He might have reminded Jacqueline of a rogue pirate, about to de-flower an unsuspecting maiden, except the brand-new cowboy hat he held in his hands, having not bothered to put it on when he had exited the vehicle, ruined the scenario.

She stood up, and he snapped, "Don't you dare move!"

Her body jerked. Nervously, she licked her lips and stood rooted in place.

He came up the three steps and did not stop until his boots touched the tips of her shoes. He opened his mouth to say something, changed his mind, and pulled her to him as he crushed her mouth to his.

Her body relaxed into his, and her hands moved up to wrap around his neck. She returned the kiss as though she were about to drown, and he was her anchor.

She had so much she wanted to say to him. So much to apol-ogize for, and yet her mind could not form a coherent thought as he devoured her mouth, and she his.

Slowly, she moved her hands away from his neck, trailing them along the length of his back, and tried to reel him in closer.

He broke the kiss on a hiss of pain as he took a step back while he favored that area that had flared up because of the small amount of pressure.

Her eyes widened. "I am sorry!" she exclaimed, having for-gotten the rest of the damage done to him not long ago.

He waved the apology away as he closed his eye and worked through the pain. "No problem," he sucked in a breath, and wiped tears from his eye, brought on by the pain's intensity. "Normally it doesn't bother me anymore, and it's healing well. But just when I forget about it, a wrong move brings the bugger to life."

"Colten," her voice broke.

He looked at her intently now that the throbbing of his rib had gone to a dull ache. "I told you, it's okay."

When he saw her tears, he moved to her. Forgotten was his physical discomfort. "Don't cry," he begged, always at a loss when a woman did that.

She cried harder. "Colten, I am so sorry I brought harm to you...."

He put a finger on her lips and narrowed his eye. "You didn't do this to me. No!" he shouted when she shook her head to disagree. "Pierre is to blame. Being in the Secret Service isn't a piece of cake. There is always danger. It could have happened anytime, anyplace. I'm not sorry we met, Jacqueline."

"In the hospital, you told me I belong in France...."

He made a sound of disgust. "The doctor had given me a sedative to put me to sleep. I was just coming out of it, and damn it, I was dazed and couldn't get my thoughts out properly." He kissed her lips. "When you walked out that door," now he cupped her cheek and used his thumb to wipe away a tear. "It almost killed me. Don't ever do that again, Jacqueline."

She wept, pressed her face more firmly into his hand, and closed her eyes as he brushed her lips with his. A sweet butterfly wing that at first was barely there, before it became more solid and more demanding.

"I wanted to be with you," she sniffed. "While you were in the hospital, I wanted to be with you because I kept thinking that if I were there, you would get better faster. But then I would remember your indifference to me, and my mind would tell me it would be foolish to be where I wasn't wanted."

He reached up, cupped her face in his hands, and a humorous smile spread across his lips. "It was probably better this way. I wasn't the best patient in the world. In truth, there were probably a dozen nurses that held a party the day they released me."

Her own smile came out as she said, "Your mother told me half the hospital would be glad to see you gone."

He stared. "When did you speak to my mom?"

"Every day," she confessed. "We talked to each other on the phone every night when she came back to the hotel where she and your father were staying. I needed to know you were doing okay."

Colten frowned. "She told me she had no idea where you were, so I better heal quickly and go look for you."

Jacqueline laughed, and its sound filled Colten with wondrous joy. He did not care they had not known each other for long. His heart opened to her that first day they met, and he knew then there was truth in the expression, love at first sight.

"I have to say something," he told her. "And it's going to sound crazy, but I've got to say it anyway. I love you, Jacqueline."

Her heart almost leaped from her chest with the joy she felt rush in. "Then we're both crazy because I love you, too."

It was his turn to laugh, and he did as he pulled her closer and once again devoured her mouth. When he pulled back, he told her, "You're going to marry me, Jacqueline Medora Grymes."

It was difficult to keep her face blank as she asked, "Am I?"

"If I have to hogtie you and carry you to the altar, I'll do it," he promised.

She smiled through the tears. "Well, if you are going to insist." She cocked her head. "But could you tell me where the altar is?"

He blinked; thought for a moment and frowned. Traditionally, the ceremony took place near or in the bride's hometown. He tried not to grimace as he said, "I suppose... somewhere in... France?"

She shook her head. "I will marry you, Colten Marshal Fisher, but only if it's there." She pointed across the short distance to the St. Mary's Catholic Church.

"I'm not Catholic." He told her solemnly.

"Good. Neither am I. But I think if we make a sizable enough donation, we'll be allowed our day."

Their eyes met. Their smiles formed slowly, and then laughter erupted and echoed off the buttes.

"I love you, Jacqueline." He reeled her in and sealed the vow with a kiss that was more filled with promise than anything else.

Chapter Twenty-one

"Five minutes," the guard's voice held the authority of someone used to giving orders and would not tolerate anyone who did not listen. "I'll be standing over there to give you some privacy." He received an icy glare from the prisoner, but he was no stranger to this kind of treatment; he had been working with convicts for fifteen years. As he moved away, he did not turn his back but stayed watchful and alert. His experience had taught him never to take any chances.

Pierre Bellefeuille sneered at the guard before sitting down at the small table in front of the wired window. His visitor sat on the opposite side. The handcuffs around Pierre's wrists clattered as he brought them up and rested them on the worn tabletop.

"Da guys a prick," Pierre's visitor said, pushing his face as close to the wire as he dared before the prick watching his every move objected. "He probably ain't been laid in a month. Stick up 'is ass is what he 'as..."

"Shut... the... fuck... up," Pierre growled low in his throat, speaking slow enough for the dimwit to understand. He hated relying on people whom he considered beneath him in intelligence. But he had no other options. The authorities were shipping him off to France early tomorrow morning. If he wanted revenge, it would have to come through someone other than himself. He detested that fact but would accept it.

The man before him spoke like an uneducated hick. Pierre suspected the guy could barely read, but his talent as a hitman was renowned.

Pierre had used the man's talent before, when that Ambassador to Italy tried to shortchange him on a drug deal.

Pierre often wondered why people thought drugs were evil. He did not believe they were. He did not use them himself, but they were an excellent way to make money. Buckets full of money, and anything that made him rich, had Pierre's full support.

"I will pay you after the job is complete," Pierre kept his voice low, so the guard could not hear this conversation; although he knew the man was straining to catch every word. "The usual method."

Eugene, feeling safe enough on the other side of this security wire, asked, "'ow do I know da money will be there?"

Pierre's face flushed red. His body vibrated with the need to reach out and grab the man by the throat. "Has there ever been a problem collecting your money?" he asked between clenched teeth.

"No," Eugene admitted, but he had never done a job for this man when he was behind bars, either.

"Get the job done before the end of the month, and there will be a bonus in it for you."

"You want both of dem? Or just your sister?"

Pierre risked a glance at the guard. He didn't appear to have heard anything yet, so he continued in the lowered tone, "You kill both of them. I want that government man to pay for coming at me from behind."

He watched Eugene walk out the door and was smiling when the guard escorted him back to his cell. His dear stepsister might think she was safe, but she did not understand the reach of his hand.

He was practically shoved into the seven-foot square cell that had been his home for the past two months and shivered with disgust. The laws of this country, and that of France, might say he should spend the rest of his life in a place like this, but he disagreed. One day, he vowed, he would have his freedom again.

He shuffled to the hard cot and sat down. The mattress provided might as well not have been there. It did not offer any comfort from the metal slats it rested on.

Leaning back, he closed his eyes. But they snapped back open when he realized he had not gotten the whereabouts of his stepsister and that fucking government man.

No matter. They would be dead soon. And when the time came, when he made his escape from whatever prison he wound up in, he had plans of revenge for someone else.

He would punish Rosalinda Vallombrosa for her role in trying to keep Jacqueline away from him and he grinned, picturing exactly what he would do to her when he finally have her in his grasp.

Chapter Twenty-Two

Colten spent the evening with Jacqueline in his parents' home in Medora, holding her throughout the night He had wanted to make love to her, but his still healing rib put a damper on that desire quick enough.

He tried, though. Having spent hours dreaming about her while lying in that hospital bed gave him incentive now that she was with him, and she was not an illusion. But fantasy and reality did not always mix. When he laid down on the bed, pulling her on top of him, her elbow hit the mending rib, and that was the end of the lovemaking idea.

When morning arrived, they headed toward Bismarck. At first, Jacqueline asked him to show her his home, south of Medora, but he told her she would have to wait a little while longer until he was ready to sit a horse again. The only way to reach the cabin, Colten claimed, was by horse.

She had laughed at that revelation, telling him he and Digger had more things in common than she realized.

During the drive to the capital of North Dakota, Colten explained he had not lived in Medora since the day he married Caroline. She had been a city girl. And, although she had enjoyed the Badlands, she had not wanted to live there year-round. So, he moved to Bismarck and hired a local farmer to take care of his horses and keep an eye on the place.

Colten cringed at the thought of living in Bismarck again. But it suddenly dawned on him that Jacqueline was from a place much larger than North Dakota's capital city.

What if she wanted to live in France?

The very idea made his stomach churn, and he must have turned a little green, because Jacqueline remarked on it. "Colten, is something wrong?"

He cleared his throat, kept his eye on the road, and said, "Will you be happy living in Bismarck?"

The silence that greeted that question had a stone lodging in the pit of his stomach.

She turned, studying his profile as the scenery rushed by through the window. "Is your cabin not livable?"

They reached the outskirts of Belfield and Colten slowed down as the highway they were on went through the town.

His heart hammered at her question, wondering if it meant she wanted to stay in this state, rather than her homeland.

Easing the car onto the nearest street, he parked before he did something foolish and caused an accident. He was not sure what she might have meant by the question, but he felt hope soar. Gripping the steering wheel, he continued to look out the window as the car idled. Dare he hope?

"Colten?" she looked around, confused. Why had they stopped?

"Jacqueline, my home is just an old cabin. Matter of fact, it was my grandfather's. It's not up to date; no electricity or running water. It's larger than Digger's tiny place, but it's still the same. I can't expect you to live there..."

"Why not?"

Now his heart truly was doing the jitterbug. He turned his head so he could see her face and determine if she really meant what she was saying. "I'll update it if I can," he promised, as though it was a vow. "Hell, I'll build you a goddamn mansion if it will make you happy." And before he realized it, he was rushing forward, telling her of his long-time dream to open a

191

place that would allow tourists to enjoy guided tours into the Badlands.

Her face lit up like sunshine breaking through the clouds of an overcast day as he spoke of his passion. "Colten, that is an excellent idea!" With all her heart, she meant every word. Living in the badlands, surrounded by the deep canyons, towering spires, and flat-topped tables, appealed to her in ways she could not explain. To have horses back in her life was like a balm to an open wound. As much as she had wanted a career working with children with special needs, she missed riding every day.

She loved this man enough to want to see his dreams come true. And perhaps there would be a way to incorporate all of it someday.

He reached out, grasped her shoulders, and pulled her to him for a kiss that left her feeling breathless. She would have sworn on the bible that her toes curled from its intensity.

"I love you, Jacqueline," he told her, and knew that what he felt for her went so much deeper than what he had shared with Caroline. Here, with her, he found his other half, and it made him whole.

The hour-and-a-half drive to Bismarck seemed to fly by as the two of them talked of the future.

Their future. The only thing to worry Jacqueline was how she should tell Colten her secret. He had the right to know before the wedding. She wanted it to take place as soon as they could make the arrangements. She did not want a vast affair. Which was a good thing, since she doubted St. Mary's church would hold over fifty people.

The first place the couple went upon their arrival in town was to Colten's parents' home high on a hill on the northern outskirts of Bismarck. Doctor and Barbra Fisher's two-story split level looked out over the ever-growing city. The first person to greet them at the door was Colten's twelve-year-old brother, Thaddeus. The kid took one look at Jacqueline and whistled a male seal of approval.

"Hey, bro. Who's the babe?" Thaddeus's eyes traveled up Jacqueline from the tips of her black pumps to the top of her head. He might have been twelve, but he was showing signs of liking women in ways that were not childlike.

Colten gave him a not too gentle push on the shoulder to move him out-of-the-way. "The babe," he grinned at Jacqueline, "is my soon-to-be wife."

"No, shit?!" Thaddeus exclaimed, then clamped his hand over his mouth when he heard his mother's outrage come from behind him.

"Thaddeus! I've told you how I feel about that language being used in my house!"

He slumped his shoulders for appearance's sake, and managed to sound contrite as he said, "Sorry, mom," but Colten knew his youngest sibling wasn't in the least bit repentant.

The two brothers shared a quick grin behind their mother's back.

Barbra Fisher's face beamed when she saw Jacqueline with Colten. Without a pause in her momentum, she reached out and hugged the younger woman close. "I have missed you so much!" She claimed.

"They're getting married," Thaddeus announced, gaining him a glare from his brother. He had to admit, even with one eye, Colten had that badass scowl down to a science.

"What?!" Barbra exclaimed, tears of joy springing to her eyes. "I can't tell you how happy that makes me!" She glanced around the foyer, seeming to be looking for something.

Thaddeus rolled his eyes. "You know what that means," he said out of the side of his mouth, low enough for only his brother to hear.

Resigned, Colten nodded.

"Now, where did I put my camera?" Barbra moved off in search of it.

Colten sighed.

Confused, Jacqueline looked to her future husband for the answer.

Colten took her hand and led her up the stairs to the living room. "Welcome to the family," he said, as he steered her to a soft leather couch. "Mom takes pictures of everything."

Thaddeus piped up with, "That's why I've been saving up. I'm going to buy stock in the Kodak Company. I'll make a mint off mom's monthly film bill."

Colten sat down next to Jacqueline, threw his head back, and laughed. He also knew his brother was not kidding about buying stock. His brother seemed to have a knack for numbers. The kid read the stock market every day in the local paper, and his subscription to the Wall Street Journal, religiously. His financial portfolio was already impressive enough to have bankers wooing him to keep his money in their banks.

Suddenly, Clinton came running into the room at full throttle. Without pause, he launched himself into Colten's arms, throwing Colten back into the couch. The impact to his rib had Colten hissing out a breath, and the pain caused his stomach to pitch.

Seeing his brother's distress, Thaddeus pulled Clinton off his father's lap. Not an easy feat, with the child squirming and chanting, "Dad, dad, dad!" He had enough photos hanging in his room of the man he was trying to reach that he recognized him easy enough. And his grandmother made sure every night he said a prayer for daddy. They might not have spent much time together, but Clinton undeniably loved his father.

"God," Colten hissed, gulping in air as his hand held his side. "It's okay," he said, not wanting to alarm the child. "It's okay." He reached out his hand, looked at his brother. "Ease him in gently."

Jacqueline's heart swelled with pride, and she fell in love with him all over again. The pain Colten was experiencing must have been excruciating—his face had even turned gray. Yet, it was obvious he desperately wanted to hold his son.

As Thaddeus lifted Clinton to set him on Colten's lap, Jacqueline took one cushion resting on the couch and placed it along the injured area, trying to shield the sore ribs from anymore impact an overzealous boy might inflict.

The moment Clinton was on his father's lap; he pressed his face into the crook of Colten's neck. "Dad, dad, dad," he whispered as though it were a sigh, and held on for dear life.

"I love you, Clinton," Colten managed in a choked voice.

Clinton sat back; his smile radiated. "I know that dad!" He looked embarrassed and ducked his head. Although it was the first time his father had said the words, Clinton never doubted his father loved him. He never asked why his father was not there with him. Or why he lived with grandma and grandpa. He just accepted it as though it were normal.

Chewing his bottom lip, Clinton studied his father's face and finally said, "You look like a pirate. Is it Halloween?" He looked up as his grandmother entered the room. "Grandma, can I be a pirate too?"

Barbra froze in mid-step. She thought she had explained well enough to the child what happened to his father.

Colten stroked his son's light brown hair, cut short in the crewcut style his mother favored. "I'm not a pirate," he said, wondering how to explain the patch was permanent.

Jacqueline watched father and son and fell in love with the boy instantly. He had the face of a cherub. Those wide dark brown eyes, eyes just like the fathers, tugged at her heartstrings. "He's a hero," she told him. "He saved my life."

The child turned his attention to her. "You're pretty," he said. "I like horses." With that, he forgot all about the patch over his father's eye. He launched into an explanation of the different horse breeds, beginning with the Abaco Barb. He would have kept on going all the way to Z, had Barbra not raised her camera and snapped a photo. The flash of the bulb had Clinton stopping in mid-sentence, wrinkling his nose, and exclaiming, "Grandma!"

Barbara smiled and proclaimed, "It stops him every time."

The room erupted with laughter.

Colten turned to Jacqueline. It dawned on him he never mentioned he planned on taking his son back from his parents and raise him as he should have done. Would she be willing to commit to both of them? And if not, would he be able to say goodbye to her? As much as he loved her, he had a responsibility to Clinton. One he pushed off for far too long.

"We're a package deal," he told her.

Jacqueline reached out, touched Colten's face, and then Clinton's. "I would not want it any other way."

Her acceptance of his son caused Colten to swallow to clear the lump that formed in his throat.

"But I have not asked Clinton if he wants me," she said and took Clinton's hand in hers. "I would like to be your mother. Would that be all right?"

Clinton studied her for a long, long while, as though sizing her up. "Do you like horses?"

"I love horses!"

Clinton cocked his head to the side. "Then, I guess that would be okay."

They heard movement in the hallway, a shuffling of sorts, and then a sound of distress. All heads turned to the ancient man holding onto the wall as though he needed it for support. His eyes, glued to Jacqueline, looked as though they had seen a ghost.

Thaddeus raced to his grandfather. "Grandpa, are you all right? Is it your heart? What's wrong?"

With a shaking hand, one that had not been steady for several years, but seemed more unstable now, he pointed to Jacqueline and whispered, "Medora?"

With more than a little confusion, Thaddeus looked toward the living room. "No Grandpa, that's Jacqueline; Colten's fiancée." Gripping his grandfather around the waist, he led him into the living room. He sat him in the chair next to the couch Jacqueline was occupying.

Howard Fisher stared at Jacqueline, then shook his head. "Forgive me. For a moment, with your face in the shadow, you looked like a woman I knew a long time ago." He smiled weakly. "But she had auburn hair, brown eyes, and wasn't nearly as pretty as you."

The old man looked at his youngest grandson.

"Thaddeus. In my room there is a photo of me with Medora, taken the day before she and her husband left North Dakota in 1886. Would you bring it here, please?"

"Sure, grandpa." Thaddeus rushed down the hall and brought the framed photo back in record time and handed it to his grandfather.

Howard Fisher looked down at the image, touched the photo behind the glass with his finger, then looked back at Jacqueline. "You have her jaw and mouth and the shape of her eyes. I see it here. How can that be?"

When Jacqueline smiled, Howard felt the uncanny recognition once again. He had to remind himself it was not who he thought it was. Some of her features were so like the other woman, and in the way she moved her hands. But up close, it was easy to see this woman was the opposite of Medora. That woman had a rugged appeal. This one was flat-out beautiful.

He shook his head. Perhaps he was finally going senile. A ninety-seven-year-old should be allowed some setbacks now and then, he thought.

Jacqueline leaned toward him, glanced at the photo where she could see for herself what the man referred to. "If I remind you of Medora Vallombrosa, it is because she is a distant relative of mine. I have had older family members tell me I have her chin and jawline, and now I can see, by this photo, they spoke the truth."

Howard blinked and thought, my God. Perhaps there really was reincarnation. Not only did the woman resemble Medora, but her voice sounded the same. However, Medora did not have a French accent as this woman did because she was American born although, she had spoken seven languages so perhaps she might have had some twang, he just could not recall it.

Colten reached for the photo.

As he held the photo in his hand and studied the image, which he had seen countless times in his life, Colten knew why he had been drawn to Jacqueline the first time he saw her. It was because of the familiarity with the photos of Medora, and Jacqueline's resemblance to her, although he believed his newly acquired fiancée was far more attractive.

"I would very much like to speak to you about Medora's time here in North Dakota," she told Howard. "I love hearing about my family's history."

And now Howard's smile beamed. "I would enjoy that very much."

"That will have to wait, grandpa," Colten told him, knowing if given the chance his grandfather would launch into a story that would take up the rest of the afternoon. "We have a wedding to plan."

Thaddeus piped up with, "You haven't even gotten her a ring yet."

Colten glanced at Jacqueline's left hand and frowned. He had not thought that far ahead. And here was his brother, his eighteen-year younger brother, bringing that fact to light.

"I didn't have time," he said defensively.

Thaddeus snorted and rolled his eyes.

Barbra set down her camera. "I know a place in town that has a wonderful selection of good quality rings. Your father has taken a few of his pocket watches there for repair. And he's been pleased with their work."

"Sounds good," Colten said. "We'll go there after a bit. What's the name of the place?"

"It's Walker's Jewelry. It's on Third Street, just up from Main. They've been in business for at least twenty-nine years, and it is still owned by the founder, Charles Walker."

Chapter Twenty-Three

The weeks passed quickly with the planning and preparations for Jacqueline and Colten's wedding taking up most of the couple's time. The wedding would take place at the end of next month, allowing time for Jacqueline's mother, stepfather, and brother to arrive from France. Colten kept busy by cutting his mother's list of guests down to manageable. The woman wanted to invite everyone she knew, along with all the relatives, which seemed to be half of North Dakota.

For maid-of-honor, Jacqueline chose Rosalinda. The actress was returning to France in a few days but would be back for the wedding.

Colten chose Cadman for best man.

By the end of the third week, Colten had enough of city life. New Yorkers, he knew, would laugh over a town the size of Bismarck being called a city. New York City's population alone was more than the entire state of North Dakota. Regardless, there were still too many people to suit. So, he packed up Jacqueline and his son and headed back to Medora. His rib was now well enough for him to mount a horse. He was eager to show his future wife his property. They would be a family soon and having Clinton along just seemed right.

He picked up supplies for their weekend stay, knowing his cabin would have nothing in it for food or water. He also telephoned the man he paid to watch the place and asked if he and his wife would mind airing out the cabin for him; at least it would not look deserted when Jacqueline saw it for the first time.

Clinton was excited about this outing with his father, not comprehending it was the first time he would accompany his father on an extensive stay. He had heard there would be horses, and that was all it took to have him continually asking, "We go now?" every half hour the entire day.

Barbra smiled at Colten when he looked about ready to pull his hair out, and said, "It takes some getting used to, but over time, you learn to tune his obsessing out."

Colten was not sure about that. It was difficult, but he was determined to love his son as he was, and not lose patience with him. If it meant clamping his jaw tight until his teeth hurt, so be it.

The three of them left early Friday morning, with Clinton clasping his favorite pillow, blanket, and stuffed horse close. The stuffed animal, Barbra informed the love birds, went with Clinton everywhere. The child felt safe and secure, as long as the animal was with him.

Arriving at the outskirts of Colten's property, Jacqueline sighed, "It is so beautiful here." Once through the barbwire gate that kept the horses in, she knew she was not lying. From what she had seen of the area thus far, this land came alive with an array of colors. Eroded by wind and water, it resembled volcanic rocks. Canyons, ravines, and gullies filled with spectacular color, alternating from dark black to blue coal to bright clays to red scoria. It would be a view she would never grow tired of seeing.

Colten eased the vehicle to a stop before a barn type structure located a short distance from the gated entrance. "We'll park the car inside to protect it from the weather. There are saddles and other tack inside." He motioned for his small group to follow him as he went to the barn door and opened it on hinges that creaked.

He turned to Jacqueline, who stood with her arms folded over her stomach, taking in the view. Her expression was one of serenity, and he knew, in that instant, she meant what she'd said. The truth was on her face. She loved this land, and if possible, he fell in love with her all over again.

He came up behind her. Wrapping his arms around her, he rested his chin on the top of her head. They stood together, taking in the peaceful and breathtaking view. Softly he told her, "The Lakota called this Makhóšiča, which means literally bad lands."

She smiled, though he could not see it, but he felt it in the way her body relaxed into his. "I believe French trappers called it, les mau-vaises terres à traverse."

"The bad lands to cross," Colten correctly translated.

She turned around, keeping within his embrace, and smiled up at him. "Mr. Fisher, have you been learning French?"

He looked down at her. "Some," he admitted, then leaned into her to whisper a French phrase in her ear that had her flushing and snapping her eyes toward Clinton.

"Don't worry," he chuckled, "He didn't hear a thing." He took her hand in his. "Let's catch those horses, saddle up, and ride out. I plan on exhausting Clinton to the point he'll be dead to the world while I," he whispered in her ear once again.

"Colten!" She had not thought her blush could deepen but knew it did at hearing his private words, yet they thrilled her as well. She would do everything in her power to join in the worthy cause of draining a child's energy.

They found Colten's dozen purebred quarter horses, ranging in colors of sorrel, black, brown, red dun, and palomino, standing sheltered together in a stand of trees, eyeing them cautiously.

Clinton could barely contain his excitement. If his father hadn't reached down and taken hold of his collar, the boy would have run straight into the herd, scattering them for miles.

"Easy, son," he said, surprised how easy the word was coming to him with each passing day.

"How we going to get them?" Clinton bounced in place like a rubber ball.

Jacqueline eyed the herd, impressed, and yet she said, "My Arabian will be a wonderful addition."

Colten placed a hand above his heart and faked a heart attack. "Please tell me you're joking."

She shook her head. "No. I've made arrangements for Prince to be brought here from Paris."

Colten groaned. "Prince?"

She grinned.

"Dad! Dad! Dad!" impatient to get to those horses, Clinton tugged on his father's pants legs.

"All right," Colten stroked his son's head and gave a shrill whistle. Within moments, a horse of about sixteen hands, with a luxurious brown chestnut coat, pushed its way from the back of the herd. The horse walked to Colten's outstretched arm, cautiously sniffing before pressing its muzzle into the familiar hand.

"He's beautiful," Jacqueline said. "What is his name?"

"Prairie Knight." He stroked the horse's neck as he spoke gently to the animal. "It's a name to honor the people who first lived on this land. The Lakota, Crow, Dakota... all the tribes. The braves protected their families, just like the knights of

England defended their lands. They, the Indians, were Knights in their own way."

Jacqueline nodded her approval of the name. She had never thought of the American Indians in quite that way. His explanation had her looking at the native people in a different light.

Soon, three horses were tacked and ready to ride. Colten could not help but feel pride over Clinton's knowledge of horses. He chuckled to himself as the child explained the proper way to saddle a horse, as though imparting words of wisdom the adults did not already know. He would nod at things Clinton would say, keeping a sober face as though considering everything as new knowledge. When Colten told his son to make sure the horse blanket and saddle were placed slightly higher up on Mouse's neck, the horse he chose for Clinton to ride because it was gentle, so that both items could be pulled gently down into the correct position, before doing up the girth, Clinton informed him in a voice of authority, "It's not a horse blanket. It's called a Numnah."

Jacqueline chuckled. "He told you, didn't he?"

Colten glowered. "That might be the fancy name for a pad used under a saddle, but around here it's just a plain ol' blanket."

"Dad! Dad! Dad!" Clinton tugged on his pants leg, shaking his head like a wet dog. "Numnah! Numnah!"

Colten held out the blanket for his son to examine. "It's a blanket. I'll show you a Numnah one day, but this isn't one."

To Clinton's mind, his dad was wrong, wrong, wrong.

"All right, it's a Numnah," Colten sighed, and Clinton grinned ear to ear. There was no reason to argue over something so trivial.

After that, tacking the rest of the horses went smoothly. They distributed the supplies and changes of clothing into saddle-bags before mounting the horses. Colten was in the lead, Clinton in the middle, with Jacqueline bringing up the rear.

The cabin was located about a half-hour on horseback from the property gates. But Colten took a few trails he had not been on for a long while to make the ride longer, knowing both of his companions would prefer it. He liked Jacqueline's gasps of pleasure at the different scenic views. And he daydreamed about tonight and making her gasp while his hands were stroking her.

It was better not to dwell on that now, as he felt himself beginning to harden in the saddle and forced himself to think of other things.

He took them splashing through the Little Missouri, past a prairie dog town, and a burning coal vein. Jacqueline and Clinton did not enjoy that part of the personal tour. The sharp sulfur oder hanging in the air caused their eyes to water. At their request, Colten turned the caravan of three west and headed for the cabin.

Jacqueline had prepared herself for the worst. She had been telling herself ever since Colten said he lived in a cabin with no modern conveniences, that she would be happy there. Except for the few times she visited Digger, she had never roughed it. But she vowed she would be a good wife to him and make the best of things. However, she was pleasantly surprised to find a well-built structure with a small porch, two small bedrooms, a room for washing, a tiny living room, and a place for cooking. She would have to learn how to cook on the ancient stove, but that did not deter her. She was up for the challenge, having always been adventurous. It would only be temporary until they built the home they had talked about.

Moreover, Colten's grandparents, having lived in this place as a married couple with their five children, made Jacqueline more determined to succeed in her journey. It amazed her how seven people, including the parents, could find room enough in such a small abode.

But they had, and so could she.

There were a few outbuildings close by. An outhouse, Jacqueline would not be squeamish, accustomed to a mansion on the outskirts of Paris with all the latest updates implemented almost as soon as they were invented. She had never been a snob, but she could not see herself entertaining any of her friends in this home because most of them were snooty.

One small structure looked as though it once had been a chicken coop. The other structure was a typical American barn, and it was in good condition.

After removing the tack from the horses, rubbing them down, placing them in stalls, giving them fresh hay and water, the threesome entered the house to put away supplies and begin the evening meal.

Jacqueline's first attempt at using the small parlor stove had not been a disaster. But she admitted it was only because Colten helped with the entire process. Had it not been for him, she wondered if she would have burnt the place down.

She admired the pioneers for their determination.

When evening arrived, they sat on the porch and watched the sun slowly descend in the western sky. Its fading light reflected off the buttes in bright oranges and reds. It was one of the most spectacular sunsets Jacqueline had ever seen. Others would be speechless when they, too, witnessed the events in the warm summer evenings. Tonight was perfect, a cloudless sky, with almost no hint of a breeze, and the temperature was in the low eighties.

"Beautiful," she breathed.

Colten wrapped his right arm around her and pulled her close. As she placed her head on his shoulder, he whispered huskily, "Not as beautiful as you," then leaned down to kiss the top of her head. When she looked up, he caught her mouth with his for a slow, lingering kiss.

Just as their tongues began to duel, Clinton said, "Eck."

Reluctantly breaking the kiss, Colten turned his head to look at his son and tried not to be frustrated with the fact the boy was sitting on his blind side. Monocular vision was not easy to accept. He would never admit to anyone that sometimes he got spooked when someone came up on his left side he had not expected to be there.

"Don't you like it when I kiss your mom?" he asked. They had been referring to her as mom since announcing their engagement. Clinton would never understand the concept of Jacqueline being a stepmom.

Clinton wrinkled his nose, shook his head quickly side-to-side. "Eck," he repeated.

Colten grinned. "Well, I kind of like it. But if that's how you feel, you don't have to kiss her."

Clinton crinkled his whole face, disgusted with the thought. He liked hugs from people but having their mouths near his freaked him out.

Jacqueline moved away from Colten's embrace, stood, and stretched with feminine grace. With a voice low and sounding seductive, she looked Colten in the eye and said, "I think I'll go inside. Perhaps read a book. In bed," she added and stroked his cheek.

"You're an evil woman, Jacqueline Grymes. I don't think our son is ready to go to sleep just yet."

She paused at the threshold, looked over her shoulder, and grinned. "Neither am I."

Female laughter followed, and as she entered the cabin, she heard Colten say, "Hey there, buddy. How about I read you The Cat in The Hat, and then you go to sleep?"

Chapter Twenty-Four

Almost two hours later, Colten decided he hated Dr. Seuss and The Cat in The Hat. By now, he had no reason to look at the words. He could recite them by heart. Now, having blown out the lantern in the room, his son finally asleep, he closed the door quietly with the words to the book running through his head.

When he opened the door to the room he would share with Jacqueline over the next few days, the rhyming words vanished and suddenly, what The Cat in The Hat considered fun, did not compare to what ran through Colten's thoughts now.

Jacqueline was sitting up in bed with a book in her hand. She looked up when Colten came in, and his mind went blank as he took her in. She had changed into a negligee the color of azure that was so sheer he could see the hint of her breasts beneath the material. She had brushed her waist-length hair until it gleamed; strands of it fell over her shoulders, to weave over the part of her anatomy that had first gained his attention when he opened the door. His eye did a lazy walk down the rest of her as his throat went dry.

"Is Clinton sleeping at last?" Jacqueline asked.

He looked back up, met her eyes. "Who?" he croaked. For the life of him, he could not think of anything but her.

She smiled and set her book on the small table next to the bed. "Clinton," she repeated, looking amused.

"Clinton," the word came out slow and foreign sounding, even to his own ears. Were they talking about Clinton? — and if so, in the name of heaven, why?

He ran a hand through his hair as he tried to jump-start his brain.

She reached for him. "Come to bed, Colten. I believe we've waited long enough."

He came to life as though someone pushed him from behind. When he reached the bed, his weight caused the mattress to dip a little, and finally, he was pulling her into his arms. A sweet cocoon of warmth, where Jacqueline felt loved and safe, as she breathed in his scent of outdoor sunshine, leather, and horse.

His lips moved to her temple, then her cheek. Finally, they slipped down to find her mouth. With his hands resting on the sides of her face, his thumbs lightly touching her cheekbones, slowly, reverently, he kissed her.

As his kiss intensified, sending warmth through her whole body, she slipped her arms around his neck and held on as though he might suddenly disappear.

"I love you, Jacqueline," his deep voice sent a warm shiver down her spine. His lips caressed her temple, then they traveled across her cheekbone to find her mouth once again.

She groaned with the sheer pleasure of having his mouth on hers. His hands moved down to cup her breasts, kneading softly, his thumb a gentle caress on her nipples; bringing moisture to her core so fast it made her gasp.

Her hands reached up to run through his thick, unfashionable, collar-length, dark brown hair. But the cord holding the patch in place was in the way.

When she went to slip it off, he stopped her.

"No," was all he said, taking her protest into his mouth. He did not want her to see the horrific scarring. "Not tonight." He wanted to say, not ever. But they would be married soon, and the chances of her never seeing the deformity were slim.

"All right," she gently kissed his jaw, moving her hands slowly down his face, then his neck, and finally to his shirt. Reaching between them, she began unbuttoning it. Then her fingers slipped inside the opening to caress him back, and he shuttered.

And when they were naked, as he once again stroked her breasts, in the back of his mind, he thought they felt fuller than they had been. But he set the thought aside. After all, they had only been together that one night, and that had been several months ago. Obviously, he had not quite remembered their texture, and blocked the thought from his mind as his hands continued to explore.

He slid down her body, his mouth and talented tongue sending shivers of anticipation through her body. When he reached the junction between her legs, she nearly jackknifed off the bed. But he anchored her hips and demanded, "Come."

Her body convulsed. As she continued to ride the waves of release, he was moving up, raising her hips and drove home with ruthless determination. "Again," he rasped.

She reached up, pulled his head down, and clamped her mouth on his. Mimicking with her tongue, what he was doing to her. Sending them both over that edge, where bodies suddenly go tight, then liquid.

They held on to each other as the aftershocks slowly subsided. Once their breathing returned to normal, and heartbeats slowed, Colten rolled over enough to take his weight off her. But he kept her close, tucking her head onto his chest as he rolled to his back.

"I love you too, Colten." Her hand absently stroked his chest.

The arm he held her with gave a quick squeeze.

As the minutes ticked by, Jacqueline warred with herself. Debating, knowing she could not keep silent forever. Sooner than later, everyone would know the secret she had been holding. Gently she asked, "Colten, how many children do you want?"

The hand he had been using to stroke her shoulder froze. "I..." Oh, boy, he thought. It was something he supposed they should have talked about a while back. But here it was, hanging in the air. But would she understand? He cleared his throat. "I'm thirty years old, Jacqueline."

She did not like the sound of that. But she had taken him by surprise, and, because of that, she pushed the foreboding aside. "And I'm twenty-three. I have always wanted a house full of children."

He gave a shaky laugh. "Well, considering the size of this house, we're full up with one kid already, occupying the only other bedroom."

She dislodged herself from his hold and slowly sat up. "You do not want any more children." It was a statement, not a question. She felt her heart squeeze in terror that what she thought she had with him would be over before it had even begun.

He continued lying on his back, looking up at her. "Jacqueline, we're just starting a life together. I've had a life-changing experience, and I'm trying to accept the one child I have. One who will never hold a job..."

"You do not know that! Clinton may very well be autistic, but he is also extremely high functioning. I have been working with him..."

Now Colten sat up. His jaw worked to keep from shouting. "Great. That's good. But I don't want to take the chance of fathering another one."

Jacqueline gasped. "I cannot believe you just said that!"

He looked away. Neither could he. It sounded shallow and harsh, and he hated himself at that moment. He swallowed, turned back, and winced at the shock on Jacqueline's face.

"Couldn't we talk about this tomorrow?" he reached up to touch a breast because, after all, it was right there tempting him.

She batted his hand away. Tears swam in her eyes. "No, we might have nothing to say to each other tomorrow."

"Jacqueline," his voice was full of exasperation.

She swiped at the tear that made it past her lashes, took a deep breath for courage, and blurted, "I am almost four months pregnant, Colten."

He stared at her as though she suddenly changed shape.

"That night in the motel room, we did not use birth control."

He made a sound, one of disbelief, frustration, and horror, before shooting out of the bed. Grabbing up his pants without stopping, he walked out the door. He did not close it behind him, but left it gaping open, like the hole he just put in her heart.

She covered her face with her hands and wept until there were no more tears, and exhaustion took over. If it were not for the fact they were, literally, in the middle of nowhere, she might have gotten dressed and walked out the door as well. But there was no place to go. She laid her head on the pillow, took a calming breath, and told herself tomorrow was soon enough to face his farther rejection. If he did not want the baby, which was more than obvious, he couldn't have her. Because no way in hell would she ever give up her child.

* * * *

The next morning, after heating water on the old stove and using it for a sponge bath for her and Clinton, she helped him brush his teeth and dress in fresh clothes. The simple tasks kept her mind occupied so she would not have to think of what would happen today whenever Colten showed up from wherever he had gone last night. She had heard no horse ride out of the yard during the night and assumed he had slept in the barn.

For all she cared. She hoped Colten had gotten a rotten night's sleep. God knew she hadn't slept well herself, tossing and turning all night, missing him despite her hurt, and hating herself for wanting him beside her.

She was feeding Clinton breakfast when Colten walked into the house. In a flash, her heart gave a leap, and in the next, she was kicking herself for feeling anything other than anger at him.

Oh yes. She was definitely an idiot.

He remained in the doorway. Jacqueline could feel him watching her interact with Clinton but refused to acknowledge his presence. What would be the point? As soon as she did, they would probably start arguing. And she did not have the energy to fight with him. Besides, she refused to make a scene in front of the child.

She glanced at Clinton and felt her heart swell. He was not merely a child. He was her son. She had fallen in love with him the moment she met him. It broke her heart to know she had no rights to him. Once they got back to Bismarck, his father and she would no doubt go their separate ways. And unless Colten allowed it, she would never see Clinton again.

His footsteps warned her he was coming their way, and she tried not to be tense. Clinton was not the least bit stressed. He bounced in the chair, waved his spoon, and said, "Dad! Dad! Dad!" with his usual gusto; utterly oblivious to the tension between the two adults he had made the center of his life.

The father reached out, stroked his son's hair, and leaned down to kiss the top of the boy's head. "Morning," was all he said, his voice sounding gruff.

The chair he pulled out scraped against the floor.

Jacqueline kept her eyes averted; finding the toast she managed to make on the stove more interesting than it had the right to be.

Colten's silence began to wear on her nerves, but she refused to give him the satisfaction of being the first to acknowledge the other.

"Five," he said, his voice seeming to boom in the house's stillness regardless of the fact he had kept it at a reasonable, conversational level.

She could not prevent her body from jerking at the suddenness of the sound. Her eyes leaped to his face in question.

"Five," he repeated, then reached over and took one slice of toast off her plate and stuffed it into his mouth.

She watched him chew, then swallow; and hated herself for finding the act sexy. "Five? What does that mean?"

He jerked his chin to indicate Clinton. "Including him, I want five kids."

She kept her eyes level with his and refused to let her heart soar. "Last night," she kept her voice calm, "you didn't want any at all."

Blowing out a breath, he rubbed a hand over his face. His hair was a mess, his face full of stubble. "Jacqueline, it was a shock, okay? I reacted badly. I know that. I've always been one to blow my cork first, then after I calm down, I generally come around. It isn't right of me to expect you to deny yourself your own dreams when you've embraced mine and accepted my son as yours."

She looked away as tears pricked her eyes. Could Colten really mean what he said? "I gave you something more," she whispered, voice raw with emotion. "I gave you my heart."

He was by her side in a flash, pulling her up and holding her tight. "I know, and last night, I threw it back at you without thought because of my own insecurities." He stroked her hair. "I'm sorry, honey. It's been a lot of events in a short few months." Colten placed a hand under her chin, tilted her face up to his. "I've told you plenty of times, I love you, and loving someone means dealing with life when it takes unexpected turns."

Because his knees shook, he sat down in the chair and pulled her into his lap. "It terrifies me," he admitted, in a voice so gruff, it made her heartache. "It terrifies me. Not because the baby might not be normal. I've already lived through someone I love dying, giving birth, and leaving me alone in the world." He buried his face in the curve of her neck. "The thought of losing you cripples me. Jacqueline, what I had with Caroline dulls compared to my feelings for you."

A tear made it down her cheek. "Do you mean that Colten?"

He nodded. "With all my heart, Jacqueline. If there hadn't been you...." He shook his head, as his own heart squeezed, and closed his eye for a moment to get his purchase. "If there hadn't been you to look forward to while I was in that damn hospital, I don't know where I'd be today." He nodded toward Clinton. "Where we would be. You've shown me that, just because people might be different from you and me, it doesn't make them less of a person."

217

He met her lips with his. A slow mending of lips, putting all he felt for her in it, leaving her breathless and loved. And cherished more than she had ever felt.

"Yuck!" Clinton exclaimed. "Dad! Dad! Dad! Yuck!"

The adults chuckled against each other's mouths.

With a glance at his son, Colten said, "It's never yucky to kiss your mother."

Clinton shivered with repulsion.

"Let's go horseback riding," Colten suggested, releasing Jacqueline with reluctance. All he really wanted to do was pull her into the bedroom and show her, with his body, how much he loved her. But instead, he said, "We'll keep the horses at a slow pace, considering your condition." He placed a hand on Jacqueline's still flat stomach. Imagining it, as it would be in a few more months, swollen with his child. At that moment, he realized he was excited about holding it in his arms. He had missed out on so much when he foolishly withdrew from his first child. This time, he would participate in parenthood.

"I think today I'll have you pick out the place you want our house built so I can get started on it. And we won't be living here this winter."

As they walked across the dirt yard to the barn to saddle-up the horses, her mouth drew downward in a frown. "Why? I love it here...."

"Honey," he drawled, "You ain't never seen a North Dakota winter. With you being pregnant, I'm not going to risk having to deliver the baby in the middle of a raging blizzard."

Chapter Twenty-Five

Together they chose land close to the main entrance of Colten's property for the house they would build, keeping in mind the dream Colten had of starting a business, offering trail rides to tourists, as Harold Schafer built up Medora. They mapped out where they thought the stables would be located and hypothesized about other buildings. Perhaps they would need a bunkhouse if their business grew large enough to hire employees, and in time, they could add guided camping trips into the Badlands for tourists who would gladly pay the fee for such an adventure. That could lead to needing a general store where people could purchase or rent supplies.

As they discussed their plans for the future, their ideas expanded until they were both laughing at the prospect of creating their own small town with such ambitious development.

It was almost noon when Clinton announced he was hungry. The adults were not ready to ride back to the cabin because of their excitement, but they knew it was better to feed a child than starve a tantrum. Clinton was a good kid most of the time but, withhold food from him and he would let you, and everyone else around, he was not happy with an empty belly.

Colten was helping Clinton onto the horse when something whizzed by his ear. The horse screamed with pain, sidestepped, and almost stepped on Clinton's toes. A split second later, the report of a rifle shot echoed off the buttes.

Colten grabbed for the horses' reins, forcing it to lie down and tucked Clinton, as close as he dared, into the wounded animals back, using the beast as a shield from the unseen threat. "Stay down!" he ordered. And prayed to God the child would understand the danger, as another report sang out, and another horse screamed.

Jacqueline. Where was Jacqueline? His heart pounded as he tried to see the world around him, cursing the fact his sight was limited.

He spotted her forcing her own mount down to the ground, mimicking what he had done, using the horse for protection.

"Colten!" she screamed, motioning behind him.

He spun around, saw Clinton getting up, and ran zigzag to his son, scooping him up, and racing to where Jacqueline huddled behind her horse.

There was not enough cover for the three of them, but right now, it was all they had.

Jacqueline's eyes were enormous as they looked at Colten. "Who is shooting at us?" she cried.

Hell, if he knew. All he could do was shake his head. "Keep Clinton's head down." His face was a mask of determination.

"Where are you going?"

"Hunting," he said, and moved away.

Heart in her throat, Jacqueline glanced around, looking for a shelter that would be better than what she and Clinton had, and trusted Colten with whatever he was planning to do.

There were few choices for shelter to choose from. But she knew that to remain where they were, if the person shooting at them gained higher ground, or circled around behind them, she and Clinton were sitting ducks.

She eyed the bottom of one butte, then another. Searching until, yes, there. Part of a butte jutted out, and if she were lucky, there would be more coverage on the opposite side.

Taking a firm hold of Clinton's hand, the boy was shaking like a leaf; she did not blame him; she got her horse up.

Jacqueline knew the animal had been wounded and prayed the injury was not life threatening as she pulled her son along with her, keeping the horse between them and the last place the shot had originated from.

"Hungry!" Clinton cried, "Mom! Mom! Mom!"

A bullet hit the face of the butte she had been moving toward, dislodging dirt and pebbles. The report of the rifle was ominous.

"Oh, God!" she sobbed, grasping Clinton's hand tighter when she felt him ready to run.

"It is all right," she soothed. "We will have something to eat soon."

"Now! Now! Now!"

He did not understand. Jacqueline's heart raced with fear, more for Clinton than for herself.

They reached the finger of the butte. She sent up a prayer of thanksgiving when she discovered it did indeed have protection on both sides, and a slab of rock above.

Forcing Clinton in before her, hoping there was not a rattlesnake lurking undetected among the foliage and rocks, she made him sit on the ground before crouching in front of him, like a human shield, as she let go of the horses' reins.

It bolted without a backward glance.

"Mom! Mom! Mom!"

She had never lost patience with a child whose mind did not function properly. But she almost did at that moment until she remembered the small bag of trail-mix she put in the pocket of her jeans before they left the cabin that morning.

"Here," she whispered and wondered why she bothered to keep her voice low when it was apparent the person with the gun knew their location. "You will like this," she promised, and ripped open the package with her teeth before handing it to Clinton.

The boy looked doubtful for a moment. But when he spotted the raisins mixed in with the nuts, he took the offering and grinned. He loved raisins.

Taking a deep breath, thankful it would satisfy him for now, she reached out and petted Clinton's stuffed horse, clenched in his left arm. "I bet horsy," not an original name, but that's what Clinton called the cherished object, "would like a story. You know how he likes stories."

For a moment, Clinton just looked at her as he munched on a nut. Then his eyes went to the animal and agreed. "Horsy likes stories."

Jacqueline took a deep breath; blew it out. For now, at least, he would be calm.

But oh God, where was Colten?

Taking a deep breath, saying a silent prayer for Colten's safety, she began reciting The Cat in The Hat. Clinton stroked horsy and munched trail-mix, as though there was nothing strange about them huddling in a crevice, pressed against its wall.

* * * *

Eugene crawled along the ground on the hill above the area where Colten and Jacqueline had been. After having missed them in Bismarck, only to find out they'd ended up in this forsaken place, put him in a sour mood. When he discovered the vastness of the land now surrounding him, he had almost given up. Regardless of having gotten directions from some cowpoke, in that piss of a nothing town, he had gotten lost five times.

He had almost given up. What did he care about whether these people lived or died? Pierre was far away in France. He, Eugene, would be safe as could be if he walked away. But he wanted that damn money. After all the twists and turns, he had had since trying to locate his prey, he deserved payment.

Another wrong turn, a few hours ago, turned out to be the right one. The road led him right up to a fence of barbwire, with a barn on the other side and a hand-painted sign attached to the gate declared this was Fisher Land and private property.

He had been afraid the couple would be in the barn. After all, there was not a soul in sight, and it was the only structure on the place.

Where in the hell was that cabin the local guy said was Fisher's place? He asked himself that question countless times over the last three hours.

Having discovered the car in the barn, he set off on foot, having been told there was no road leading to the cabin and that he would have to take a horse. That was not going to happen. He did not know the first thing about the damn filthy beasts.

So, he took the canteen filled with water from his car, grabbed his rifle, and started walking. He kept track of the time and counted steps. After walking one way for a half-hour, he would turn around, retrace his route, and take another direction. He had been told that cabin was thirty minutes from the gate, but he had not found it yet.

He almost decided to go back to his car and wait for them to come to him when he spotted them below. He grinned. A broad smile people would describe as sinister if they saw it.

He couldn't have asked for a better location than being above his prey. Raising the rifle, sighting through the scope, he pulled the trigger - just as some gopher-like creature popped up from its hole, and gave a shrill whistle, startling him.

He missed his intended target. That alone made him livid enough to turn the rifle on the animal, fire, and hit that mark.

The animal keeled over with a squeal.

By then, the people below knew there was something amiss and had taken cover behind a horse. Not that he could not have picked them off. But after the trouble he had finding them, he wanted to play a bit. He enjoyed terrorizing. Imagining their fear was a balm to his senses.

When the man made a mad dash away from the others, Eugene raised his rifle and fired.

And missed. Again.

With no little amount of frustration, he looked at the scope. Obviously, the site was off. He must have bumped it on something while taking it out of the car and not realized it.

Damn it!

He sat down and went to work, trying to correct the accuracy. When he saw the woman and boy using the horse for a shield, as they moved toward the face of a hill, he used the horse as a target to test the adjustment.

Closer this time. With a couple more turns on the elevation, Eugene raised it and fired as the woman reached the rock finger.

It gave him great pleasure to see the woman jump when the shot came within inches of her. One more turn and..."

Now, he could not see her or the boy, but it mattered not. He would just have to go to them.

He started to crawl his way there but as thorns, thistles, and ground-hugging cactus embedded themselves into his clothing, pricking his skin, he gave that idea up quickly enough.

Why in the hell, he wondered, would anyone want to live in this abyss?

So, he stood up and went sprawling back down as a weight landed on his back.

"Who the hell are you?!" the person on his back raged, grabbing his hair, lifting his face, and slamming it back into the dirt.

Eugene bucked, dislodged the weight from his back, and came up swinging.

Colten ducked, gave an uppercut to the stranger's jaw, forcing the man's head back with the impact.

Eugene was stronger than he looked. He came back with a punch to Colten's stomach before he could block it, knocking the air out of him and it came out a whoosh through his mouth.

They grabbed each other's shirts, each fighting to unbalance the other.

What seemed like hours, but was only a few moments, the two men grappled, swung, missing blows, connecting with others.

At last, Colten got his opponent on the ground. Leaping on him, he pummeled the man's face until he no longer fought, and his body went limp.

It took every ounce of willpower for Colten to stop and not beat the man to death. He wanted to. He vibrated with the want, and it scared him.

He stood up, tasted blood, and spit it out. He eyed the man, wondering how to tie him up so he could go to Jacqueline and Clinton to make sure they were okay.

He looked around, knowing there would be nothing of use, but still tried before taking off his shirt and tearing it into strips. Flipping the man over, Colten secured his hands and feet.

Then he used the last remaining bits of cloth to tie a strip between both knots so that hands and feet were tied together.

The guy was not going anywhere.

Picking up the rifle, Colten made it down the incline, calling out when he reached the bottom. They were not where he left them. When he saw them coming out of their hiding place, his heart swelled with pride. His woman was not dumb. She looked for shelter where others would not think twice about using it for protection.

She ran to him, launching herself into his arms. Sobbing his name, kissing him on the lips, the cheeks, the neck, as her hands ran over his skin, looking for injuries, and gasping when she found them.

"It's all right," he soothed, stroking her hair, kissing her back.

Clinton came running, too. Seeing the adults kissing, he said, "Yuck!" Pulling on Colten's pants, he all but screamed, "Hungry! Dad! Dad! Dad!"

On a sigh, Colten pulled away. "Seems we have a little dilemma," he said, looking into Jacqueline's eyes. "Our son thinks he's going to starve to death, and there's some guy hogtied up there." He motioned with his head toward the butte he'd come down.

"Who is he?"

Colten shrugged.

"Well, as far as I am concerned, our son comes first."

Colten whistled, and Prairie Knight came at a run. "Take Clinton to the cabin," he told Jacqueline. "Feed him. I'll stay here and keep an eye on our unwanted guest."

"What are we going to do with him?"

"I'll think of something while you're gone."

She touched his face. "I love you.

His smile brought a flutter to her heart. "Go on before Clinton pulls my pants off me."

Jacqueline looked down, and sure enough, Clinton's continued tugging had moved Colten's pants almost past his hips.

Taking Prairie Knight's reins, he waited while Jacqueline mounted, then handed Clinton up to her. "Take it easy," he told her, referring to her pregnancy. "You're sure you know the way?"

She nodded and got the horse into motion, turning east and away from the man she loved beyond anyone she had ever known.

Colten waited until they were out of sight before climbing the ridge. He found the man awake, frantically squirming around, trying to loosen his bonds.

Striding forward, he stopped within inches of Eugene and pointed the rifle at the man's head.

"I think it's time we have ourselves a conversation."

"Fuck you."

Colten smiled, but not pleasantly. "No, thanks. I prefer women."

Squatting down, he said, "You going to make this easy on yourself by telling me why you're here?"

Eugene spit. The saliva landed on Colten's face.

"Well, now, that wasn't nice." Colten said, wiping the offensive liquid away. "I take it that means we will have to go about this the hard way."

"I ain't tellin' you nothin'."

The expression that crossed Colten's face had Eugene sweating. "Oh, yes, you will." The words were spoken so softly, Eugene had to strain to hear.

"One last chance. Why are you here?"

Eugene's lips pressed together, and he glared.

Exhaling, Colten reached out, grasped Eugene's balls, squeezed and twisted, and held on tight while Eugene withered and moaned and cursed Colten to the depths of hell. Not that Colten cared. He kept adding pressure, harder and harder, until Eugene was singing soprano; not dropping a single note, as he spilled the beans on Pierre Bellefeuille's hired hit.

When Colten was satisfied, he released his grip on Eugene's nuts.

The man promptly rolled over and puked.

Colten ignored him.

If Pierre could hire someone from behind bars to continue tormenting Jacqueline, he was more dangerous than they had thought.

Chapter Twenty-Six

Getting the hitman back to civilization had not been easy.

When Jacqueline came back from finding something for Clinton to eat, Colten send her back to the cabin. He needed some items from the barn so he could make a travois. He would have gone himself, but he had not wanted to leave her alone with the man, still lying on top of the butte, regardless of the fact he was hogtied tight.

Jacqueline retrieved the items incredibly quickly. She even brought an extra shirt for Colten to replace the one he had ripped apart to tie up the mysterious man.

She had grit; Colten would never deny that. She did what needed doing and did not complain. But then, a woman who could hold a loaded gun in a man's belly, without shaking like a leaf, would have a backbone.

Despite the situation, Colten smiled at the memory. He had probably fallen in love with her at that moment.

Jacqueline helped Colten construct the A-framed device and attach it to Prairie Knight. They were down to two horses. The first shot fired severely wounded Mouse, the mount Clinton had been riding, and Colten used the rifle he had acquired from the mystery man to stop its suffering.

It was not easy to keep Clinton away from the carcass. He was curious and wanted to know why it was lying on the ground.

The second horse fared better. It was grazed along its front leg, but Jacqueline and Colten could still use it.

Colten got Eugene on the travois by practically picking him up and dragging him onto it. The guy was in no shape to help; even had he been obliging enough to do so. After he came too,

Colten knocked him back out when he began throwing insults and threats at Jacqueline.

Clinton's reaction, seeing some guy being hoisted onto the thing his dad made and hooked to the horse, was to stare, bewildered. It made him nervous. He clenched Horsy as tight as he could, close to the curve of his neck.

They made it to the main property gate in a little more than a half-hour. Jacqueline helped Colten pull the man from the travois and drag him into the back seat of his vehicle. Once that was done, the two of them leaned heavily against the car, catching their breath after the exertion it took to lift what felt like dead weight.

"Now what?" Jacqueline asked.

"I'll drive his car since he was nice enough to leave the keys in the ignition, and you'll drive mine. The nearest jail is Dickenson. We'll get him locked up. Then I'll call Cadman."

Jacqueline's eyes widened. "You want me to drive your car?"

He nodded, but as a thought struck, he asked, "You know how to drive a car, don't you?"

"Of course, I do," she snapped indignantly.

"Then why do you look so worried?"

She ducked her head, chewed on her bottom lip. "I do not have an American driver's license."

He blinked. "You don't have a-" he trailed off, his laughter almost choking him. That would be the least of their worries.

Later, once Eugene was locked up at the Dickinson police station, Colten made a call to Cadman to fill him in on the day's events. Then he had Jacqueline drive back to Bismarck so that Clinton would have comfort in known surroundings. Colten stayed to guard Eugene. Not that he did not trust the Dickinson Police. The officers appeared competent to him. But, with anything relating to Pierre Bellefeuille, no matter how minor, he would personally see to the problem.

Jacqueline had not been happy with having to leave Colten but understood his reasoning. Clinton came first. The child was upset and, understandably, wanted his grandmother. No matter that Colten was in his life to stay, and he already considered Jacqueline his mother, it was not the same. There was nothing like the comforting arms of his grandmother to soothe him when she was the one to have been there for him over the years.

So, Jacqueline drove back to Bismarck, keeping the speedometer at precisely 55 miles per hour. Lord knew the last thing she needed was to be pulled over by a highway patrol officer and be arrested for not having an American driver's license.

* * * *

That was over two weeks ago.

Now, at Colten's parent's home, another day was passing, as slow as a snail, with still no word from the man she loved. Jacqueline knew he was not in Dickenson. He phoned her the day after they took Eugene to the local authorities to let her know the man was being transported somewhere else but would not say where for security reasons.

Colten went along as an added escort. She had not heard from him since then, and with each passing day, she worried something had gone terribly wrong.

She glanced down at her hands and frowned. She had never been a nail biter, but that seemed to have changed over the time her lover had been absent.

"He's coming back," she heard Thaddeus comment from behind her, and she turned from the window she was gazing out, watching the driveway for any sign of Colten. "He'll be here. Don't worry."

Said with the faith of a twelve-year-old who had complete confidence in his big brother.

She managed a faint smile, reached out, and ruffled his short-cropped hair. "Thank you, Thaddeus."

He grimaced. "If you don't mind, call me TJ. I've decided I hate my name."

And, she thought, what kid did not hate their name at some point in their life? "All right. But why the J?"

He looked away and grumbled, "It's for my middle name."

She raised a brow. "What is your middle name?"

He shook his head. "I'd rather not say."

"It cannot be all that bad."

He snorted. "Oh, yes. It can. I think my mom was on drugs when she named me."

Now Jacqueline laughed. "Thad... er, TJ," she amended. "Truly, It cannot..."

"Julius!" he blurted, daring her to laugh.

She could not help herself. She stared. "Your middle name is- Julius?" she had not meant for her voice to squeak on a refrained laugh, but it did, and he glared.

Thaddeus Julius... oh... my. "Well, that isn't... bad," she tried.

"It's awful!"

She sighed. "It is awful," she affirmed. "From now on, you have my word. From this moment forward, I will refer to you as TJ."

He visibly relaxed and shoved his hands into his pockets. "Just promise me; you won't give any of the children you and Colten have some stupid name."

232

Instinctively, her hand went to her stomach. Colten's family still did not know she was expecting. She had not mentioned it because she wanted him to be with her when they let the news out.

"I will try to keep that promise," she declared as the front door opened and closed.

From the basement where Clinton was playing in the family room, they heard, "Dad! Dad! Dad!"

Jacqueline would have sworn her heart stopped upon hearing the refrain. And when she heard his voice in the foyer, speaking low to his son, it came to life with a shuddering start.

Home. He was home! Before she could get her legs to move forward, he was coming up the stairs, with Clinton in his arms.

At the top of the steps, he paused when he saw her. Her heart gave a leap. He seemed to her more handsome than ever, standing there in tight hip-hugging jeans and a black shirt tucked into the waist. He had not taken off the Stetson, and it, combined with the black patch covering his left eye, caused her mouth to go dry.

She was the luckiest woman in the world, she thought. She went to him slowly, with a seductive stride that had him putting Clinton down, and grabbing her close, as a low growl sounded in his throat.

Mouths fusing, they clung desperately to each other. Others were forgotten. Only their need to feel, to touch, to know the other was all that existed.

Until "Yuck!" was all but screamed and reverberated through the room. Colten's pant leg was being tugged with abandon.

They came up for air long enough to hear Thaddeus say, "Come on, buddy. Let's go see if grandma has a cookie for you, so mom and dad can be alone."

Obviously, the thought of getting a cookie outweighed Clinton's desire to be picked back up again. He gladly allowed his uncle to take him by the hand and lead him into the kitchen.

Colten gave his brother a thankful wink. Then, he reached up to wrap strands of Jacqueline's long, dark blond hair around his fingers as his other hand stroked her cheek. "I missed you," he said and sealed the statement with another kiss. This one was so tender; it almost made her weep.

She reached up, took one of his hands in hers. "What took so long? I was worried..."

He led her to the sofa. "I'm sorry for it. I simply wasn't able to contact you." They sat, and he pulled her close, tucking her head onto his chest, and stroked her arm absentmindedly.

"We took good ol' Eugene to a select location. The place has a way of making people talk. I won't go into details about how. But Cadman and I were concerned that, if Pierre could hire a hitman from within the prison, then there had to be a way for him to know if the hit had been successful."

He took off the cowboy hat; tossed it carelessly onto the coffee table in front of them. "We found out that once the hit was made, Eugene would receive money from another one of Pierre's pawns in New York. If Eugene didn't pick up the money, that man would contact Pierre."

Jacqueline gasped. "But Pierre's in France; under maximum security!"

Colten shrugged. "If you'll recall, earlier this year, and around the time we met, four men escaped from Alcatraz Island. No one ever thought anyone could successfully escape from there." He shifted. "We don't know what connections Pierre has, or where they end. We had to make him believe the two of us were dead–if, somehow, word could reach him."

She sat back. Eyes huge. "We will never be safe!" she exclaimed, fear gripping her heart. "My God, Colten. If Pierre truly has that amount of power...."

"That's why we made sure Eugene picked up his money."

Staring at Colten, her mouth slowly fell open. "He agreed to keep his mouth shut about us being alive?"

"Certainly," Colten chuckled. "Eugene had six guns trained on him from rooftops, while he was collecting his money. He wasn't about to take the chance of one of those men getting itchy fingers. He collected the money; his contact believes the job is done and will report to Pierre we have been taken care of."

"And Eugene?"

"He's tucked away in another prison, here in the states." Then he sighed. "There is something else, honey. We have to allow your family to believe you are dead."

Jacqueline gasped. "Why?!"

"As I said. We don't know who might tell Pierre that we are alive; his father is married to your mother, so..." He let the sentence hang in the air as he shrugged.

"But that means my mother and brother cannot be at our wedding!"

Colten looked at her, saw the tears forming in her eyes, and felt his heart break for her. "I'm sorry. It's the only thing we can do for now. Cadman is trying to figure out something, so you will have some type of communication with her, but for now, having your family believe we are dead is the only option."

She buried her face into her hands and wept. This was her fault. All of it. If she had never taken that diamond from Pierre, none of this would be happening.

"Don't cry," he told her, even though he knew it was useless. "It won't be forever. I promise. Cadman will figure something out." Then he asked, "Do you want to call off the wedding until you mom can be there?"

She shook her head. Of course, she wanted her mother to attend the wedding, but she had to accept what they could not change.

Wrapping her arms around him, she told herself this new life she was about to begin would be as happy as they could make it, and knew Colten would keep them and their new family as safe as possible from the monster named Pierre Bellefeuille.

* * * *

Miles away, across the endless ocean, in Flury Mérogis prison, south of Paris...

Lying on the hard mattress of his cell, Pierre considered his bloody lip and aching body a badge of accomplishment. The authorities had been so displeased over their failure to keep his stepsister alive that the French guards felt the need to beat him in punishment.

As though anything they could inflict on him would change the fact Jacqueline was dead. And so was that miserable government man.

Oh, how he wished he could thank Eugene personally. But the man would have to be satisfied with the money.

Despite his body's soreness, Pierre closed his eyes with a smile on his face and dreamed of his next revenge. He would get out of this hellhole. Eventually, he would find a way, and freedom would be his.

Then she would pay for her part in all of this. The authorities had done him a favor by moving him back to France because France was precisely where he wanted to be.

Epilogue

Twenty miles south of
Medora, North Dakota.
1965

Colten stood near the corral, watching Clinton saddle up the horses, getting ready for the day. There were already a few tourists who wandered onto the property, looking forward to taking an hour's ride into the Badlands.

He was proud of Clinton. The boy was now ten. When he was around the horses, he blossomed. No one watching would ever suspect that the child was diagnosed with autism years earlier. There were still traces of the handicap, of course. Though they seemed to fade with each passing day. Colten knew it was not something a person outgrew, but he would be happy with whatever progress Clinton made each year.

Some kids were not so lucky. But, having witnessed firsthand what being around horses could do for a child with disabilities, Colten had been mulling over another aspect to this ranch he and his wife were slowly building up.

The thought of his wife had him looking toward the main house. The three-story, eight-bedroom, stone-faced chateau had been a gift from Jacqueline's mother as she paid to have it constructed. Three months after their wedding, Jacqueline's stepfather died unexpectedly from a brain aneurysm and Cadman decided it would be safe enough to tell Jacqueline's mother the truth. However, everyone agreed she could never visit Jacqueline here because people might wonder why the woman suddenly started spending time in North Dakota when she was not known to enjoy traveling outside of France.

But the woman wanted her daughter to have a home close to the one she grew up in, and Colten had not objected. Besides, he did not have to do any of the work, and Jacqueline deserved the European-style home.

It amazed Colten that the design blended into the landscape.

The home had fireplaces in almost every room for those long North Dakota winters; in the event the furnace ever went out during a storm. Each bedroom had its own private bath; the master suite included a sunken tub, large enough for two people to share.

It was Colten's favorite place in the entire house, as long as his wife was in the water with him.

The garage could hold four vehicles. Although currently, it only had two to keep it company. Perhaps as their family grew, they would need the extra space.

"Daddy!" He heard his daughter's cry, and turned to see her sitting on the railing, swinging her legs fast. He feared the three-year-old would fall off.

"Careful, Donny!" he yelled, feeling his heart leap to his throat as she jumped off, as though she were a bird.

He felt his wife's arm encircle his waist. She had come upon his left side, so he had not known she was there. "Colten," she chastised, "Your daughter's name is Donna. If you keep calling her Donny, she will think she is a boy."

"I know my daughter's name," he grumbled. "Besides, it's my nickname for her. If I called her kitten, would she think she was a cat?"

Jacqueline scowled at his logic.

He smiled, leaned down, and kissed her, then placed his hand on her swollen belly; another child soon to be born. He marveled at the wonder of having children in his life. If this one was a boy, his wife gave him permission to name him. She had named their daughter, Donna Athenais Fisher, in honor of the de Morès family's daughter.

Jacqueline conceived the child in her womb while they were visiting some of his relations in Sundance, Wyoming—nearly eight months ago. They did not leave North Dakota often, not wanting the risk of anyone in Pierre's circle reporting to him they were alive, but now and then they would travel to Wyoming, or within North Dakota, to visit friends.

"You know," he said, looking around the land, remembering when there had been nothing here, except their excitement and determination, "I think we did all right."

She leaned against him. "I love you, Colten Marshal Fisher," she sighed, watching Clinton chasing his sister away from the horses, so the three-year-old would not get kicked in the face from a horse she walked behind. Clinton watched his sister like a hawk and took his responsibility as a big brother seriously.

"And I love you, Jacqueline Medora Fisher. If there hadn't been you, where would I be now?"

She looked up at him, humor showing in her eyes. "Probably having some woman's gun stuck in your belly. It is a good thing I saved you from such a horrible fate."

He chuckled, leaned in, and nipped her nose.

"Hey!" she grinned, punching him lightly in the stomach, then stepping away. "We do not have time for fun and games," she abolished. "Tourists are arriving, and the church youth group from Bismarck should be here any moment."

He wiggled his brows. "We can have fun and games tonight, right?"

She gave him a level look. "Is sex the only thing you think about, Colten Fisher?"

He placed a hand on his heart. "Did I say anything about sex?"

A car driving into the yard saved him from any retaliation on her part.

As one, they looked toward the approaching vehicle. "It is the Davidson's!" Jacqueline exclaimed and, taking Colten's hand, walked with him toward the incoming car. They were expecting them, but not until noon. Anytime the family came was a welcome visit.

They reached the vehicle as it rolled to a stop in the visitor's parking area. Before they turned the motor off, the three Davidson children were opening the back door and rushing out to hug Jacqueline, and then Colten.

"I am so happy to see you!" Jacqueline cried, wiping at her eyes, to remove tears she was unashamed to shed.

Colten grinned when Digger stepped out from the car. "I'll be damned," he said and walked forward to give the older man a bear hug. "How in the hell did they manage to get you out of your cave?"

"Do I know you, young man?" Digger asked and got a hoot of laughter out of Colten. To this day, Digger continued with his scatterbrain act. Everyone kept the truth to themselves, allowing him to gain extra attention from Jacqueline. Although Colten suspected his wife knew it was a ploy, and went along with it anyway, just because she loved the old man.

"You all go up to the house," Colten nodded toward the structure. "Gary, you can move the car into the drive. It will be easier to bring in your luggage." The cottage behind the house allowed guests to have their own place, and the Davidson's loved it there. Digger would stay in the primary residence, and Colten was looking forward to visiting with the man. They both enjoyed swapping stories of their days working for the government.

A bus coming through the gate gained Colten's attention. "I'll be along later. Jacqueline can get you all settled in. I've got a youth group to entertain for a while." He walked off to greet the want-to-be-saints; suspecting they were more sinners than anything else.

As the young adults began alighting from the bus, Colten shook hands with the youth pastor and was going over the details for the day's outing, when he heard a muttered, "Shit!" from behind him.

He turned his head to see which one of the boys voiced a word that seemed out of place within a church group. But all he saw was a leg as it disappeared behind the bus.

The youth pastor grimaced, apologized, and called out, "López! Come here."

"I'd rather not!" came the reply, which was followed by laughter from the group.

The youth pastor's face flushed red.

"Trouble in the ranks?" Colten asked, enjoying himself.

"New kid from New York," the man explained. "He and his mother recently moved to Bismarck; she's got relatives there. He's spent most of his life on the street. She finally moved away from the bad influences he's been around. The problem is, he will be eighteen soon, and I'm afraid the move didn't sit well with him. The only reason he's with us on this trip is the mother threatened to have the cops put him in juvenile detention because he keeps stealing."

Bad apples, Colten thought. They were everywhere. "He a problem? Dangerous, I mean," he clarified, thinking of the tourists and his family.

The pastor shook his head. "Nah. He just likes to steal. He's an expert at pickpocketing."

Colten's mind seemed to stutter for a moment, remembering another time, and another pickpocket.

He shook his head. It couldn't be.

But he couldn't be sure, so he excused himself and made his way to the back of the bus, stopped, and stared.

Older now, teetering on the verge of manhood, but still a boy. He sat on the bumper of the bus while his leg bounced with nervousness.

And Colten grinned. "You, López?"

The seventeen-year-old's head jerked up and his eyes were as wide as the prairie. He looked left and right, as though looking for a place to escape. He was out of his element here. There was nowhere to go, so he tried a semi-cocky smile and said, "Mr. Government man," his voice was shaky, "Haven't seen you for a while. How's it going?"

Colten took off his hat, hit it on his pants leg, and replaced it on his head before he said, "Well now, I don't think I've ever been better. I've wondered about you from time to time, thinking about the wallet you lifted from me a few years ago." He scratched his chin. "What was it I said I would do if I ever caught you?"

Juan López's face drained of color.

It was difficult to keep his face grim when inside Colten was having the time of his life, toying with the kid. "Nice to see you understand the situation."

Juan swallowed, hard.

The youth pastor came around the corner of the bus. "Do you know each other?" he asked.

Juan yelled, "No!"

Colten laughed, "Hell, yes!" He saw one of his summer employees crossing the yard, called him over, and gave him instructions to get the horses ready for the youth group, before turning toward the pastor and Juan.

"Let's go on up to the house. I'd like to speak with López's mother. You got a phone number for her?" Colten asked the pastor.

The man nodded.

"You're going to telephone my mother?!" the kid exclaimed, indignant. "What in the hell for?"

Colten reached out, fisted his hand in the boy's shirt collar, and hulled him up until their faces were two inches apart. "I lost three hundred dollars when you lifted my wallet," he hissed, then spun him around and began marching him toward the big house.

"Three fifty," the kid mumbled, then clamped his hand over his mouth.

Colten chuckled. "Glad you remember the exact amount, 'cause if I can get your mom to agree, you're going to work it off for me this summer."

The pastor kept pace, nervous as a cat in a dog pen. "I find this very high handed. You can't treat him like this."

Colten didn't break stride. "What? Make him pay me back for what he stole from me?"

The man stumbled a bit, unsure what to say to that.

Once inside the grand and massive house, Juan had the nerve to say, "You've done okay for yourself. What's three hundred fifty dollars to you?"

Colten pushed him into a chair in the spacious kitchen; the housekeeper was looking on with wide eyes, and shock on her face. "It will be worth every cent to see you working your ass off to pay me back."

Juan tried to get out of the chair. "I'm not going to work for you!"

Colten gave him a level look. "Would you rather me cut off your balls?"

The boy blanched, turned green, and sat down.

"Thought you might see it my way." With that, Colten got the phone number for Juan's mother and dialed. A half-hour later, with the pastor assuring the single mother the person wanting to employ her son was on the up and up, the Fisher Ranch gained an employee.

That turned out to be the best thing to happen to Juan López, Pickpocket from New York City. Over time, he discovered he enjoyed cooking. And the following year, when Colten and Jacqueline added a mess hall for employees and tourists, he took pride in being its head chef.

He never stole another wallet after that first day on the ranch, not that he hadn't had plenty of opportunities but the threat from Colten, that his balls would find themselves cut off, held weight and detoured him whenever he felt his palms itching to hit an easy mark.

Author notes

This story is a work of fiction based on historical facts, although some events may not have taken place in the exact time frame of the story.

Harold Schafer was a North Dakota businessman. He founded the Gold Seal Company, whose products included Glass Wax, Snowy Bleach, and Mr. Bubble. Harold's enthusiasm for hard work propelled him into the national limelight, making the Gold Seal Company the success it was. Harold's love for the mostly forgotten town of Medora, and his passion for the badlands, prompted him to begin preserving the rich history of the sleeping village.

Russell Reid was a member of the State Historical Society of North Dakota and a member of the National Conference of State Parks. Some of his outstanding accomplishments included The creation of the nation's first national memorial park, in memory of Theodore Roosevelt, in the North Dakota Badlands. Because of his friendship with Louis, the eldest son of the Marquis and Medora, Reid was able to secure, for the state, the Chateau de Mores State Historic Site. The International Peace Garden, and other historical sites throughout the state, are also accomplishments of Mr. Reid.

Tony (Antoine) Vallombrosa was the grandson of the Marquis and Medora. As a child, he would visit Medora with his father, Louis. He visited the area in 1962, 1967 and the 1970s and early 1980s, after his father's passing. Tony died in 1982. He never married or had children. He was the last of the direct family line.

While researching the history of the town of Medora, I went through the genealogy of Antoine-Amédée-Marie-Vincent Manca de Vallombrosa, the Marquis de Morès, and his wife, Medora Von Hoffman Vallombrosa, Marquise de Morès. Once a person looks back far enough, sometimes a story can be told that weaves history and fiction together.

Richard, Duc de Vallombrosa, who married Geneviève de Pérusse des Cars, did found the Yacht Club of France, and the Society of Racing, in Cannes.

Richard and Geneviève's descendants are as follows: Antoine-Amédée-Marie-Vincent Manca de Vallombrosa, the Marquis de Morès was their firstborn. Six years later, a son, Odet, was born. However, he only lived for a few months. In 1868, a daughter, Claire, was born. Then, in 1880, another son, Amédée, was born. (Amédée Joseph Gabriel Marie Manca-Amat de Vallombrosa was a French organist and composer.)

When I discovered Richard and Geneviève's son, Odet, had not lived, I wondered what his family line would have been like, had he survived. That is where the imaginary line of the

Vallombrosa family begins. I felt Odet deserved to have his own Legacy, and this is from where Rosalinda was born. The fabricated family line is— Odet, born 1864; Victor, father of Albert, and Albert, father of Rosalinda.

Medora Vallombrosa was a daughter of Athenais Grymes von Hoffman and Louis A. von Hoffman, a New York banker and one of the founders of the Knickerbocker Club. Medora's maternal grandparents were Susanna Bosque Grymes, third wife and widow of William C.C. Claiborne, the first American Governor of Louisiana, and John Randolph Grymes, the United States Attorney for Louisiana, and personal counsel to Andrew Jackson, during the Battle of New Orleans. He resigned from his post to represent the pirate, Jean Lafitte. Medora was named for her maternal aunt, who was the second wife of Samuel Ward, an acclaimed Washington lobbyist, whose first wife was Emily Astor, daughter of William Backhouse Astor. Ward's sister, Julia Ward Howe, wrote The Battle Hymn of the Republic.

Researching Medora's mother's family tree was interesting. I was amazed by the connections to other famous people in history. When forming Jacqueline's link to Medora, North Dakota, I went through Medora's mother's line to bring it forward.

If you have never visited Medora, ND, I encourage you to put it on your bucket list. It is full of history, and the scenery is breathtaking

One final note: De Morès's last name was not Vallombrosa;
Manca was. De Vallombrosa was a title which I took liberties
with.

.

About the author

Janette Walker, writing under the pseudonym J.R. Zimmer, is an author and artist. Born in Bismarck, ND, she is drawn to creative pursuits, and her passion for both literature and visual arts keeps her busy. The Badlands of ND are a source of inspiration for her. Her love of history and the fascinating characters of Antoine-Amédée-Marie-Vincent Manca de Vallombrosa, the Marquis de Morès, and his wife, Medora, inspired her to write the Fisher/Lafayette Series. You can visit her online at www.jrzimmer.com. Email: jrzimmer17@yahoo.com.

Keep Reading for an excerpt of Book Two in the Fisher/Lafayette Series. Rosalinda's story: *Now and Forever.*

Now and Forever
by J.R. Zimmer

Prelude

Paris, France 1965

It was her birthday. Her twenty-seventh birthday, to be exact. As always, her parents planned a grand party for their only daughter and held the event at the family home. A medieval-styled, 18-bedroom Chateau west of Paris. It sat on 30 acres, and included a stable for horses, a small lake, and several out-buildings surrounding the home, all of which had a view of breathtaking landscapes.

Rosalinda was of French, Spanish, and Italian descent. She had always known wealth and luxury. Her second great grand-father, Rich-ard, Duc de Vallombrosa, had founded the Yacht Club of France, and the Society of Racing, in Cannes. Before that, at twenty-two years of age, he led an expedition across In-dia and earned the Cross of the Commander of the Or-der of St. Maurice and St. Lazare.

Richard Vallombrosa had married Geneviève de Pérusse des Cars, the daughter of the Duc de Cars, who had been one of the top com-manders in the conquest of Algiers.

Despite their noble titles and wealth, Rosalinda's family was not aloof. Her parents taught their five children to have com-passion for those who had not been fortunate enough to have riches of their own. They encouraged their children to give back whenever possible, whether it be volunteering at a local soup kitchen or donating to charities that offered assistance to the less fortunate.

1

That did not mean that Albert Vallombrosa and his wife were afraid to spend their money on outlandish parties. And this birthday bash for their youngest child would be the talk of the Paris elite society for a long time.

Rosalinda should have been having the time of her life. The musicians were one of France's most popular and famous groups. They sang and played their instruments on stage, and the people danced and laughed in the ballroom, enjoying the evening.

Among the guests were celebrities of film and the live theater. They were there to congratulate Rosalinda, who quickly rose in the ranks of popularity because of her exceptional acting abilities, as well as for winning the Best Actress award for her performance in the movie Love in The Spring last year.

However, Rosalinda was not enjoying herself and was not exactly sure why. Perhaps it was because she realized she was closer to thirty years of age than she would have liked to be. Or it could be she was saddened because her best friend, Jacqueline Fisher, could not attend the festivities. Even if Jacqueline wasn't pregnant, and scheduled to give birth in about a month, the woman would not have been able to attend; no longer able to travel freely to Paris. Because even though the woman's stepbrother thought she was dead, no one could take the chance that someone in France would recognize Jacqueline and report it to Pierre. He had hired a hitman to kill her three years ago and, as far as he knew, his directive had been successful.

Rosalinda's green eyes scanned the ever-increasing crowd. Until recently, she would have been scoping out a handsome man who would catch her fancy and then seduce him into a quick fuck. She'd always had a strong sexual drive and never wanted for willing partners who were happy to scratch her itch with no further demands or commitments.

But she was not interested in sex at the moment. At least, no one had struck her fancy or aroused sexual desires in her for the past four months.

Rosalinda wondered if something was wrong with her.

Her eyes went back to scanning the ever-growing crowd. What, or who, she was seeking; she wasn't certain.

She felt someone come up behind her. Turning, she found the Ameri-can agent who helped escort Jacqueline's step-brother to Fleury Mérogis prison three years ago, standing be-hind her. He was a handsome man, a little over six feet tall, with a wide chest and muscular arms. Arms that held her a few times over the past three years. The first time she had gotten him into bed was the day she first met him. After that, he vowed it wouldn't happen again, and she'd viewed that as a challenge. The next time she saw him, at Colten and Jacquel-ine's wedding, she seduced him in his hotel room.

It had been a glorious night for both of them. So much so that each time he came to Paris, they would meet at her home and make memories, until it was time for him to catch the plane back to the United States.

Cadman Benson was a sexy-looking man and a superb lover. Yet, looking at him now, she had no interest in tearing his clothes off.

He smiled at her, that small dimple at the corner of his mouth she had always enjoyed sucking and licking peaked at her, and yet, tonight, it was nothing more to her than what it was. A dim-ple that was just there.

Obviously, she was coming down with something. Perhaps she should visit the doctor to find out if there was something wrong with her.

Cadman leaned in, kissed her cheek. "You are as beautiful as ever." When she made no move to make his kiss into anything more, it surprised him, but he shrugged it away. The on again, off again sexual relationship they shared satisfied him in ways no other woman could. Although he was half in love with her, he never fooled himself into thinking she would ever be his exclusively.

Besides, he was beginning a new career soon, for the United States government, which wouldn't leave him time to pursue any permanent relationship with anyone. And he was happy enough with the arrangement he had with Rosalinda.

"Thank you," she murmured, her eyes going back to the crowd.

"Are you looking for someone in particular?" Cadman asked, stepping up to stand beside her, as his eyes, too, scanned the crowd. He wondered if her indifference to him was because of her having her sights set on some other man tonight. Which actually bothered him. If she was looking for a sexual encounter, he was more than willing to be her slave.

"Umm?" Rosalinda's response wasn't an answer at all.

Shaking his head, he decided that whoever the starlet was searching for wasn't any of his business. He told her, "I'll be flying back to the United States tomorrow. Next month I'll be starting my vacation. I'm going to spend a week with Colten and Jacqueline in North Dakota, on that horse ranch of theirs."

Rosalinda glanced up at him and smiled. "I am jealous of you, Cad-man. But I will travel there the moment Jacqueline sends word that the baby is born." She patted his arm. "Although I will miss seeing you ride a horse. The first time I witnessed it, I laughed for hours."

"Ha, ha," he said with a scowl. He hated horses, but every time he visited the Fisher ranch, which offered tourists a chance to horseback deeper into the Badlands of North Dakota, Colten somehow talked him into getting on one of those four-legged things he called a quarter horse.

Rosalinda's eyes moved to the entrance of the ballroom. They stopped when they landed on Charles Lafayette as he entered the room. The talented movie producer seemed to hesitate in the doorway for only a moment, before moving to where Rosalinda's parents stood next to the food table and refreshments.

Rosalinda's breath caught in her throat the instant she saw him enter the room, and she did not realize she was holding her breath until her lungs forced her to breathe.

The man was eleven years older than herself. She had used the age gap as an excuse for ignoring whatever feelings he evoked in her, but something seemed to be shifting inside her concerning him. Changes she wasn't sure if she wanted to admit.

A few months ago, she noticed he lost the small amount of extra weight he always carried around his stomach. And, although his balding head had some sections of hair trying to remain behind, it never distracted her from thinking he was attractive- and kind- and gallant. And why couldn't she allow herself to love him? She knew the man loved her. He showed her so many times over the years that he did not look at her as a sexual conquest and treated her as though he cherished her. He never suggested she sleep with him. Though Rosalinda saw the longing in his eyes whenever she caught him looking at her.

5

She never tried to make him a conquest; she respected him too much. And knew, too, that with him, he did not want a one-night stand. He would want more than she was ready to give one man.

He would want marriage and commitment.

Watching him now, speaking with her parents, she felt a familiar tug at her heart. She did not know what to do with these damn emotions that wanted to propel her to him.

As usual, he was alone. Rosalinda had never seen him with another woman, and her heart twisted. He deserved someone in his life who would understand he was worth loving.

In her eyes, he appeared lonely, and the urge to go to him was almost strong enough to cause her feet to move in his direction.

Ruthlessly, she pushed the desire down. She knew that if she went to Charles now, she would not want to let him go, and she was not ready to give up her freedom.

When the band played another number, she grabbed Cadman's hand and pulled him onto the dance floor, determined to forget about Charles Lafayette and the feelings his mere presence stirred within her.

Fisher/Lafayette Saga

If There Hadn't Been You

Now and Forever

Someone Like You

Spitfire

Something Magical

Coming Home (Free Ebook when signing up for my newsletter at www.jrzimmer.com. Not available anywhere else.)

The Dreamer

Eagle's Wolf

www.ingramcontent.com/pod-product-compliance
Lightning Source LLC
Chambersburg PA
CDIIW000413180028
46817CB00007B/2560

* 9 7 8 1 7 3 4 5 7 8 9 8 0 *